JAMES AXLER

DEATH LANDS®

Bloodfire

A GOLD EAGLE BOOK FROM

WORLDWIDE®

TORONTO • NEW YORK • LONDON
AMSTERDAM • PARIS • SYDNEY • HAMBURG
STOCKHOLM • ATHENS • TOKYO • MILAN
MADRID • WARSAW • BUDAPEST • AUCKLAND

First edition December 2003

ISBN 0-373-62574-X

BLOODFIRE

"Dark night, there's a land tank over there!"

"Alone?" Ryan demanded pointedly.

"No, wait, there's two of 'em! Big as anything I've ever seen. Some smaller wags, too. Couldn't get a good look."

"Is the war wag an APC?" Krysty asked, squinting to try to see past the conflagration.

"Converted trucks," J.B. said, lowering the longeyes. "Machine gun blasters, rocket pods on the roof, and what sure as shit looks like a radar dish."

"Just sitting there, or is it turning?" Ryan asked.

"Turning steadily."

"That means it's probably working," Ryan muttered, a hard smile crossing his face. "That's gotta be Trader."

"Indeed, logic dictates it to be so," Doc rumbled, and then added, "How can we assist him in this internecine battle?"

"Their fight is about as civil as a jihad, ya old coot," Mildred shot back. "This unknown Trader may be somebody we can trust, or not. But we know for a fact that Gaza is a mad dog and the sooner he's wearing grass for a hat the better."

Other titles in the Deathlands saga:

Power, like a desolating pestilence,
Pollutes whate'er it touches; and obedience,
Bane of all genius, virtue, freedom, truth,
Makes slaves of men, and, of the human frame...
—Percy Bysshe Shelley, *Queen Mab* (1813)

THE DEATHLANDS SAGA

This world is their legacy, a world born in the violent nuclear spasm of 2001 that was the bitter outcome of a struggle for global dominance.

There is no real escape from this shockscape where life always hangs in the balance, vulnerable to newly demonic nature, barbarism, lawlessness.

But they are the warrior survivalists, and they endure—in the way of the lion, the hawk and the tiger, true to nature's heart despite its ruination.

Ryan Cawdor: The privileged son of an East Coast baron. Acquainted with betrayal from a tender age, he is a master of the hard realities.

Krysty Wroth: Harmony ville's own Titian-haired beauty, a woman with the strength of tempered steel. Her premonitions and Gaia powers have been fostered by her Mother Sonja.

J. B. Dix, the Armorer: Weapons master and Ryan's close ally, he, too, honed his skills traversing the Deathlands with the legendary Trader.

Doctor Theophilus Tanner: Torn from his family and a gentler life in 1896, Doc has been thrown into a future he couldn't have imagined.

Dr. Mildred Wyeth: Her father was killed by the Ku Klux Klan, but her fate is not much lighter. Restored from predark cryogenic suspension, she brings twentieth-century healing skills to a nightmare.

Jak Lauren: A true child of the wastelands, reared on adversity, loss and danger, the albino teenager is a fierce fighter and loyal friend.

Dean Cawdor: Ryan's young son by Sharona accepts the only world he knows, and yet he is the seedling bearing the promise of tomorrow.

In a world where all was lost, they are humanity's last hope....

Chapter One

On through the night they rode, seven people on six horses, the unshod hooves of the animals pounding against the hard-packed sand of the desert.

Streaks of light were starting to brighten the overcast sky as dawn slowly came to the Deathlands. Thunder rumbled in the distance, lightning flashing bright as a gigavolt of electricity slashed into the planet like fire trying to cauterize an open wound.

Suddenly, a ravine yawned wide in the ground before the companions, the edges sparkling with a residue of salt that infused the entire landscape from the crashing ocean tidal wave caused by the nukecaust so very long ago. Digging in their heels, the companions urged the animals to go faster and jumped the pit, landing hard. The horse with two riders went to its knees for a moment, then, struggling erect once more, it continued after the others.

The seven friends were red-eyed and hunched over, exhausted from the race for survival. The bridles of the horses were sopping wet with saliva and flecked with foam. The humans and horses were all drenched in sweat, the chill of the night slowly passing as the fiery sun exploded over the horizon, bathing the world in its fire.

Moving to the steady motion of the powerful stallion he rode, Ryan Cawdor fought his exhaustion and tried to stay in control of the beast. Tiny particles of sand and salt hit his scarred face like invisible sleet, getting underneath the leather patch that covered the ravaged hole of his left eye. His clothes were stiff with dried sweat and caked with blood, thankfully none of it his. Escaping from Rockpoint had been a nightmare of snipers on the walls and savage cougars running wild in the streets. The weapons he had stolen from the local baron's secret arsenal were long gone, and now Ryan carried only his personal blasters, a 9 mm SIG-Sauer at his hip, and a bolt-action Steyr SSG-70 longblaster strapped across his back. The blasters had been with him a long time, and in his expert hands usually proved more than deadly enough for anything the Deathlands could throw his way. Not everything, but most.

Following a swell in the sandy ground, the group of people slowed as the horses galloped up the sloping side of a large sand dune. As the panting animals crested the top, Ryan saw that the dune stretched hundreds of feet and offered the friends a good panoramic view of the desert in every direction. Perfect. If that damn APC came their way again, its headlights would give away its approach in plenty of time for them to ride off again.

"Give them a rest!" Ryan shouted, his voice a throaty growl from thirst and exhaustion. "We stop for five!"

Pulling back on the reins, the companions allowed their mounts to slow to a canter, then walked them to an easy stop. As the dawn steadily grew brighter in the east, the others could now see that the dune was covered with green plants of some kind. Hungrily, the horses sniffed at the vegetation, then snorted and turned away in disgust. The reek of salt from the mutant weeds was strong enough for the humans to detect. The plants were as inedible as the sand itself.

Sliding off the rear of the mount he shared with a boy, J. B. Dix stretched a few times to work the kinks out of his sore muscles. Dark night, he thought, it had been a mighty cramped ride sharing the horse, and more than once he'd been sure he'd lose his grip on the saddle and go flying off.

Short and wiry, John Barrymore Dix was dressed in a loose shirt and trousers, a leather pilot's jacket and fingerless gloves. An Uzi machine pistol hung across his chest, and an S&W M-4000 shotgun was slung over his back.

"Just in case I forgot to say it before," J.B. said, offering a hand to the boy, "thanks for saving my ass back there."

Still on the horse, Dean Cawdor stopped massaging the neck of the big Appaloosa stallion and looked down at the adult. Appearing many years older than his real age of twelve, Dean had a bloody streak across his face where some hot lead from a sec man's blaster had just grazed his cheek during the escape. The son of Ryan, the youth was growing rapidly, and there was little doubt that he would be even taller than his father some day.

A veteran of a hundred battles, Dean had a Browning Hi-Power pistol holstered on his hip, and a home-made crossbow and quiver hung across his chest. The bulky weapons had been in the way a lot during the ride, but he needed the room behind to fit J.B. on the horse.

Reaching down, Dean took the offered hand and the two shook before breaking into weary smiles.

"No problem," the boy replied.

J.B. released his grip and turned to walk to the edge of the dune. Tilting his fedora to block the wash of growing sunlight, the man studied the sprawling landscape to the north, then reached into the canvas bag hanging at his side, rummaging through the fuses and black powder bombs to unearth a brass cylinder about the size and shape of a soup can. With an expert snap, he extended the antique telescope to its full length and swept the distant horizon to the north.

"Looks clear," J.B. announced, adjusting the focal length of the scope. "I think we lost them."

"Thank Gaia for that," Krysty Wroth exhaled, reaching into the backpack tied just behind her saddle. The rawhide lashings were loose from the wild ride, but the pack of food and ammo was thankfully still there.

Sticking up from the gun boot attached to the saddle was the stock of a recently acquired longblaster called a Holland & Holland .475 Nitro Express. It was the biggest weapon the woman had ever seen, and firing it almost wrenched her arm from the socket. But the big-bore rounds did a hell of a lot worse to the sec men they hit, blowing one man clean out of his saddle and beheading another. She was down to only a few more rounds for the monster, after which it would become a liability and not an asset.

Tall and full breasted, with an explosion of fiery red hair and emerald-green eyes, Krysty more looked like a baron's plaything than a tough survivor, and many fools had died learning the truth of the matter.

"No more than one drink apiece," a stocky black woman directed, pouring some water from her own canteen into a cupped hand and offering it to her panting horse. "We need to conserve until we reach fresh water again."

Eagerly, the animal lapped at the fluid, its rough tongue seeking every drop. Dr. Mildred Wyeth was in a red flannel shirt and U.S. Army fatigue pants, her ebony hair fashioned into beaded plaits. A patched satchel hung from her shoulder, and the checkered grip of a Czech ZKR target pistol poked out of her shirt where she had tucked the weapon away for safekeeping. Mildred had almost lost the blaster twice from the rough ride over the irregular salt flats, and had no intention of challenging fate a third time.

Although she rarely spoke of the matter, Mildred considered her personal portion of luck long gone. Back in the twentieth century, she had gone into the hospital for a routine operation on a cyst, but there had been complications and they froze her to save her life. Ryan freed her from cryogenic suspension a hundred years later, a stranger in a new and desperate land.

"We'll find water," Krysty said, pulling out a canteen from her backpack. "That pipe under the temple had to come from somewhere. And the Grandee River isn't that far."

Then she paused for a moment until the throbbing in her temples subsided. Her hair had been cut by an arrow in the fight at the ville, and the pain still lingered. As she stroked the filaments, they coiled tighter, almost protectively about her hand, and as the dull agony eased somewhat the animated hair relaxed once more into a crimson cascade about her shoulders.

Taking a very small sip from the canteen, Krysty carefully washed out her mouth before taking a long drink. Born and raised in Colorado, she had learned early in life to always cut the dust from your mouth before drinking, or else you remained thirsty and wasted precious water taking a second, unnecessary drink.

Finally lowering the canteen, Krysty wiping her

mouth dry on the sleeve of her bearskin coat, and tightly screwed the cap back onto the container. Waste not, die not, as her mother always used to say. Tucking the battered tin canteen safely away, Krysty then fingered her S&W Model 640 revolver to make sure it was still with her after the wild ride. Then kneeling, the redhead checked the knife tucked into one of her cowboy boots.

"Best not ride for a while," Jak Lauren stated. "Horses rest or die."

"That's why I stopped here," Ryan said, brushing back his wild crop of hair with stiff fingers. Sleep tugged at his eyes like deadweights, and he jerked his head to try to stay awake. This wasn't the time or place to catch some sleep. Soon, though, they'd find someplace to make camp, and he'd get some rest then.

Grunting in acknowledgment, Jak awkwardly easing himself off the roan mare with his good arm, the other tucked inside his shirt stained dark with blood. He had caught some flying lead in the fight to get out of Rockpoint, but there had been no spurting of blood to show a major artery had been hit. It was only a flesh wound, the small-caliber round having gone clean through his arm without even hitting the bone. Soon it would be just another scar on the albino teen's body, lost amid the dozens of others.

"My dear Ryan, are you quite all right?" a silver-haired man asked, sitting easily in his saddle as if born there.

Dressed in a frock coat and frilly white shirt with an ebony walking stick thrust through his belt like a sword, Dr. Theophilus Algernon Tanner seemed to be a refugee from the nineteenth century. A WWI web belt encircled his waist, the closed pouches bulging with ammo for the colossal handcannon resting on his hip. The large blaster was a Civil War–era LeMat revolver, a 9-shot .44 that used black powder. Though Doc looked deceptively old, he could wield the LeMat with authority.

Fighting back a yawn, Ryan scowled at the other man, then shrugged. "I could use some coffee," he admitted in frank honesty. "Got an MRE?"

Doc nodded in understanding. MRE stood for Meal Ready to Eat, and the pack included a main course, snack, gum, cigarettes, candy bar, dessert, coffee, sugar, moist towelette and even toilet tissue for afterward. The companions found the MRE packs regularly in the redoubts, often with the protective Mylar wrapper ripped open, the food inside dried and useless. But they had a few of the precious rations saved away for when they couldn't hunt for meat or trade for food at a ville.

Against his will, Doc had been an experimental test subject for Operation Chronos, the use of the mat-trans units for time travel. He had been abducted from his quiet university home in Vermont in the late 1880s and thrown rudely into the nuclear wastelands of the Deathlands. For a very long time his mind had been shattered by the event, memories lost and reason gone. But the episodes of madness were less and less frequent these days, which the scholar took to mean that he was slowly becoming adjusted to the present. He found this oddly disturbing. Doc was still grimly determined to find a way to go back in time to his beloved wife, Emily, and his children. They were long dead and buried, in the present, but still alive and well in the past. Someday, somehow, Doc would return to them, and God help anybody who got in his way.

"Indeed I do," Doc replied, and slid off his mount to rummage in his backpack until he found a foil-wrapped package and tossed it over. "What's mine is yours, my dear Ryan."

"Nuke me, but coffee sounds like the best idea I've heard in years," J.B. said, compacting the scope to tuck it back into the canvas bag, nestled between a thick coil of homemade fuse and several jars of grainy black powder.

"Has to be cold," Ryan said, fumbling with the envelope from the MRE pack. "Still too dark for a fire. Up here, we'd be seen for miles. Might as well shoot off a bastard flare."

"They go sleep?" Jak asked.

"Makes sense that they'd sleep during the day," Dean stated, breaking in two a granola bar from another MRE pack and eating one part while giving the other to his horse. "Sunlight on APC, be acing hot by noon."

The huge animal gobbled down the tiny morsel in less than a second and impatiently shifted its hooves, hoping for more. The others whinnied and nickered for food, hungrily glancing at the weeds again.

"Lethally hot, you mean," J.B. corrected, straightening his fedora. "I remember traveling with the Trader, we would sometimes find deaders sitting behind the controls of an armored wag, the stink of roasting flesh filling the air inside."

"How delightful," Doc said with a frown, revolving the cylinder of his LeMat to inspect the load in each chamber. "Thus the only question is who is in the infernal contraption chasing us, Gaza, or Hawk."

As carefully as mixing explosives, Ryan poured the hundred-year-old coffee crystals into his partially filled canteen, then screwed the cap on tight and sloshed it about for a minute before taking a sip. It was cold and strong, but he could feel the caffeine wash away the fog from his mind, and after another swallow, Ryan passed the container around to the rest of the companions. Each took a measured swig, and the canteen was passed around twice before it was drained.

"Needed that," Jak said, shifting his wounded arm inside his shirt, the dried blood making the material as stiff as old canvas.

"I really should look at that wound before it becomes infected," Mildred said, opening the flap on her satchel and going to the teen.

"No time," J.B. replied, gazing toward the eastern horizon. "We got to keep going. Too damn visible on top of this dune."

The pinkish glow of true dawn was expanding across the sky. Soon, night would be over and the heat would really start to increase.

Wiping the crumbs of the granola bar off his face, Dean added, "Sunup will bring out the millipedes and scorpions."

"We water the horses one last time and then ride," Ryan ordered, a touch of his old strength back in his voice. Fatigue still weighed down his bones, but he felt good for another couple of miles. More than enough for them to find some shelter from the heat and the bugs. There were supposed to be some ruins to the southwest of there—those would do fine, if they weren't too far away.

There was hard wisdom in his words, so the weary companions saw to the needs of their mounts with what supplies could be spared. Draining off the last of her canteen, Krysty refilled it from the big leather bag she had grabbed in the corral when they stole the horses. Cupping a hand, she pooled some water in the palm and offered it to the chestnut mare. Eagerly, the horse lapped it off her skin and nudged her for some more. But as she refilled her hand, the animal sharply inhaled, then trembled all over. As the horse suddenly fought for breath, blood began to trickle from its mouth, its eyes rolling upward until only the whites showed.

"Gaia!" Krysty cried in horror, dropping the canteen.

Weaving about as if drunk, the animal unexpectedly dropped limply to the ground and went into violent convulsions before going very still.

"It's dead," the woman said softly, then jerked her head to stare at her wet palm as a horrible realization filled her with gut-wrenching dread.

Chapter Two

Rumbling and clanking, the battered APC rolled along the irregular landscape of the Texas desert, its cracked headlights throwing wild columns of splayed light ahead of the war wag as it rose and fell.

Crouched in the driver's chair, Baron Edgar Gaza stared hatefully through the small rectangular slit of an ob port, his hands clenched hard on the steering yoke of the preDark vehicle. Once there had been periscopes for the driver and gunner to see through without exposing themselves to enemy fire, but those had been broken long ago, and now the only way to see was through small rectangular vents.

In the rear of the war wag, four of his wives were sitting near the gun ports, their pale hands expertly cradling 9 mm Uzi machine pistols. Spare clips were thrust like knives into their belts, and each bore fresh wounds from their recent battles, bloody bandages covering their legs and arms.

Sitting in the middle of the deck, his first wife was clumsily working on a .50-caliber machine gun, trying to figure out how to unlink the ammo belt to make the big-bore blaster feed properly. The turret and gunner's nest rose directly behind the woman, but those periscopes had also been smashed. The 25 mm cannon had survived intact but had been removed for use in the ville keep, and now they only had a .50-caliber machine gun to mount on the pintel stanchion. It didn't have the sheer destructive power of the explosive 25 mm shells. On the other hand, it didn't eat ammo as fast and the brass cartridges could be reloaded.

Gaza glanced at her, more pleased with the amount accomplished than the wealth of skin exposed from her position. Bending over the way she was, her full breasts were nearly coming out her blouse, the dark nipples clearly visible. Returning to the driving, Gaza felt vastly pleased with himself for choosing Allison. Sex was great, but a wife who could fire a blaster was worth a hundred times more than some dumb slut as beautiful as the moon but whose only talent was spreading her legs.

Suddenly, Allison snapped her fingers for his attention.

"What is it?" he demanded gruffly.

The mute woman gestured to the east and flipped over a hand until it was palm up.

Gaza frowned angrily. Dawn was near, eh? Nuking hell, they hadn't traveled anywhere near the number of miles he had wanted. But the APC had broken down several times, and once during repairs they had been attacked by a swarm of millipedes. Damn mutie insects were harder than hell to chill, and only their rapid-fires had held them off long enough for Gaza to fix the diesel engine and get the APC rolling again. Little bastards still tried to get in through the air vents and had to be shot off with precious ammo. Damn the Core and their pet muties!

"Okay, I'll find us some shade to rest in during the day," the baron said, squinting through the ob port. "In the lee of a sand dune, or something."

From experience he knew that driving the metal vehicle in the desert sun made it hot enough to ace a norm. They would have to drive only after sundown, and sleep during the day. That would put them at a disadvantage, since the headlights would give away their position for miles, but there was nothing he could do about that.

On the other hand, it would make tracking the outlanders a lot easier. His original idea had been to drive north into New Mex and take over some ville as their new baron. But Allison had vetoed that plan and insisted they go to the south, directly on the trail of Ryan and the others. Actually, this pleased Gaza greatly. As much as he wanted to be a baron again, revenge on the outlanders would be even better. Besides, the man knew it was always wise to follow the advice of the doomie.

Soon enough he would find the outlanders. Gaza only hoped that Allison had the machine gun operational by then. He didn't want Ryan and the others merely dead; he wanted them torn into pieces too small for even the scorpions to eat. Mutilation, rape and bloody torture would have been better, but there was no time for that. Even as he hunted for the people on horseback, the sec men from his former ville might be hunting after him, as well. And they would want to do to Gaza exactly what he wanted to do to Ryan. However, his wives would never allow that to happen.

As if sensing these thoughts, Allison turned away from the gun port she had been watching and nodded at her husband. Gaza felt his skin crawl slightly at the idea that the mutie could be reading his thoughts, and turned to concentrate on the driving. The removal of their tongues had been done simply to protect his secrets, yet it also made each of his wives oddly loyal to him, as faithful as dogs, and he trusted their judgment implicitly.

Spewing great columns of bluish smoke, the APC angled away from the salt flats and into the rolling dunes seeking shelter from the oncoming daylight. Soon enough Gaza would find the others. Horses had to rest, but the APC could drive nonstop all night long. There was no possible escape for the outlanders from his war wag, the deadly machine gun and his doomie wife.

By tomorrow midnight, they should be dead at his feet, and then he could get back to his plan of seizing another ville to rule and continuing his war against the Trader.

AS THE REST of the companions rushed to her side, Krysty bent to sniff at her hand. There was no odor of any kind, but there could be no other logical reason for the horse's violent death except poison.

"What in hell happened?" Mildred demanded, approaching the corpse with a drawn blaster. If the physician had learned anything living in the Deathlands, it was to approach every situation as if it was a life-or-death battle. All too often it was.

Ryan covered the animal with his 9 mm SIG-Sauer, while J.B. knelt by the animal and checked its neck. There was no pulse.

"It's dead," he stated, standing. "But this doesn't look like exhaustion, and it's not hot enough for heat stroke."

Dean glanced upward. "Screamwing get it?"

Instantly, the other companions raised their blasters and scanned the lightening sky for any movement. Screamwings were tiny flying muties that could send a person on the last train west in a split second with their needle-sharp beaks. Small and fast, screamwings were harder than hell to shoot down and died trying to take its victim with them.

"No, it wasn't a screamer," Krysty stated, throwing away her canteen. "I think the water is poisoned."

"All canteens?" Jak asked frowning deeply, his own blaster resting comfortably in his good hand. The blued steel shone like polished violence in the dim morning glow.

She shook her head. "No, I drank from that before, and so did my horse. It's the big water bag."

"Must be incredibly powerful toxins to cause this severe a reaction in so large an animal," Mildred said in a clinical manner. "My guess would be a neurotoxin of some kind. Heavy metals and such would never work this fast."

At those words, Krysty froze in the process of wiping her hand dry on her leg. Now the women knelt and scrubbed her palm with the salty sand until the skin was bright pink. Then she spit in her palm and wiped it clean again. Seeing the actions, Doc handed her a spare moist towelette from the opened MRE, and she cleaned both hands thoroughly.

"Calm down, it's okay," Mildred said, holstering her piece. "If the chemicals haven't been absorbed through the pores by now, I'd say you're safe."

"Are you sure?" Krysty asked anxiously, her fiery hair relaxing back into gentle waves.

Kneeling by the dead animal, Mildred peeled back an eyelid to examine the pupils. They were fully dilated, but the creature could have glanced at the rising sun before dying. Drawing a knife, she pried open the mouth to inspect the tongue. There was no discoloration or marked lividity. Interesting.

"Am I sure?" she said honestly. "Not without an autopsy. Maybe the horse had heartworms."

Jak snorted at that. "Dog get, not horse."

"People, too," Mildred corrected.

Tucking away his LeMat, Doc bowed his head and muttered something in the preDark language he called Latin that sounded like a poem or a prayer.

Keeping his weapon in hand, Ryan went over to the leather water bag lying in the sand beside the dead animal. "That was the bag we took from the stable," he said, scowling, nudging the bag with the bulbous tip of the silenced blaster. The fluid inside sloshed about like water, and there were no telltale secondary motions of anything alive inside the sack. It had been a long-shot idea, but it never hurt to check.

"Can't be the same. I drank from that bag," Dean started hesitantly, then pointed and said. "No, wait, it was the smaller bag on Doc's horse."

"You triple sure?" Ryan asked sternly, squinting his good eye.

"Yeah, Dad, I'm sure."

"Good. Then that water is clean," J.B. said gruffly.

"Jak, what about your water?" Ryan demanded.

"Not used mine," Jak said, patting the heavy bag hanging from the rear of his saddle. "Drank canteen before."

Grabbing her satchel off the pommel of her mount, Mildred strode to the other horse and removed the bag as if it were a ticking bomb. Pouring some of the water onto the ground, she sniffed, then removed a small swimming-pool testing kit and ran a sample. It wasn't much, but all that she had and it did give accurate results within a limited spectrum. Filling a plastic tube,

Mildred added a few drops of chemicals and the water promptly turned a bright orange, and then went clear.

"Damn, the water neutralized the acid immediately," she reported, holding the vial to the sunlight. "This is contaminated with a base chemical of some kind. There's no way to tell for sure, but I would guess it's scorpion venom."

Doc raised an imperious eyebrow. "Ridiculous! Venom strong enough to kill a horse, madam?"

"These things like the daylight, instead of the night like a normal scorpion," she reminded him. "And the ones caged back at Rockpoint were the largest I've ever seen. Who knows what other attributes may have mutated since the nukecaust?"

"Egad," Doc rumbled, worrying the silver lion's head of his swordstick. There was a sharp click, and the decorative head slid back to reveal several inches of shiny steel hidden inside the stick, then he slammed it back into place with a locking snap. "By the Three Kennedys, this is why those water bags were hanging near the horses!"

"A trap," Dean said solemnly, scratching at his cheek.

"Makes sense," Ryan grunted. "A bag of water just hanging there for anybody to take in a town where folks were killed over a thimbleful? It was just bait for horse thieves to take along. Then the locals could simply watch for buzzards in the sky and get their horses back."

"Along with the blasters and other possessions of the thieves," Dean added thoughtfully.

"Smart," Jak drawled in wry acknowledgment, brushing back his snowy white hair.

"Millie, anything we can do to clean the water?" J.B. asked hopefully. "Boil it or something?"

"Too bad not have bread," Jak said. "Drain radiator fluid through stale bread and make drinkable. Not know if work this."

"Piss might do it," Ryan said calmly.

J.B. made a rude noise at that, but Mildred agreed.

"That might work," the physician said. "Urine neutralizes scorpion venom in an external bite, so logically it should also work on tainted water. Basic chemistry there, bases and acids." Then she paused and frowned. "However, for water this strongly polluted, it might require so much urine that the resulting mixture would be rendered totally undrinkable afterward."

"Well, I would certainly think so," Doc muttered softly, trying to contain his revulsion.

Titling her head, Mildred smiled. "I agree. Tobacco also works on scorpion bites, but with the same results. The water might be safe, but nobody would willingly drink it until absolutely necessary."

"Which might become the case," Krysty said. "We're low on water now, and have no idea how much farther it is to reach the lowlands where the Trader travels."

"Couple of hundred miles at least," Ryan growled, looking into the distance. "From now on, we piss in that bag and save it for boiling later."

"Much much later," J.B. said.

"We can only do this once," the physician warned. "We're already dehydrated, and the ammonia content of our urine will be dangerously high."

"Better that than death," Ryan said grimly.

"Okay, do we have anything else that hasn't been checked over yet?" J.B. said wryly, hooking both thumbs into his belt. "We could be hauling a dozen more boobies among our stolen supplies."

Quickly, the companions laid out their belongings and checked over every item carefully, but no other traps were discovered. That was good news, but it was tempered by the fact that the companions were now dangerously low on water and reduced to only five horses for seven adults.

"Mebbe take turns riding," Jak suggested hesitantly, rubbing his wounded arm. "Horses too tired for double riders."

Just then a large black scorpion scuttled into view from under a rock, snapping its pinchers happily at the heat of the morning sun. Standing nearby, Dean moved fast and crushed it under his combat boot, grinding the heel to make the little killer was thoroughly aced.

"Okay, no time to waste. We leave on foot," Ryan commanded brusquely. "We need shelter and we need it bastard fast! We're all going to walk for a while. That will let the horses get some rest in case serious trouble arrives and we have to ride again. If that comes, Dean goes with Jak on the stallion, J.B. with Mildred on the big gelding.''

Krysty stepped to the man and rested a hand on his shoulder.

''Correction, lover,'' she said sternly. ''We walk, but you ride. Each of us caught some sleep yesterday, but you haven't in days. We're alive now because of that, but right now I doubt if you could shoot the side of a barn with your longblaster even if you were fragging inside the building.''

Inhaling sharply, Ryan felt his hair-trigger temper flare at the words, but then found himself too bastard weary to even argue. She was right. Even with the coffee working, he was on his last legs. Nodding assent, the man forced himself to climb into the saddle and squeeze his feet into the small stirrups. This had to have originally been a woman's horse. Mebbe one for the baron's many wives. Unless Gaza himself was a very small man. It was well trained and bridle-wise, but didn't really seem to like a rider as large as Ryan.

''Okay, I'm on point,'' J.B. said adjusting his fedora and swinging his Uzi around to the front. He worked the bolt, chambering a round for immediate use. ''Two-yard spread. Jak and Dean, take turns leading your mount. Doc, you're rear guard. Stay razor.''

"I am honored! And shall remain as sharp as the Sword of Damocles!"

Annoyed, J.B. glanced at Mildred.

"That means yes," she stated.

Guiding the horses by the reins, the companions started across the dune and down the other side. Ahead of them stretched the endless vista of the desert, the salty ground rippling from the gentle morning breeze.

Allowing his tense muscles to slowly relax, Ryan swayed in the saddle. Slowly stooping his shoulders, Ryan expertly leaned forward, his hands crossed at the pommel, with the reins looped securely over twice. Slowly allowing himself to succumb to the sweet siren call of sleep, the big man's eyes soon closed.

Walking close by, Krysty smiled as she heard a soft sound of snoring. Brave didn't make a warrior bulletproof, and even men of iron needed to eat and sleep.

AS THE COMPANIONS disappeared over the southern horizon, the salt and sandy ground of the big dune broke apart and strange figures rose from its depths, shaking off the loose debris. Standing taller than any norm, the beings were bipedal, but impossibly skinny, with every inch of their bodies wrapped in dirty rags that completely hid any possible view of their anatomy.

More of the creatures arrived from belowground, as their leader, who carried a long spear, bowed once to

the sun, then gestured violently at the dead horse. Now
the others pulled curved daggers from within their rags
and began to dissect the corpse, the tainted blood flowing in rivulets down the slopes of the dune.

Chapter Three

Fleeting visions of a bad mat-trans jump boiled in Ryan's dreams, constantly punctuated by distant blasterfire. Or great preDark war machines charging after the man with their cannons clicking on shells no longer there. Or sec hunter droids snapping deadly scissors, or...

With a start, Ryan awoke to find both hands tied to the pommel of the saddle. For a split second, he thought they had been captured and his blood surged with adrenaline, his wrists breaking apart the twine as he clawed for the blaster on his hip. But surprisingly, it was there and as the mists of sleep faded away, Ryan saw the other companions leading their horses along the brightly lit desert. Fireblast, just a bad dream.

"Good afternoon, lover," Krysty said, glancing sideways. "Nice to have you back."

Afternoon? Had he really slept that long? The dull ache in his back from sleeping in the saddle seemed to confirm that, and the sun was high overhead, the air stifling with heat.

Licking his dry lips, Ryan started to reply when a faint clicking sound reached his ears. When he realized that his usually silent rad counter was the source, he flipped his lapel and took a look, recoiling in shock when the counter revealed they were in a lethal zone. They were walking directly into a nuke crater!

"Everybody freeze!" Ryan roared, grabbing the reins and bringing the horse to an abrupt halt. "We're hot!"

"What?" J.B. replied gruffly, turning. Placing a thumb behind his lapel, he flipped the cloth. "See that? Mine is— Dark night! I put it in my backpack at the ville for safekeeping!"

J.B. hurriedly snatched the pack from the saddle pommel, rummaged inside for a moment and removed a small lacquered box. Inside lay the precious rad counter. "Hard at the edge of the danger zone," J.B. announced, his voice strained.

Suddenly, the companions went pale, each person straining to sense the invisible death pouring from the featureless ground around them.

"Which way?" Krysty asked, climbing onto her horse.

Taking the rad counter in hand, Ryan turned about in every direction until pointing due west.

"That way!" he said, kicking his horse into a trot.

Scrambling onto their mounts, the rest of the companions moved with a purpose and galloped after the man as if their lives depended on it. Nothing was said for almost an hour as they raced for safety away from the lethal rads, the featureless landscape flying beneath the pounding hooves of the animals. No predator was visible to the horses, but they seemed to be able to sense the terror of their riders, and were putting their hearts into a desperate race for life.

Reaching an embankment, the companions slowed their mounts to hurriedly walk down to the lower desert floor. Now patches of rock could be seen amid the salty sand of the desert, and Ryan called a halt to check his rad counter.

"This is far enough," Ryan said in relief. "We're clear."

Exhaling in relief, the companions brought the horses to a ragged stop, then walked them about until facing one another.

"Out rads?" Jak demanded, slipping to the ground from behind Dean. During the long morning walk, Mildred had taken the opportunity to clean and bandage his bad arm. It was sore, but he could use it again to fire a blaster if necessary.

"Seems so. I'm reading only normal background count," Ryan said, aiming the rad counter around just to double-check.

When satisfied, he attached it to his collar again.

Gazing back the way they had just come from, J.B. removed his hat to fan himself. "Damn good thing you woke up when you did. I was strolling us smack into a rad pit hot enough to chill us all."

"Radiation," Dean growled. "Hot pipe, I'd rather fight stickies."

Stickies were the curse of the Deathlands. The size of a norm, stickies had sucker pads on their fingers and feet, and could walk walls and ceilings like insects. They attached their suckers to a person's flesh and ripped off pieces until the screaming victim was only a mass of still beating organs. Ryan had once seen a sec men attacked by a swarm of stickies take a blaster and put a round into his own heart rather than be savagely torn apart by the muties.

"Gotta go," Jak said, hitching up his belt. "Give bag."

Krysty passed it to him and the teenager went behind a dune to answer the call of nature. A few minutes later he returned and passed her back the sloshing container.

"Here," Dean said, offering his canteen.

Jak nodded in thanks and took only a sip, then passed the canteen back and placed a smooth pebble in his mouth. It helped a person to lose less moisture by keeping his or her mouth shut, and the salvia generated eased the pangs of thirst.

"Which way now, my dear Ryan?" Doc asked, shifting in the saddle.

His long hair ruffling in the dry wind, Ryan checked the rad counter carefully.

"West and southwest are clear," he said in a measured tone. "I'd say south by west as that heads us closer to the Grandee."

"River means fishing and means villes," J.B.

agreed, pulling out his minisextant from under his shirt to shoot the sun and check their position.

"Okay, we're about four hundred miles from the redoubt on the Grandee," he said, tucking the priceless tool away. "Might as well make that our goal, and we can expand our search for the Trader from there."

"Hell, he might be there," Ryan growled, chucking the reins to start his horse trotting.

As the companions rode their mounts at an easy pace, the sun reached azimuth directly overhead and started to turn the world into a searing crucible. The sparkling sand reflected the heat until it was difficult to see from the reflections, and the salt infused the atmosphere, making it difficult to breathe as every breath tasted of salt and leached moisture from their flesh. Knives were used on spare clothing to form masks, and the companions regularly wet a rag and wiped down the faces of their horses. The animals were starting to heave deeply, near total exhaustion, but until shade was found, there could be no respite.

As they walked the horses, Mildred reached into her satchel and pulled out a small leather-bound notebook to jot down the location of the radiation field. The notebook was a recent acquisition, and she often wrote her thoughts into the journal. Someday when she had the chance, Mildred planned to organize the material to leave behind a sort of legacy for others: medical knowledge, a true history of the Deathlands and its people, danger zones, etc. Perhaps nobody would ever read her words, but she felt compelled to record her observations.

The hours passed under the baking sun, and then cool relief came as a swirl of storm clouds expanded across the sky, blotting out the sun with unnatural speed. Now lightning crashed amid the purple-and-orange hellstorm above the world, and the companions paused for a terrifying minute as there came the strong smell of sulfur on the wind. Quickly pulling out the heavy plastic shower curtains taken from the redoubt a few days earlier, the companions braced themselves for an acid rain storm, but the reek faded away with the dry desert breeze and they relaxed. Muties and sec men could be fought, rad pits avoided, but when the acid rain came only stone, steel or heavy plastic could save a person from burns. And if the acid was strong enough, the plastic would be useless.

Doc suddenly gasped in delight as he spied a touch of green on the side of a small dune almost hidden from sight behind a much larger mound.

"Eureka," Doc cried, and started to gallop in that direction.

With only his eyes showing through his makeshift mask, Dean scowled. "Trouble?" he demanded, the words muffled by the cloth.

"Good news," Mildred translated.

Gesturing grandly, Doc cried out in delight. "Behold, ambrosia!"

Slowing his horse, Ryan looked over the area then checked his rad counter just to be sure. In the lee of the rocky dune was a small stand of cactus—Devil Fork, they were called because they resembled a fork with its handle stabbed into the ground. Some barrel cactus were mixed in, but mostly it was all Devil Fork. The husk of the desert plants was as hard as boot leather and covered with needles that could stab through a canvas glove. Dangerous stuff, but their roots went down for hundreds of feet into the sand, and the delicious pulp inside was a sponge filled with sweet water.

"We're saved. That's more than enough to replace the poisoned water," Mildred said in relief, and climbed from her horse to walk to the cactus stand.

Pulling out a knife, she debated where would be the best place to start to cut when a breeze shifted the sand in a small whirlwind and the glint of steel reflected from amid the lush greenery. Now Mildred found herself staring at the bleached white bones of a human skeleton. Only a few tatters of clothing covered the body, and a scattering of brass cartridges and a homemade blaster made of bound iron pipe and wooden blocks lay near the hand.

Leaning forward, Ryan scowled from his horse. "He died fighting," he said slowly. "Must have been an animal, something too big to reach him behind the cactus needles."

"Why an animal and not a person?" Mildred asked,

then she answered herself. "Of course. Because a man would have taken the rounds afterward. Check."

"Doesn't really matter, chilled is chilled," Ryan stated pragmatically. "More importantly, those rounds look intact to me. Might be live."

"Any chance they're .44 calibers?" Doc asked hopefully. He was well stocked with black powder and miniballs for the LeMat, but he was dangerously low on bullets for the Webley.

J.B. adjusted his glasses. "I'd say those were .45. Sorry, Doc."

The old man shrugged in resignation.

As J.B. started divesting himself of bags and weapons, Mildred walked over to the plants.

"Don't bother, John," Mildred said, starting to reach between the cactus, "I'll get them."

But as she knelt in the sand, there was a whispery sound and the companions turned to see an incredibly thin figure rise from the desert sand and lurch forward to hurl a spear directly at Mildred!

Caught by surprise, the woman didn't react in time and the metal rod went straight past her, coming so close she could feel the wind of its passage. Then she dived aside and rolled over, drawing her .38 ZKR when there came a high-pitched keen and the cactus burst apart, writhing green tendrils streaming into view from inside the plant. Moving like uncoiling snakes, the tendrils stabbed for Mildred, and she cut loose with her blaster just as the rest of the companions did the same.

The Devil's Fork screamed even louder as the hail of lead punched a dozen holes through its stalks and branches, one of the tendrils getting blown off the main trunk. Thin pink "blood" gushed from the wounds, and the mutie went wild, every tendril thrashing about and grabbing for the nearby norms.

A horse was caught in the throat by a tendril, its barbed needles embedding deep in the flesh like fishhooks and dragging the screaming animal closer. Doc slashed out with his sword and cut through the ropy tendril, a well of pink ichor gushing from the wound. Another grabbed Jak around the neck, but as it tightened its grip, the tendril fell apart, severed by the razor blades hidden in the camou covering of the teenager's jacket.

J.B. aimed and fired his shotgun as the companions moved away from the bizarre killer, the keening plant jerking as it was hit by another barrage of lead. Then a deafening report split the day and the main trunk erupted at ground level, the booming echo of the explosion rolling along the dunes like imprisoned thunder.

Lowering the smoking barrel of the Holland & Holland Nitro .475 Express, Krysty broke the breech, the two spent shells popping out to fall away as she thumbed in two more.

Revealed amid the smashed skeleton and torn pieces

of the cactus was a pulsating wound of exposed organs, ligaments and tendons. Ryan fired two more rounds from his SIG-Sauer directly down the gullet of the creature and it went still, the pumping ichor slowing to a mere trickle and then stopping completely.

"Another mutie plant." Dean scowled, dropping the spent clip from his blaster and slipping in a fresh one.

"Animal, not plant!" Jak cursed, using a knife to pry away the needle covered bits of the creature still clinging to his jacket. Oddly, it reminded him of the hellish ivy-covered town in Ohio where they nearly lost Krysty.

"Damn good camouflage," Mildred said, shakily reloading her blaster and pocketing the empty brass for later reloading. "Certainly fooled me into thinking it was merely a plant."

"But *he* knew," Ryan said, the barrel of his blaster now aimed rock steady at the stranger wrapped in rags.

Doc swung the LeMat's barrel in the same direction. The skinny person said nothing at those actions, simply standing there in silence, the dry wind tugging at the tattered ends of its wrappings.

"He saved Millie's life with that spear," J.B. said, racking the pump on his shotgun to chamber a fresh round.

"Unless he meant to ace her and that was a miss," Ryan pointed out.

"Until proved otherwise," Doc pronounced, "the enemy of my enemy is still my goddamn enemy."

Thumbing back the hammer on her .38 ZKR target pistol, Mildred briefly gave the old man a puzzled look, then returned to the matter at hand. This wasn't the time and place to find out where that paranoid quote had come from.

Just then the horse attacked by the underground mutie fell to its knees and started to shake. Ryan never took his eye off the stranger, but since it was his horse Doc rushed over to see what was the problem. As he got close, the scholar could see that the needles of the mutie were still sunk deep into the throat of the horse, red blood flowing from the severed end of the tendril. By the Three Kennedys, he thought, the piece of the dead mutie was acting like a tap and draining all of the blood from the horse!

Whipping out his eating knife, Doc tried to figure out where to begin trying to remove the needles in the horse's throat when the animal gently lowered its head to the sandy ground as if it were going to sleep, then simply stopped breathing. Almost immediately, the blood ceased to flow on to the salty ground.

Standing helpless near the dead beast, Doc blinked moist eyes at the sight for a moment, then drew in a sharp breath and turned away.

"I am impressed. Drinkers are very hard to kill," the stranger spoke unexpectedly, his words dry and raspy as if spoken through a long tunnel. "If I had known your iron weapons worked, I would not have revealed myself.''

"So it could drag us all down for dinner?" Ryan growled in a voice like granite. "It lived underground, and so do you. This seems pretty straightforward to me. So what was the deal? It hauls us down and you share in the food?''

The being tilted his head. "You walk the surface," he said. "Does that make you friends of the rattler and the stickie?''

"Fair enough," Ryan said, easing his stance but not turning away the blaster. "So who are you?"

As if in reply, a thrilling whistle came from the stranger, and the sand behind him shifted as more of the beings rose into view from belowground. Even as the companions aimed their collection of blasters at the newcomers, dozens more of the wrapped people came from the sand, then even more on both sides. Turning about slowly, Ryan and the others saw they were now surrounded by an army of the beings, every one of them armed with a needle-tipped metal spear or sicklelike longknifes. The ebony blades were worn from constant use, the handles stained with dried blood.

The figures stood at average height, sporting two legs, two arms and head, but each was so heavily wrapped in strips of loose cloth it was impossible to tell if they were men or women, even if they were norms or muties.

"I am Alar," the first stranger said, "the leader of the Core."

Even through the thick wrappings, Ryan could hear the capital letter being used. The Core, eh? That could mean anything. But there was something oddly familiar about how the being held the short spears in his bandaged hands, and Ryan grunted softly as he recognized the military postures from the guards at the Anthill. These were the descendants of army troops, copying the port arms and such of drilling troops. Only they were armed with spears instead of longblasters. The Core as in U.S. Marine Corps, or a nuclear core? Could be either way, and there was no way of telling.

"I'm Ryan," he said gruffly, then introduced the rest of the companions.

Alar bowed to each, the rest of the Core copying the gesture. At the end, the masked people put away their weapons, and the companions hesitantly did the same. Since they were outnumbered by a fifty-to-one ratio, it seemed prudent to stay on smooth terms with these…people?

"Here you go," Dean said, walking up with the spear from the Drinker and offering it to the Core leader.

Nodding his head, Alar took the weapon and stabbed it twice into the ground to clean the tip of the sticky pink blood.

"Thank you, small one. A weapon returned is a

bond of peace with my people. I grant you free passage through our desert until the next moon.''

"The blessings of Gaia upon you, great leader," Krysty said, making a gesture in the air too quick to be described.

With a scowl, Ryan asked, ''And what happens if we're still here by the next moon?''

Alar shrugged. ''Then you must leave or join the Core forever.''

''Yeah? Nothing more?''

A warm breeze tasting of salt blew over the crowd, making the horses shift about to hide their faces.

''No, Ryan of the horse riders,'' Alar said calmly, the sand dancing at his feet. ''We are a peaceful people with only one enemy. We welcome all to join the Core.''

Or else you prefer to strike from behind, Ryan thought to himself.

''Sounds good,'' J.B. admitted, rubbing his mouth on the back of a hand. ''How about we go to your ville and talk. Any chance you got water to trade? We have a few spare blasters that are better for acing a Drinker than those pig-stickers you're carrying.''

''Ville?'' Alar muttered, crouching so that he rested on his heels. ''We have no stone place. The desert itself is our home. We live in the sand, on the sand. We are of the sand!''

The entire crowd of masked people shouted a word in an unknown language.

Doc, Mildred and Krysty exchanged glances. They didn't know the language, but the tone was familiar. The Core was chanting like a choir in a church. This Alar was more than their leader; he was probably also the local high priest.

"However, we can offer you drink and food," Alar said, gesturing at the crowd.

Scurrying to obey, another being stepped forward to hand Ryan a clear plastic jug. The fluid inside was blue in color, almost a topaz.

"Doesn't look like water," Ryan said suspiciously.

"There is no water here," a tall member of the Core announced sternly, thumping his spear twice on the ground at the word. "We drink *jinkaja*."

"Drink," Alar said in a friendly tone. "Drink and live forever!"

That stopped Ryan cold. "What do you mean, forever?" he demanded hostilely.

Still holding the spear, Alar spread his bandaged hands wide. "We do not die with the passing of the decades like you norms. The members of the Core are as ageless as the sands!"

"Right," Mildred said slowly, taking the container from Ryan. The physician didn't know whether that was a sales pitch, but either way she wanted no part of this *jinkaja* stuff.

While the others waited, Mildred inspected the blue fluid carefully. It was thick with a high viscosity, almost like a British beer. Removing the cap, she took a careful sniff. The smell was very pleasant, slightly citrus in nature.

"How is it made?" Dean asked, copying the squatting position of the Core leader.

"From the essence of the Holy Ones," Alar said, bowing his head. "Once consumed you can take no other nourishment, not animal flesh or water. But you live forever!"

"As long as we keep drinking it," Ryan said, feeling his temper rise like a red madness. With a major effort of will, he forced it under control for the moment.

Since Alar was covered in the cloth rags, it was impossible to read his facial expressions, but his body language was that of a parent explaining something very basic to a child. "Of course. To live forever you must drink forever. It is the way of the Core."

Pale red ants had discovered the dead mutie and were now covering its remains, carrying away tiny pieces of its flesh. Then a scorpion appeared and began to feast upon the ants using both pincers. In a flash of movement, a Core member thrust out a spear and impaled the scorpion, lifting it high for the others to see until the mortally wounded creature went limp. Now he lowered the spear and shook off the tiny corpse so that it fell amid the ants. Without hesitation, the bugs swarmed over their dead enemy and began tearing it apart along with the mutie.

"Made from Drinker?" Jak asked scowling. "That Holy One?"

Throwing back his head, Alar actually laughed. "No, top-walker, it is made from the essence of the night-walkers, whose numbers are greater than their legs. Greater than the grains of sand!"

So the Holy Ones had a lot of legs, eh? Suddenly, Krysty recalled where she had seen blood almost the exact same color as this *jinkaja*.

"Millipedes," she said in disgust. "It's made from triple-cursed millipede blood."

The crowd of masked people began to mutter at that, and more than one shifted their grip on a weapon.

"How dare the filthy top-walkers to defile the Holy Ones!" the tall Core member shouted. "Punishment!"

For a moment the world seemed to spin, and Ryan felt nauseous as if he had just emerged from a bad jump. As his vision cleared, he could see the others were also reeling slightly, Dean and Doc having both dropped their blasters onto the burning-hot salt. Only Krysty seemed unaffected, but her hair was writhing like he had never seen before.

"Stop!" Alar shouted, and the word seemed to resonate in both mind and ears.

Instantly, the queasy feelings were gone as if they had never existed and Ryan pulled out the SIG-Sauer again, the handle slick with the sweat from his shaking hand. The damn Core was ruled by doomies of some sort! Muties with mental powers. Mildred sometimes argued that they weren't actually muties, but the next step in evolution unlocked by the cataclysm of sky-dark.

"Silence, Kalr," the leader demanded. "It is not for you to decide."

"It is the law!" Kalr shouted. "All drink or they must die!"

Doc and Dean bent to recover their weapons, but the rest of the Core seemed to be paying no attention to the outlanders. The group was splitting apart into two groups of about the same size.

"The law says they must drink or leave," Alar corrected sternly as he pressed the shaft of his spear. With a metallic sound, razor-sharp blades snapped out along the entire length. The mirror-bright steel reflected the harsh sunlight like tortured rainbows. "And I have given my personal word they have until the next moon!"

"Useless! Pointless!" Kalr shot back, his own staff blossoming with similar razors. "They drink or die!"

"That is not what the law says."

"Then the law is wrong!"

"You challenge the law!" Alar said in a flat tone, the crowd of beings behind the leader muttering angrily as more shafts snapped out blades.

Moving as carefully as if in a mine field, the companions were edging closer to their horses. This had every mark of a civil war, and those staffs could tear a norm apart with their razor teeth. On top of which a fight of doomies was something nobody wanted to be near.

"I challenge you!" Kalr shouted, throwing his staff into the ground.

A dry breeze blew over the rocks as Alar stared at the younger being, then with slow calculated care, the leader raised his staff high and also plunged it deep into the ground.

"Accepted!" he roared.

Now the rest of the Core moved away from the combatants, and the horses started nickering in fear. Without comment, the companions retreated from the two beings only seconds before the whole world seem to whirl once more, and the companions fell helpless to the ground, their minds exploding with visions of violent death and chaotic madness.

Chapter Four

Rockpoint was melting.

Holding a large duffel bag in both arms, Alexander Hawk struggled through the waist-deep water. The man was wide with muscle, not fat, his features oddly flat as if there were a lot of Oriental or American Indian blood in his heritage, or just a touch of mutie. His long black hair was held back in a ponytail with a ornately tied length of rawhide, his boots were some kind of lizard skin and a brace of pistols rode protectively behind the buckle of his gun belt, the handles turned out for a fast draw. The blue head of a scorpion tattoo peeked from under his shirt, and the scars marring his body were too numerous to count.

Towering high above the ville was the water spout rising from the destroyed temple of the Scorpion God. Scowling at the sight, Hawk sloshed around a corner of a sagging building as he headed for the front gate. As the chief sec man of the ville, Hawk had known the water shortage was a lie concocted by Baron Gaza to control the ville's population. They had to obey his every command, or else he cut off their water ration.

The plan was brilliant, simple and brutal. It had worked for years and would have for a lot more.

Then those damn outlanders came riding into town and blew the temple, cracking open some sort of a preDark pip large enough to drive a truck into! Now the entire ville was flooded, the houses and buildings and barracks made of sun-dried adobe brick were literally dissolving under the never-ending rain from the gushing water column in the center of the ville. Most of the people had already fled into the desert, but the ocean of water was right behind them, pouring like a river through the gaping hole in the ville wall, and spreading out across the Great Salt in every direction. Rivulets of trickling water were becoming shallow creeks, and several nearby depressions had filled into small ponds. Hawk had no idea when the torrent rising from the temple would stop, mebbe never. Mebbe the preDark river was connected to some freshwater sea and would continue pouring into the Great Salt until it was an inland ocean again the way the wrinkles said it had once been in ancient times, millions of years before skydark.

Tripping over something unseen below the muddy surface, Hawk almost dropped his bundle and tightened his hold on the heavy bag. The clouded water was filled with loose floating items from the disintegrating ville—straw, wooden spoons, some bits and pieces of preDark plastic and a lot of drowned scorpions. The little bodies bobbed about like veggies in a soup, and it broke the man's heart to see so many of his beloved servants lifeless in the swirling muck.

Then he saw a large black scorpion perched precariously on a dead child. With a shout of delight, he scooped up the tiny desert dweller and it instantly stung him, the barbed tail struck deep into his hand. Hawk grunted at the pain and put the creature on a shoulder for safekeeping. The scorpion dug in its legs and grabbed his shirt collar in self-preservation.

Ever since he was a child, Hawk knew he was different from most folks, maybe a mutie of some kind, because he was completely immune to most poisons. He used this ability to make others fear him by always carrying around a lethal black scorpion, the giants of the desert who were five times bigger than their little red cousins. More than once that had saved his life, and it was how he became the sec boss in Rockpoint. People were terrified of a man who got stung a dozen times and it didn't even faze him. As always, fear meant power, and now that the baron had fled, he had been their first choice to be the new baron.

It was a bitter victory, though, since soon there would be nothing to rule. Not here anyway, but he would find another ville, and with the bundle in his arms and his few remaining sec men, Hawk would rule as baron yet! Then someday he would find former Baron Gaza and chill the man with a knife, twisting it slowly in his guts until he begged for death, then twist some more.

With a groan, another building tilted sideways, and Hawk splashed hurriedly out of the way as the gaudy house fell apart, the crashing wall forming a wave that pushed the sec boss helplessly along until he slammed into the base of the keep. The impact knocked the breath from the man, and a sharp stabbing pain pierced through his shoulder, the bandaged wound in his chest suddenly leaking red blood.

Struggling to stay erect, Hawk lurched away from the keep, still holding on to the heavy bag. Made of preDark brick and cinder blocks, not dried mud, the keep was the only structure still standing undamaged. It also used to be the home of the baron and was armed with a 25 mm cannon in perfect working condition. Not even the Trader in his armored war wags wanted to face the Scorpion's Sting, as Hawk liked to call the gun. It tracked fast and could chew through any mobile armor, treads or tires. Once a war wag was motionless, it could be easily covered with loose tree branches, or anything else that burned, and set on fire. The crew would cook alive if they stayed, or be shot the moment they crawled outside. Either way meant death.

Recalling the last time he had been inside the keep, hot rage flared in Hawk. Gaza had betrayed him, gunning down his sec boss because Hawk discovered that the baron was really a coward. Unfortunately for Hawk, he was a coward with a very fast gun and got the drop on the sec boss, but failed to finish the job properly. Now Hawk was back and hungry for revenge.

Reaching the area near the front gates, Hawk found the rest of his sec men sitting on their horses and kicking away the occasional person who begged for a ride, or for food. One man tried to take a longblaster from the boot alongside a saddle of a riderless horse, but another sec man caught the motion and fired from the hip. The would-be thief staggered backward to flop limply into the dark waters, and his companions descended upon the dying man to yank off his boots, knife and other possessions.

Since they were robbing a thief, Hawk paid no attention to them and splashed directly to the empty horse and carefully placed his bundle across the saddle. The horse whinnied at the tremendous weight and shuffled its hooves about unhappily, while Hawk lashed the bag firmly in place with lengths of rope and a few leather belts.

"All set," Hawk declared, hurrying to a second horse and climbing into the saddle.

Twelve other horses stood before the open gate of the ville, and a small wooden cart. Eight men and two women were in the saddles, all of them heavily armed with blasters from the former baron's private arsenal, the woman also carrying bulky packs of food and assorted supplies. Everything was soaking wet from the constant rain of the water plume, the roar muted to a low rumble.

"Black dust, I can't believe you got it," a sec man said, shaking his head.

"Gonna need it when we face the Trader," Hawk growled, pulling a longblaster from the boot and checking the load. "Did you get the stand?"

A burly man with a full beard grunted in assent. "Yes, sir. It was bitch and a half to drag through the mud, but we got her here."

"Good job, Mikel," Hawk said bluntly. Always compliment your troops on a tough job. It only made them work harder on the next task. Gaza was a fool. Dogs and sluts should be whipped until they obeyed, not valuable property like horses and men.

Hawk had gone after the 25 mm cannon from the keep himself. He couldn't trust anybody else not to run away with the blaster. A man could almost buy a ville with a weapon like that. Unfortunately, it couldn't be fired by hand. The recoil would have torn off a person's arms, but there was a tripod from a .50-cal that had been altered by a blacksmith. Mebbe that would work, mebbe not, but it was the only hope of controlling the monster rapid-fire.

Hawk sheathed the longblaster. "Ammo?"

"In the cart," one of the women said, jerking a thumb. "Got all we can carry from the junkyard without busting an axle. Almost a thousand rounds."

"Well done. Let's ride," Hawk said, shaking the reins. "We got some chilling to do."

"Gaza?" Wall Sergeant Henny asked, shaking the water from his face.

"For starters," Hawk growled.

As the armed sec men splashed through the sagging front gate of the dying ville, they entered a shimmering saltwater plain that spread to the distant dunes, the searing heat of the sun causing it to steam into mists as if this were the birth of a new world.

Even more than Hawk wanted Gaza screaming under his knife, the new baron needed to meet up with that black bitch who traveled with the outlanders. He had felt she was going to be trouble the moment they entered the ville, and he'd been right. Now the ville was gone, and while Ryan may have pulled the trigger, it was that bitch Mildred who loaded the blaster. Hawk planned on keeping her alive for a lot longer than Gaza, and in a lot more pain. He had once heard about some old sec men called Nazis, real preDark hardcases with some twisted ideas about revenge. Hawk liked their style and remembered some of the really good parts. Yeah, trees would grow, fed by the blood and screams of the hated woman before he finally let her go into death.

SLUGGISHLY, the companions awoke in cool shadow with a steady wind howling in their ears. Blinking at the darkness, Ryan realized it wasn't shade, but night. Craning his neck, the man saw a scattering of stars peeking through the roiling clouds of tox chems high overhead. Fireblast, how long had they been unconscious?

From what he could see, the companions were sprawled in the corner of a piece of building, the brick wall forming a triangle, with the desert wind howling around the sides. They had been moved from the dead Drinker and could be anywhere by now. Reaching for his blaster, Ryan was consoled to find the weapon still at his hip, his Steyr SSG-70 stuck through the lashings of his backpack, the saddle nearby. However, there were no signs of the horses.

Squinting against the windblown sand, Ryan could vaguely see that ahead of them lay more pieces of preDark building, the smashed windows looking across the desert like the eyes of a corpse. A thick layer of sand covered the paved street, and no structure rose more than a few stories until abruptly ending in ragged destruction. Beyond these few tattered remnants of the lost civilization, only a flat, endless desert stretched to the distant horizon.

Forcing himself to stand, Ryan shuffled over to the other companions and shook each one to rouse them from sleep. Everybody stirred easily enough, and once figuring out where they were located, immediately ran a check on their possessions. To Ryan's eye, it seemed as if their packs and bags hadn't been touched. Even the water bags were present, including the poisoned leather pouch from Rockpoint.

The wind kicked up sand and salt, and it howled

straight through one open window. Going to the empty window frame, Jak took one of the plastic shower curtains they had salvaged from the Texas redoubt as a makeshift rain poncho and used four knives to tack it in place, covering the opening. The force of the wind lessened noticeably, and the companions could fully open their eyes now without salt being blown into them.

"A plastic shower curtain is the most massively useful thing a hitchhiker can carry," Doc rumbled in amusement, deliberately misquoting an ancient novel.

"Check your things," Ryan demanded, his words making him wince. Once, very long ago, he and Finn had been involved in a drinking contest that stopped only when the ville bar ran out of shine. The next day Ryan was so sick he thought death was near and welcomed it with open arms. This was worse.

"Looks like everything is okay," Dean whispered, running his hands over a backpack. Checking his blaster, the boy used a bowie knife to open a round and inspect the greasy cordite inside. Nope, the blasters hadn't been tampered with and the ammo was live.

"Why did they take the horses?" Doc queried. "If it was to keep us here, then surely they could have bound us prisoners instead."

"Mebbe got do by choice," Jak muttered, using his good arm to run stiff fingers through his unruly mane of snowy hair. "Why do hard way, when got no choice?"

"That makes chilling sense, Mr. Lauren."

The teenager shrugged as he made sure his collection of knives was intact hidden in his clothing. His wounded arm had come out of its sling, but was still otherwise okay.

"Passive-aggressive recruitment techniques." Mildred snorted in disdain, fingering a rip in her flannel shirt where a button had come off somewhere. Probably while they were being transported to this place. "Well, that's a new one on me."

"Shh, not so loud," J.B. said, holding his glasses in one hand while massaging the side of his face. Then he noticed Krysty sitting quietly by herself. "How you doing, Krysty? You don't look so good."

Hunched over, Krysty said nothing in reply, her limp hair moving freely in the wind.

"You okay, lover?" Ryan asked gently, kneeling by her side. "I'm surprised you didn't pass out before the rest of us, since you have some mental abilities."

She glumly nodded, moving as if every atom of her body was in agonizing pain. "Worse," the redhead muttered, hanging her head.

"What do you mean?"

"I stayed awake," Krysty said woodenly. "I…saw everything. They fought each other with nightmares, demons in the mind. Alar aced Kalr with visions that drove him insane and cracked his mind until he died."

She looked up with tears streaming down her face.

"Gaia, help me, I saw it all! Everything! The things they did to each other...the...I..."

The woman began to shake violently and Ryan comforted her in his powerful arms, rocking slightly as if she were a child while the woman wept unashamedly on his chest.

"I got a pint of shine," J.B. said quietly.

"Get it," Ryan ordered softly.

"Just a minute," Mildred countered and, rummaging through her satchel, Mildred dug out a battered tin canteen and passed it around to the others. Doing a jump through a mat-trans unit always made them ill—headaches, nausea, muscle cramps, which she attributed to a disruption of the human nervous system for that split nanosecond they were pure energy being shifted from one redoubt to another. The physician had been working a cure to counter the jump sickness using alcohol, herbs and what painkiller she could scrounge in the ruins or trade spare ammo for from other healers.

The companions relaxed and slumped gratefully against the brick walls. Mildred hadn't found a potion that worked yet, but this batch seemed to be effective in countering the aftereffects of surviving a death battle between two mutie telepaths.

"Good batch, Millie," J.B. said, passing her back the canteen.

"Thanks," she replied, screwing the cap back on the empty container. "I grabbed some things back at

Rockpoint to use at the Grandee redoubt. Came in useful sooner than expected.''

Ryan agreed, and the brew had to have even worked on Krysty as her hair started to revive, and soon the woman was limp against him breathing deep and regularly.

"She should be okay," Mildred said. "Just let her sleep for as long as she wants."

"Then we get fuck out," Jak snarled, fixing the sling on his arm.

Ryan fixed the teenager with his one eye. "That loads my blaster," he agreed. "The sooner we leave the better. Don't know if I could take surviving another of their mind fights."

"I wonder if the only reason we're in this good a condition is because of the hundreds of jumps we've made," Dean said, leaning his back against the brick wall. "Sort of hardened us to getting our brains scrambled."

"Excuse me," a new voice said. "What a redoubt?"

Caught by surprise by her sudden appearance, the companions said nothing to the member of the Core standing in the doorway, holding a sagging bundle of horsehide. For a brief moment, Ryan debated chilling the masked girl, but where could they hide the body from people who traveled underground? But something had to be done and quickly. The existence of the redoubts was the greatest secret of the preDark world, and they had no intention of sharing it with anybody.

"This is a redoubt," Mildred said with a smile. "It means a fort, or a protected place, and this brick wall protects us from the wind."

"Oh," she said softly, then added, "My name is Dnal and I have some food for you. May I enter?"

Doc waved her inward. "Come in, child. This is your town after all."

Hesitantly, she did so. "You are wrong, old one," Dnal said. "This building has been given to you for your stay. None of the Core are allowed within a spear's throw."

"That looks like horsehide," Dean said. "Are our horses aced?"

"Yes," the masked girl replied, placing down the bundle. "Their minds could not handle what they saw. We carved them into food and brought the very best to you."

Unwrapping the flap of hide, J.B. found a stack of thick steaks, the flesh still dripping with fresh blood.

"I thought you folks didn't eat real food," Ryan asked.

Dnal turned to face him. "We do not, but the Holy Ones do. They can eat anything, but prefer fresh meat." Then she untied a small gourd hanging from her rag belt and placed it alongside the pile of meat. "I thought you might like some *jinkaja* to have in case you change your mind and wish to stay with us."

Trying to hide his disgust, Ryan's first impulse was to shoot the container and kick the mutie girl out of the ruins. Gaza had forced the obedience of his people by controlling their water supply; Alar and the Core did the same thing. Either way, it was just another form of slavery, and that was completely unacceptable.

"Thank you," Ryan said politely. "However, we are still considering the offer."

"If—" she paused and then rushed forward with the words "—if you're going to cook the flesh, may I stay and watch? I have never eaten food before."

Mildred patted the ground nearby, and the girl sat with the effortless grace of a ballerina. The physician wanted a better look at the Core, and this was a prime opportunity.

"First we dig a hole," Mildred said, drawing her knife, "so the wind doesn't put out the fire." And protected within the ruins, nobody should be able to see the flames. Mildred knew Gaza was still somewhere out there. Perhaps he had given up hunting the companions, but maybe not, and it was always wiser to plan on what an enemy can do, instead of what he might do.

The girl watched excitedly while Mildred got to work digging the cooking pit. Meanwhile, the rest of the companions went to check the other buildings, soon coming back with armloads of fuel, wooden tables and chairs and bookshelves to build a respectable fire. Soon the campfire was going, and Mildred roasted the meat well to prevent any parasites from being conveyed to new hosts. The smell was thick and greasy and sent waves of hunger through the companions. Their last meal had been MRE rations, and before that, cold dog stew at the ville.

"By the way," Ryan asked, turning the steaks with a whittled stick, "ever heard of a norm called the Trader?"

"Yes," came the surprising reply from the girl, who seemed as fascinated as much by the fire as what it was doing to the slabs of meat. "He is the enemy of our enemy."

"Ah, Gaza," Ryan said, taking a shot in the dark. He was local and utterly ruthless. That made him a prime candidate.

Staring into the flames, Dnal nodded. "Yes! He controls scorpions, we worship the Holy Ones. They dislike each other greatly and always battle to the death."

Well, not always, Ryan thought to himself. But here in the Great Salt it was probably true.

When the meat was dark brown and sizzling with fat drippings, Ryan carved up portions and served them. Using their U.S. Army mess kits, the companions filled the steel plates with juicy steak and started eating. The meat was stringy and difficult to chew, but it filled their stomachs and eased the growing pangs of hunger. That was more than enough for the moment.

Dnal watched their every move as if it was brand-new, and timidly accepted a roasted morsel to nibble on the edges. Through the slit in her bandages the girl had a very human-appearing mouth, tongue and teeth. Of course that meant nothing these days; muties came in every shape and size.

She inspected the food, sniffing at it for a while before taking a tiny nibble, and then popping the rest into her mouth. Chewing experimentally, Dnal almost immediately started to gag. Spitting the half-chewed meat onto the ground, she then grabbed the small gourd and deeply drank the *jinkaja* to cleanse her mouth.

"Hideous!" Dnal cried, wiping some blue juice from her mouth on the back of the wrappings covering her arms. "It was like consuming hot waste straight from the backside of some animal!"

"Definitely needs more salt," J.B. said languidly, glancing at the Great Salt desert only yards away from the ruins. If the girl understood the joke, she didn't find it amusing.

"You okay?" Mildred asked, touching Dnal's shoulder. The bones under the coverings felt human, as did the muscle play. As far as the physician could tell, this was a perfectly ordinary fifteen-year-old girl. Maybe only the minds of the Core were unique, amplified a millennium into the genetic future of humanity.

Shying away from the steaks spitting on the fire,

Dnal nodded vigorously. "I am undamaged," she said, moving her mouth as if trying to get of the terrible taste. "Merely…wiser now."

Rising, she started for the open doorway, then turned and paused, pulling a spear into view from where it had been hidden, leaning against the other side of the brick wall.

"I thank you for the hospitality," Dnal said solemnly, and gave a small bow.

Somehow it reminded Ryan of when they had jumped to Japan and tangled with those samurai and the shogun king. Each bow meant something different to them, and no outsider ever really understood what the gestures fully meant.

"We thank you and your father in return," Ryan said, giving a even smaller bow from his sitting position.

At that, Dnal tilted her masked head. "How did you know Alar was my father?" she asked quizzically.

Ryan continued eating and said nothing. As if a chief would have sent anybody else but blood kin to palaver with the outlanders visiting the tribe.

"If I may, I would like to ask a question, dear child," Doc said as casually as possible, patting his greasy mouth clean with a grayish linen handkerchief. "Can we really leave whenever we wish?"

"Of course!" Dnal answered, sounding slightly insulted that the word of the Core should be questioned, especially by meat eaters. "Go anytime, and anywhere."

Then she turned and pointed. "Except to the south. That is the blessed land, the origin of the Core and none may go except for the leader of the Core. For any others, it means death."

J.B. shot Ryan a glance, and the Deathlands warrior subtly nodded in agreement. The land to the south was probably radioactive, he thought, glancing at the rad counter on his lapel. But the device indicated that they were in a safe zone. If so, why did the Core mutate into telepaths? Was it the bug juice? Merely another reason never to touch a single drop of the stuff.

"What about those?" Dean asked, waving at the nearby ruins.

"This is where we mine for the metal of our weapons and the clothing that protects us from the sand," she said. "Explore all you wish, take anything you find."

Turning on a heel, Dnal started to walk away into the wind, the loose ends of her wrappings jerking with whipcrack snaps. Then over a shoulder she added, "It doesn't matter what you do. There is no water for a hundred miles. When your thirst is great enough, you will return to drink and join the Core." As the girl walked, she soon vanished into the darkness and the windblown sand.

"Yeah?" Jak growled, easing the safety back on the blaster in his holster. "Like hell will."

"Indeed, my taciturn friend," Doc rumbled, placing aside his mess kit. "I do believe that it would be preferable to put lead in my head then join these antediluvian freaks."

"How much water do we have?" Dean asked, wiping his hands clean on the sand and then on his pants.

"Three days," Mildred answered promptly. "Not counting the poisoned stuff we're saving for an emergency."

"How far away?" Krysty whispered in a strained voice.

Looking at the stars overhead, J.B. hazarded a guess. He wouldn't be able to shoot their exact position until the sun rose. "To reach the Grandee?" he said, rubbing his chin, "I'd say about three days on foot. If we move fast and head straight south."

"Across the forbidden zone?" Dean said, casting a glance over a shoulder at the featureless blackness stretching behind them.

"Yep."

"Damn," Mildred murmured unhappily. "We have no choice, then."

"Agreed. We better cook all of the meat tonight," Ryan said, returning to his meal. "Gonna need it when we start running for our lives at dawn."

Chapter Five

The rough brick pressed uncomfortably against Dean's cheek as he peeked through a crack in the wall. The companions had risen just before dawn and hidden themselves in the maze of old preDark ruins. His father figured that since a lot of large sections of pavement and sidewalk were still lying about, the Core wouldn't be able to travel through the sand under the dead city and would have to walk on the surface. He proved to be right when Dean spotted a group of the Core eerily rise from the loose sand a hundred yards away and then head for the location that had been their campsite.

Without the horses to carry the heavier supplies, the companions had been forced to abandon a lot of their excess possessions, the saddles for starters, extra blankets, rope tools, some of the roasted meat and most of their spare blasters, along with the large leather bag of poisoned water. His father thought that would make it look as if they were only exploring the nearby ruins for a source of water.

As the companions zigzagged into the crumbling array of structures, Krysty had found a perfect spot where they could watch the campsite and see what the Core did. Shifting his position, Dean heard a sprinkle of crumbling mortar fall to the ground and tightened his grip on the iron framework jutting from the side of the destroyed warehouse. Since he was the lightest and the smallest, Dean got the job of climbing up the smashed building and snuggling into a crack in the wall where he could sit and keep a watch.

Sure enough, a short while after dawn the Core arrived. The masked beings came in force and marched straight into the camp. Now they were going through the abandoned items of the companions, inspecting the saddles and tossing bits of spare wood onto the campfire to watch them smolder, then burst into flames. Only one Core member stood by itself—man or woman, it was impossible to tell with the thick wrappings—and surveyed the campsite critically, turning over small items with a spear. Squinting to try to see better, Dean could only guess that it was Alar from the respectful way the others acted. Then the leader of the Core pulled out a small vial from within its rags and the rest got busy.

Sons of bitches! Dean thought. So that was the plan, eh? Wiggling free of the crevice, he walked along the tilted floor until coming to a large hole, then jumped through, falling a few feet down to the next level and running along a stronger concrete floor until coming to the ragged end of the building. This entire side of the warehouse was gone, sheered and crumbling into the desert sands. However, a large dune was piled high against the outer walls and Dean skipped down the slope, using speed to stay ahead of the loose sand disturbed by his passage.

Near the bottom, Dean jumped clear of some rocks and landed on his boots near Ryan. His father had been standing guard with his longblaster at hand, ready to give cover fire if the Core spotted Dean. At the noise of his landing, the others came out from behind the rusted shell of a locomotive engine, weeds growing between the wheels, and a buzzard's nest cresting the long cold smokestack.

"Well?" his father demanded.

The boy nodded. "You got it, Dad. They come with the first light, poked around our stuff some, then poured that damn *jinkaja* stuff on the leftover horse meat and in the water bottle."

"Our own free will, my ass," Krysty snorted. She had spent a bad night fighting the demons in her memory, but the training she had received from her mother pulled her through and she had the nightmares under control. Mostly, anyway. But if the hammer fell, she was going to blow away Alar with the first round. That perverted twist was never going to be allowed access to her mind again.

"Yeah, thought so," Ryan said through clenched teeth. "I don't care if that bug juice grew me back an eye, if they catch one of us, best to do a mercy chilling rather than take a drink."

"Having to ace one of our own. Dark night!" J.B. swore.

Keeping a watch on their nest, a flock of buzzards circled high about in the cloudless sky, the morning sun already feeling ten times hotter than it did the previous day. Drawing his blaster, Ryan jacked a round from the ejector and rubbed the oily cartridge on his lips to help ease the growing thirst.

"Let's move out," he said gruffly, dropping the clip to thumb the round back in with the others. "Stay close and quiet, two-yard spread. Dean, keep that crossbow ready, Doc your sword and Jak a throwing blade. Use blasters only as a last resort. Any noise could put us in a world of hurt."

Nobody commented on the orders, as they had done such things before many times. Darting from one pile of bricks to the next, the companions stayed low and fast, keeping to the sidewalks, pieces of pavement and fallen walls for as much as possible until a few hours later they finally had reached the southern edge of the ruins. Twice along the way they discovered a hidden scorpion, and once a huge millipede. Each time, Dean tracked the muties with his crossbow, but they left the creatures alive. A fresh kill would only attract the buzzards, which could in turn summon the Core.

Now flat, open sand stretched before them, with only some angled dunes rising low on the horizon. The air still carried the sharp tang of salt, and it mixed unpleasantly with the faint stink of the rancid sweat of the companions clothing.

Placing a hand to his forehead to block the bright sunlight, Ryan studied the ground, but there were no more chucks of concrete to use to hide their tracks, not even rocks. From here they had to walk on the bare sand, even though it was the home for the Core.

"Make sure you don't fragging walk in unison," he ordered brusquely. "Stop every few yards and pat your boots softly as if it they were hot. These muties can probably hear things from underground and we gotta sound like animals. If they detect marching, they'll come in force."

"Especially with the direction we're taking," Mildred added, using a cloth to tie back her riot of beaded hair. "I just hope the land to the south actually really is forbidden for them to travel."

"Only one way to find out," Dean stated, wiping his neck with a pocket rag. "Once there, we might be safe from attack."

"If they come, spread out in a circle, not a pack," J.B. directed, checking the ammo clip in his Uzi machine pistol. "They'll be striking from underneath, so we need room to track and fire. We bunch up, and we all buy the farm."

"No prob," Krysty said, then added, "And if anybody has to piss, do it on your boot to break the force of the stream."

Testing the point of his Spanish sword on a thumb, Doc chuckled softly at that remark.

"What?" the redhead demanded.

"I beg your pardon for my uncouth laughter, dear lady," Doc said, sheathing the sword back into the ebony stick. "It had simply occurred to me that if anybody from my time had uttered such a sentence in polite society, men would have gasped, ladies fainted, children screamed, then probably been arrested and hauled off to jail."

"So nobody pissed back then, eh?" Krysty asked in a teasing manner, resting a fist on her hip.

Doc feigned horror. "Not and admitted to such an action, no, madam. Never! It was unthinkable."

"And still want go back?" Jak asked, arching a snow-white eyebrow.

"To be with my wife again, yes. But there were many good points, too, Mr. Lauren. Clean beds, hot meals and no muties." He shrugged. "But no place is perfect. Sadly for us all, there is no Shangri-La, and Brigadoon does not exist."

"But there are a lot better shitholes than this place," Ryan said bluntly, tightening the straps on his backpack. It was bastard heavy, but he had added a third belt that went around his hip to help distribute the weight. Hip straps, the pinnacle of preDark science.

"And worse, too," Ryan continued. "You know that for a fact, Doc. We found you in Mocsin, and you've been to Front Royal, which is paradise on Earth in comparison.''

Every trace of humor drained away from his features as Doc recalled the horrors done to him in that truly evil town. ''Truth indeed, old friend. I shall forever be in Trader's debt for what he did to Mocsin.''

''Yeah, Trader cleaned out that pesthole,'' J.B. added, setting the brim of his fedora against the sun. ''And he'll do the same to the Core once we link up with him.''

Pressing her canteen to a cheek, Krysty savored the coolness trying to ease her thirst without taking a drink. It was too soon to have another sip, and sucking a pebble wasn't helping much today. ''If it is the Trader,'' Krysty countered, forcing herself to lower the water container.

''It's him,'' Ryan stated with conviction, stepping onto the hot sand and starting forward at a broad gait. ''Nobody else can make so many folks so pissed off at same time.''

The brief rest break over, the companions broke ranks and spread out in a ragged line across the burning sand, the tiny salt crystals crunching underneath their boots. As the day wore on, the weary travelers stopped talking, almost ceased to think, trying to concentrate solely on placing one foot ahead of other, then break the pattern with a pause and shuffle. Sweat ran down their faces, soaking their armpits, their backs roasted dry from the blazing sun. Each tried to ignore the chafing of their backpacks and their growing thirst, savoring a delicious vision of the cool of the Grandee.

The day wore on in mindless drudgery as the companions went up and down sand dunes like driftwood riding the ocean waves. Occasionally, they would walk across black weeds to muffle their steps. Curiously, they were finding more and more local plant life, some real grass mixed in with the weeds, and a few real cacti dotting the barren landscape. While the rest kept him covered, Doc prodded the first cactus with his sword to make sure it was only a plant, and when nothing happened, the man happily cut off chunks. Badly dehydrated, the people greedily sucked the spongy pulp for every drop of sweet moisture, then very carefully placed the rinds on sloping dunes to roll far away and hide in which direction they were going. The dry wind was efficiently filling their footsteps, and even Jak wasn't sure that he could have followed anybody into the heart of the desolate land.

Refreshed from the cactus juice, the companions kept moving. The heat of the sun seeped into their bones and made their blasters almost too hot to touch with bare hands, so socks were wrapped around the grips for protection. Then Dean had to unlock his crossbow out of fear the string would break. On they moved, like cyborgs on a programmed task, heedless of anything around them, seeing only the ground before their feet.

Less than a mile later, Ryan whistled softly as he

found some more cacti. But the welcome sight turned bitter when it was discovered the plant was really a Drinker, the bones of its victims lying in plain sight.

Traveling up a gentle slope, the companions took a short break and allowed themselves a single capful of warm water.

"And take some salt," Ryan directed, grimacing at the thought.

Opening a few MRE packs, they shared the little envelopes of iodized powder. It was unpleasant, but vitally necessary. Their clothing was becoming stiff from the salt they lost by sweating so much. If it wasn't replaced, soon they would get weak, then sleepy and eventually die. Water was all a person wanted in the desert, but salt helped keep a person alive.

Pulling out his minisextant, J.B. took a reading on the sun.

"Nowhere," he announced, returning the minisextant under his stiff shirt, salt residue marking a white band across the material. "We're in the middle of nowhere and heading for abso-fragging-lutely nothing."

"I could have told that," Jak muttered, brushing his snowy hair forward to help shade his pale face from the painful sunlight.

As they stood on the crested ridge, ahead of them stretched an impossibly flat land utterly devoid of any features whatsoever. Not even a rock or a tumbleweed was in sight. Yet thick tufts of weeds and some sort of bracken lay thick along the very top of the break, almost as if marking the line of transition between the desert and the flatlands.

"E. A. Abbott, beware," Doc muttered in wry humor.

"Yeah," Mildred said, thoughtfully chewing the inside of her cheek. She recognized the reference to the 1886 fantasy novel about two-dimensional creatures discovering the 3-D world. "But this is almost too flat. Seems artificial somehow."

"Rad counter reads clean," Ryan said, aiming the lapel pin about in a slow arc for a full scan.

Pulling a compass out of his jacket, J.B. tapped the device with a fingertip. "No mag fields, either."

"Salt-fall," Jak said simply, as if that explained everything.

"Makes sense," Krysty agreed. When the nukes were coming down everywhere during skydark, quite a few of the bombs and missiles missed their coastal targets and hit in the ocean. The thermonuclear detonations created boiling tidal waves that washed inland for miles, forming flat, featureless vistas very similar to this. Yes, that seemed reasonable. This was merely a carpet of dried salt covering the desert underneath.

Stepping down from the embankment, Mildred tested her weight on the salt, then jumped a few times. Unlike the desert sand, this material neither yielded nor cracked in any way.

"Solid as rock," Ryan declared. "Just stay razor,

and go around any domes.'' Often when a salt-fall hit, there were pockets of air trapped underneath, forming low domes that would crack apart when walked upon and send a person falling for yards. Ryan never heard of anybody getting aced by a salt dome, but there was always a first time. Besides, sometimes the domes were inhabited. Mebbe that was where the Core lived, in a big dome somewhere.

''In plain sight miles,'' Jak complained sullenly, flexing his hand. A blade slipped from his sleeve at the gesture, and he absentmindedly tucked it away again. ''Not like that.''

''But we'll make better time,'' Krysty countered.

''Besides that,'' Dean added, ''if we're in view, then anybody coming after us is, too.''

Smearing a dab of axle grease from the satchel on her chapped lips, Mildred watched as Doc winced, flexing his shoulders. Jak took his bad arm out of the sling and flexed it a few times to help the circulation and keep the limb from going stiff.

''How's the back?'' she asked, tucking away the tube of grease.

''Itches like the dickens,'' Doc said, gently making a fist.

''Good. That means it's healing.''

Furrowing his brow, Doc merely grunted in reply. Pain was part of life. When it stopped, they buried you.

Climbing down the embankment, the companions

started across the flatland and found the walking much less tiring with a hard surface underfoot. As their speed increased, spirits rose. The sun was past azimuth now and the day was ebbing. Soon it would begin to get cool, and they were making good time. Even if the Core knew where they were now, it would be impossible for them to strike from below through the hard plain.

Everywhere around the companions the ground sparkled with hidden diamonds, salt crystals sometimes as large as a fist. Dean found some rusted bits of unidentifiable metal embedded in the hard ground. At a distance Mildred spotted a half-buried car tire arching up like a crochet hoop, then J.B. tripped and fell to the sound of shattering glass. Getting off the ground, the Armorer knelt again to see what he had broken.

"Nuke me, it's plastic," he said, running a hand across the satiny smooth material. "With neon lights lining the edge. I must have stepped on an intact bulb. I'd say it was some kind of a big electric sign."

"Could be an entire building buried under this," Krysty said in amazement.

"If it happened fast enough, then most of the place would be in good condition," Mildred said excitedly. Salt was a good preservative. One of the best. "Machinery, clothing, and all we have to do is dig."

"Yeah, for about a month, with our bare hands in sunlight hot enough to ignite ammo," Dean said scowling, hitching the heavy crossbow on his back. "No, thanks."

The crossbow was becoming a real burden to the boy, as the heavy weapon kept hitting him in the kidney, and he was giving serious thought to dumping the crossbow and quiver. A blaster and clips weighed a lot less, and required less maintenance, too.

"J.B., mark it on your map," Ryan directed. "Mebbe the Trader would be interested. But for right now, pulling air into our lungs is my main concern. Keep walking. We rest at night."

Stepping over the buried sign, J.B. turned away and started walking when there was a crackling sound and his leg went into the ground all the way to the knee. Panic hit the man, and as he tried to yank the limb free, cracks spread outward from the small hole with more pieces of the white ground falling away to enlarge the opening with frightening speed. Suddenly coming loose, J.B. attempted to dive away from the expanding gap, but not fast enough, and he fell into the blackness below.

"John!" Mildred screamed, reaching for the man.

Throwing himself forward, Ryan hit the cracking ground and thrust out a hand to try to grab his friend, even though he knew it was totally hopeless. Incredibly, Ryan touched cloth and he grabbed the back of the wiry man's jacket in an iron grip. Then the Armorer stood, the top of his hat only inches below the salty plain.

"Good Lord!" Doc rumbled, taking a half step forward.

In the afternoon light angling into the crevice, the companions could see that J.B. was standing on the roof of a preDark building with a rotary ventilation fan nearby. The unit was normally on top of skyscrapers to use the natural force of the wind to drive fresh air deep into the immense structures. The plastic J.B. had stepped on could now be seen as part of a rooftop billboard, the faded picture advertising some vid about a flying war wag covered with scantily clad women. The colors were faded, but otherwise the sign was in perfect condition. Beyond the edge of the roof, was stygian darkness as impenetrable as outer space.

"Only fell five feet," J.B. said with a shaky laugh. "Damn near thought I was taking the long ride."

"Climb onto the billboard," Ryan told him. "I can hoist you up from there."

But before the Armorer could move, a faint vibration shook the entire desert, and a hundred tiny puffs of dust rose from different locations across the flatland. Now a horrible stench welled from below, increasing as the cracks began to widen. Visibly, the salt-fall was shifting position, huge sections rising and falling slightly, with a crackling sound that steadily got louder.

"Oh, Christ, the pressure dropped!" Mildred cursed, in sudden realization. "When we broke the crust, it let out the ancient gases supporting the dome.

Like popping a balloon! The whole salt land is starting to collapse!''

Ryan started to speak when a hundred feet away a huge section of the sparkling white ground shook and plummeted out of sight.

"Get on the roof!" the man ordered, jumping into the hole. He landed hard, sprawling near the ventilation fan. A foot to the left, and he would have been gutted by the salt-encrusted blades.

The others were only a heartbeat behind, the white landscape crumbling under their boots. Now the crackling noise seemed to fill the world and the entire area began to quake, thin cracks shooting in every direction. Then the cracks yawned wide and the white dome broke apart completely, huge pieces of the landscape tilting sideways to expose the underside crystalline deposits, bits of fish and seaweed clinging to the irregular bottom. Coming loose, myriad pieces dropped into the reeking hurricane from below, and the crackling grew into a strident roar that steadily increased in volume and power until the companions were forced to cover their ears.

Rancid winds buffeted them from every direction, and the building violently shook, the stone and steel groaning as if in pain. It was as if the world were dying. The tempest was worse than any earthquake they had encountered, louder and more violent than the eruption of a South Seas volcano. Almost as if skydark had returned to finish the job of destroying the scourge of humanity.

Now billowing clouds of pulverized salt rose over the edge of the building, covering them in a sparkling blizzard. Desperately, the companions clenched their eyes shut, while the thunder of destruction rattled their bones from its sheer force. With the sound of splintering wood, the stout supports of the billboard crumpled, and it came hurtling down to slam onto the roof, missing the huddled friends by only a few feet. Lost in the tumultuous noise and hurricane winds, the companions never even noticed.

Now there came another exhalation of fetid gas. Pulling the collars of their shirts over their faces, Ryan and the others fought not to vomit, knowing that to open their mouths now would mean death from whirlwind of flying salt.

Helpless in the maelstrom, the companions clustered together, fighting to stay alive through the savage pounding and rampaging chaos of the collapsing salt dome.

The noise and destruction seemed to last forever, then slowly an immense white plume rose into the sky and began to form a horrifying shape of a dreaded mushroom cloud.

Chapter Six

At the top of the sand dune, Hawk plunged his hand into the pile of dried horse shit and fingered the crumbling material. It was stiff, but moist inside, and live with the tiny red ants that were everywhere in the Deathlands. His father had called them the only winners of skydark, and Hawk agreed.

"Ryan and the others were here less than twelve hours ago," Hawk announced, casting the dung away and glancing out across the shimmering expanse of the hot desert. "No more than a day max."

"Think the Core got them?" Mikel said, opening a canteen to pour some water on his head and down his neck. The day was hotter than a gun barrel, but they had plenty of water. Hell, there was still some sloshing about in his boot from the ville.

Wiping his hands clean in the sand, Hawk stood slowly, the scorpion perched on his shoulder scuttling around to keep its balance. He had simply put the creature there to get it away from the water. Scorpions drowned easily. But it seemed to like the high vantage point, and Hawk was pleased with the unnerving looks he got from the sec men. Fear was always the corner-stone of obedience.

"Mebbe," Hawk admitted, scowling at the bare skeleton lying in the sand. The bones were scraped with some sort of curved blade, very similar to those razor-sickles used by the Core. If the sand muties had harvested a dead horse to feed their bugs, then the outlanders might be prisoners, or even already converted. One sip of the bug juice and a man was perm addicted. A traveler had tried a sip once and then escaped. The next day he was burning hot with fever, covered with blisters, vomiting and crapping blood and screaming the craziest things. Never liking to waste ammo, Gaza had used an ax to chill the poor bastard, but then the pigs refused to eat the corpse as if the madness had remained inside the flesh. Triple weird. Rumor said that only long cooking purged the taint of the bug juice from food, but that wasn't something Hawk wanted to put to the trigger. Whatever the bug juice did to a person was something just this side of Hell.

"Well, nukeshit," a sec man drawled, hunching his shoulders. "Know what I think, Chief?"

"What?" Hawk demanded, squinting into the bright sunlight.

The man opened his mouth to speak, but never spoke. Then he violently threw himself off the horse to the ground.

Turning at the waist, Hawk scowled as the sec man

landed in a tangle of loose limbs, with one of his boots coming off. That's when the baron noticed the gaping hole in the man's chest. A split second later, the muted boom of a high-power longblaster rolled from the desert.

"Ambush!" Hawk cried, hitting the ground and pulling out his handcannon.

The rest of his troops did the same and hauled out their weapons. However, there was nobody else in sight, the bare ground clear for miles in every direction.

Since the body had fallen to the east, Hawk studied the west, trying to find some movement in the sand from the hidden sniper. At any range it was a hell of a shot and the coldheart had to have a scope. Probably expected the rest of them to run away in panic so he could jack the goods left behind. But that scam wouldn't work today. Soon, he would be wearing their guns in his belt.

"Jones, gimme a recce!" Hawk ordered, sweeping the sand with the barrel of his gun.

Rising up on his elbows to peer down the slope of the dune, Jones jerked backward as his throat exploded and his head came off. A grisly spray of dark blood gushing from the ragged stump of his neck. Fingers twitching, body wiggling, the deader seemed to still be alive as the echoing blast of the big-bore sniper rifle washed over the high dune once more.

Now the sec men opened fire randomly, shooting at

anything that moved. The sergeant lit the fuse of a black-powder gren and heaved it far and high toward the west. Seconds later, the bomb detonated in a thunderclap and hot shrapnel rained upon the desert.

"Again!" Hawk commanded, approving of the tactic. If there was anybody hidden behind those dunes, they had a hundred holes in them now and were in a lot worse shape than Jones.

As the sergeant sent another gren airborne, Hawk grabbed a rib from the horse skeleton, jabbed it into the base of the dead man's head and lifted it up. As the force of the explosion dissipated, there was no response.

"We got the fucker!" Hawk shouted, casting away the ghastly prop. "Okay, saddle up and let's ride him into the ground!"

The remaining sec men cheered at that and scrambled for their horses, just as a thick plume of gray smoke puffed up from a dune, and a section of the sand seemed to avalanche away in a clump. It took a moment for Hawk to realize it was a disguised vehicle draped with sand-covered cloth, but even at this range he could clearly spot the long ventilated barrel of a .50-cal sticking through the covering.

"Gaza!" Hawk cried, leveling his blaster blowing flame at the approaching APC. "Get the 25 mm mounted, and ready more pipe bombs!"

"Fuck that, we gotta run!" Mikel roared in reply,

then flew sideways off the dune to roll down the sand slope, leaving a grisly trail of entrails and organs.

Reloading, Hawk glanced up in time to see a thin puff of smoke disperse from the fifty. Nuking hell, they had a scope on the fifty and were using it as a longblaster? Was that possible? Guess so, because here he was splattered with the blood of dead men who said that idea worked just fragging fine. Then Hawk gave a grim smile. If Gaza was using the fifty as a longblaster, then he had to be shit low on ammo. Perfect!

Dashing for the cart, Hawk ripped off the canvas sheeting over the 25 mm cannon and hauled the big blaster to the edge of the dune.

"Ammo!" he commanded, awkwardly opening the breech of the deadly rapid-fire. The recoil might break his arms, but this was the best chance to get Gaza so he'd pay that price.

A sec man rushed to the cart and used a knife to force open the wooden box where the oily linked shells were stored. Grabbing the top coil, the sec man ran to Hawk and they started to insert the fat shells into the cannon.

Suddenly, a growl shook the air. The horses screamed and sec men fell as the big fifty began to spit flame, the heavy combat rounds hitting flesh and sand with wet smacks as the hot lead chewed a path of destruction through the massed troops.

The sec man carrying the ammo belt cried out and

clutched the ruin of his face. Dropping the useless cannon, Hawk looked around frantically for the sergeant with the pipe bombs, but couldn't find him anywhere. Had the cowardly son of a bitch run away?

Then a hot sledgehammer slammed Hawk in the right thigh, and he went down in confusion and pain. Shitfire, shot by Gaza again! Crawling backward from the others, Hawk pulled off the sweaty cloth from around his neck and tied it tight just above the wound in his leg. The hole was clean and tight. It had to have been an armor-piercing round to leave this little damage. And his toes still curled, so it hadn't hit the bone. As long as Hawk was still sucking air, this fight wasn't over! Gotta find those grens...

Rummaging among the dead and the dying, Hawk discovered the canvas satchel of homemade explosives trapped underneath a dead horse. Straining with all of his might, the man couldn't free the pinned bag, and started to dig with both hands, frantically scooping away the loose sand when a rumbling shook the world and something large blotted out the burning sun.

"Freeze right there, asshole," a familiar voice commanded. "Move and I ace ya on the spot."

Filled with the conflicting urges to keep fighting or surrender and try for a deal, Hawk fought a silent battle within himself for several long seconds. Then he slumped and turned from the traitorous corpse to raise both of his hands.

Silhouetted by the sun, the APC was only a black

shape. But Hawk could hear the internal hatches being opened. Several people walked out carrying rapid-fires. As his eyes became adjusted to the light, Hawk could see it was Gaza and his wives, the women looking as if they just got fucked long and hard from the pleasured expressions on their faces. Obviously, the bitches liked to kill, and Hawk now debated the wisdom of surrender.

Walking closer, Baron Gaza looked as if he had just strode out of the keep to review the troops. His boots were shiny, clothes crisp, and he was freshly shaved with his hair slicked back shiny. Stepping over a headless torso, Gaza put a spray of lead into a corpse that moved and now swung the smoking barrel toward Hawk. To the former sec boss, the barrel looked as large as a bazooka and filled with the infinity of eternal night.

"Find any other survivors," Gaza demanded, grinning down at his captured foe, "and line 'em up alongside the mighty Baron Hawk here."

Whistling and grunting in reply, the women spread out through the fallen men, finishing off the badly wounded with a knife in the throat. The rest were stripped of their weapons and marched over by Hawk. With their hands on their heads, the four sec men formed a ragged line in the dirty sand, the stink of death already spreading from the recently deceased.

"Traitors," Gaza muttered hatefully. Then he shouted, "All of you are traitors!"

"My lord!" a cringing man pleaded. "We didn't know it was you!"

"We thought it was the Core, or coldhearts!" another added.

"Just get it over with," Hawk retorted, lowering his hands.

Grinning in pleasure, Della fired a round at the prisoner, and Hawk felt the lead hum by his cheek it passed so close. Damn, they were good with those! But aside from a tiny flinch of surprise, the big man refused to move.

Minutes passed in silence. Hawk could feel the blood trickle down his leg, and sweat poured off his face, soaking his shirt and making the earlier injuries itch fiercely. As if waiting for something to happen, Baron Gaza did nothing as the desert breeze ruffled his clothing, blowing loose sand over the living and dead alike. Then the baron pulled a handcannon from his belt holster and tossed it to the first sec man in the line. The trooper stared at the weapon and then at Gaza in confusion.

"My lord?" he asked, swallowing hard. Was he expected to chill himself now?

"Prove your loyalty," Gaza said as the women behind him racked the bolts on their weapons, driving home the point. "Redeem your oath to me by taking the weapon and killing Hawk."

He was going to live! In a rush of exhilaration, the man eagerly nodded and grabbed the blaster to swing it toward Hawk. But Hawk was ready and ducked as he threw a fistful of sand into the sec man's face. Temporarily blind, the man pulled the trigger only to find the safety was still engaged. No! As he fumbled with the weapon, Hawk dived forward and wrestled it away. Then rolling over, Hawk held the sec men before him as a living shield and thumbed off the safety to aim and fire at Gaza.

Or rather, he pulled the trigger, but there only came the solid click of the hammer falling on a spent shell.

Throwing back his head, Baron Gaza let loose a bellow of laughter as Hawk desperately dry-fired every chamber.

"Such a waste." Gaza sneered, lowering the barrel of his rapid-fire. "Haven't I aced you already?"

"In the keep!" Hawk screamed, gesturing with the empty weapon. "I saw it all! He—"

Sitting in the gunner's seat of the APC, Allison burped the .50-cal once, and Hawk flew backward, his last words torn from his exploded lungs by the hail of hardball round before they could be formed.

With the sand crunching every step, Gaza walked over to the still corpse and looked at the black scorpion crawling madly about the body as if trying to rouse its master. Muttering a curse, Baron Gaza stomped on the creature, cracking open its shell, and then ground his boot back and forth until its squeals ceased.

"All hail the Scorpion God," he said with a guttural laugh, then spit on the dead man.

"Wh-what about us, Baron?" a sec man asked nervously. "How…how c-can we prove our loyalty to you?"

Baron Gaza looked at the man coldly.

"You can't," he said, and the women cut loose in a volley of lead, cutting down the rest of the sec men on their knees.

The sound of the blasterfire was still echoing among the dunes as Gaza went to the fallen 25 mm cannon and lifted it from the filthy sand. As gentle as stroking a lover, the man caressed the satiny smooth barrel.

"Now we're a match for the Trader," Gaza said with feeling, and started walking to the APC with his prize. "Load the rest of the ammo, and loot the bodies of weapons or anything else useful. I'll see to the installation of this personally."

Impressed at the display of raw strength, his wives preened in pride as the man walked the staggeringly heavy weapon over to the LAV 25 and started attaching it to the pintel mounting. Then shouldering their blasters, the women started stripping the men and horses when Victoria suddenly stood straight up and pointed to the south, making loud grunting noises.

Scowling, Allison turned and gasped, dropping the bloody boots in her hands. There, rising high above the world, was a white mushroom cloud.

EVENTUALLY, the rumbling winds passed and the companions slowly eased hands away from their faces to fill their aching lungs with the clean fresh air blowing in from the desert.

Dusted white from the billowing salt, Ryan blinked hard to clear his vision and could finally see again. The building under their boots still shook slightly, but the salt dome was gone, exposing something from another world.

It was a preDark city. The companions were standing on top of a skyscraper that rose above a perfectly preserved town that appeared to stretch for dozens of blocks in every direction. Mebbe more! The city filled a circular depression in the ground, edged by a sheer rock wall that rose to the desert floor above them. For a moment the man had a rush of vertigo as he adapted to the fact that he had fallen down to land high in the sky.

In the distance the remains of the dome crumbled along the rim of the cliff, the huge pieces falling into the city to smash cars and buildings. White salt clouds moved like fog along the streets, and a raging fire burned out of control in an intersection where a gasoline tanker had been flattened by the plummeting tons of the falling dome.

"By the Three Kennedys," Doc whispered in unabashed wonder, turning in a circle. "It is as if we have traveled backward in time."

"A preDark city," J.B. said, recovering his hat from the rooftop. "Not a ruin, but the whole damn thing."

Walking to the corner of the roof, Ryan looked out across the nameless Texas city. The skyscraper they were on was in the middle of the sprawling metropolis, near some sort of an open stadium, dust clouds still billowing inside resembling a winter snowstorm.

"A sink hole," he said. The one-eyed man had seen similar before, but never anything on this scale. It was staggering! "Must have been caused by the first nukes. Sometimes the land just cracks apart, sometimes it rises into new mountains or mesas, and sometime falls into the earth like this."

"I remember seeing pictures in *Time* magazine about a mining village in Pennsylvania," Mildred said, shifting the satchel on her shoulder into a more comfortable position. "Almost the same damn thing as this happened. A section of ground dropped out from under the folks like an elevator, removing the heart of the city. Only it didn't drop nice and even like this, it was sharply titled. Took the Army Corps of Engineers a week to rescue everybody while it continued to slowly descend."

"Is that happening here?" Dean demanded, suddenly alert, hands splayed for balance. "We still going down?"

"No, we're stationary," Krysty said, her fiery hair slowly uncoiling from the startling sight of the city. She kept starting to call them ruins, but the buildings were in perfect condition, aside from some minor damage caused by the falling dome. A few of the larger chunks had hit the streets below and not broken apart, the slabs of pristine white salt scattered about like pieces of an eggshell amid the homes and office buildings.

"But how do you know for sure?" the boy demanded, a touch of fear in his young voice. Ever since Zero City, and then the cliffs of the Marshal Islands, he had been developing a hatred of high places.

"No elevator feel in gut," Jak stated. "Remember how feel in redoubt when go fast? Not here."

Dean frowned as he concentrated inside himself, then nodded as he eased the tension from his face.

"Gotcha," he said, exhaling deeply. "Right. No problem."

Turning slowly to recce the roof, Ryan paused and pulled out his SIG-Sauer. "Who the hell is that?" he demanded, pointing at a pair of legs sticking out from behind the brick kiosk of the rooftop stairwell entrance.

Drawing weapons, the companions advanced fast, then holstered their blasters when they saw the face of the person. The skin was dried like jerky, eyes gone and lips pulled back in a rictus of death. Yet the clothing was in good shape: leather shoes without holes in the soles, pants and shirt, and a shiny wrist chron along with a gold wedding ring.

"Well, I'll be damned," Mildred said, crouching

alongside the desiccated being. The flesh was wizened and now dark brown in color from sheer age, the original race of the person hidden by the passing on the long decades. The clothes appeared to be casual, but with matching stripes on the sides and cuffs. Some kind of a uniform, but not the police or firefighters. Maybe a paramedic? There was a tool belt with a cell phone and an electronic clipboard and some weird pliers that were vaguely familiar to the physician. Then she saw a plastic name tag pinned to the shirt, the photo and card inside the clear material was easily readable as the day it had been issued.

"It's a cable repair man," Mildred said, for some reason a shaky laugh bubbling up from inside. Of all the people to find from the lost world it would have to be a damn cable TV guy. Then she looked again at the photo ID.

"Excuse me, cable TV woman," Mildred corrected, then addressed to the corpse. "Sorry."

"Somebody important?" Dean asked, inspecting the wrist chron. But the timepiece was digital, the powerful long-life batteries inert for a century.

"Depends on your priorities," the stocky woman replied, standing. "She was a television technician."

"Woman?" Jak asked, wrinkling his brow. "Hard to tell."

Mildred shrugged. "Everything shrinks with age."

"Dark night, there's more," J.B called out. "Hundreds, thousands of them!"

Standing at the cornice of the building, one boot resting on the low ledge, J.B. was using the telescope to scan the metropolis below.

"The streets are littered with people," he announced. "They're behind the steering wheels of the cars, and trucks, in the shops. They're everywhere."

"The entire population of a preDark city," Ryan said aloud, rubbing his jaw. "As well preserved as the city itself."

This was something horribly new to him. He had seen death a thousand times, and killed that many in battle. But this was beyond imagination. The sheer scope of the death toll was unnerving, staggering. A hundred thousand corpses? A million? There was no way to tell. He had known since childhood that billions died in skydark, but to now see them laid out on the ground all around like autumn leaves brought the volume of the destruction alive in his heart. What kind of madmen had brought about this level of destruction to their own people, their own world?

"Gaia rest their souls," Krysty said softly, spreading her arms as if to embrace the entire city.

"Amen," Doc said, then added some phrase in Latin, which Mildred repeated solemnly.

Staying resolute, the rest of the companions said nothing. They were also affected by the city of the dead, but refused to be rattled.

"Well, this certainly caused the stink," J.B. said, rubbing his nose, trying to change the dark mood.

"When the salt dome cracked, it released the grave-yard fumes of a million corpses, stored for a hundred years."

"I'm surprised we survived," Mildred agreed grimly. "The methane levels alone should have killed us."

"The irregular cracking of the dome must have forced most of the dead air skyward, channeling it away from us," J.B. suggested. Explosions of any kind were home turf to the Armorer.

"That would explain it," she relented.

Just then, Ryan gave a sharp whistle and pointed to the north. "We got company," Ryan said gruffly, brushing back his black hair. "The Core just arrived."

Facing that way, the companions could see small figures moving along the edge of the rocky cliff.

"Bet they're triple angry over this," Dean said, pulling his Browning Hi-Power and briefly checking the blaster. It was dusted with salt, but the rack worked fine and the clip slid in and out without hindrance.

"They had told us not to enter the forbidden zone," Doc rumbled, then he hawked and spit the salt dust from his mouth. "Their chief must be insane with rage over this transgression."

As if in reply, one of the Core threw a spear, but it traveled less than a block, then arched down into the street and out of sight.

"Think that's Alar?" Dean asked, hitching up his belt.

Krysty frowned. "Sure as hell isn't Kalr," she stated.

On impulse, Ryan brought up his Steyr and worked the arming bolt. Almost immediately, the Core scattered, diving into the loose sand and out of sight.

"Think they read my mind?" Ryan asked, still looking through the crosshair scope of the Steyr. The walnut stock felt gritty beneath his cheek, and his view of the desert was misty from the still rising salt mist. He could taste the air, and it was thick and foul as swamp water.

"I think they just saw the sunlight glint off the long-blaster and figured out lead was headed their way," J.B. said. "Any doomie able to read thoughts at this range would have known we were planning on escaping and have stopped us."

"Fair enough," Ryan said, then fired twice at a movement below the sands. "But now they're not so sure, and that could buy us some time to get off the roof."

Heading to the door of the rooftop kiosk, J.B. checked the lock and found it was open. The stairwell beyond was pitch-black, and the air carried a stale, almost metallic, odor.

Readying their weapons, the companions lit candles and entered the kiosk to start descending into the bowels of the dark skyscraper.

Chapter Seven

With Ryan in the lead, the companions started down the stairs in single file, the flickering candles throwing distorted shadows in the walls. Almost immediately they encountered another dried corpse, this one wearing a silk suit with a PalmPilot personal computer still clutched in its hand.

Kicking aside the body, Ryan kept onward, the SIG-Sauer steadily searching for targets. Just because everybody in the city was long chilled sure as hell didn't mean the place was safe. Mebbe the bodies weren't desiccated from the radiation and salt, but from some mutie that sucked them dry.

A soft moaning could be heard, and Ryan froze in the darkness as his combat instincts flared. Then he felt the gentle breeze moving against his face and realized it was only the desert wind moving through the city, and blowing into the broken windows. What glass hadn't been broken when the nuke quake dropped the city down a couple of hundred feet had to have sure as shit broken when the dome collapsed.

Reaching the tenth floor, the door to that level was propped open by a woman in a flower-print dress. Beyond they could see an office with cubicles and desks. A rustling noise, very reminiscent of bats, could faintly be heard.

At the noise, J.B. swung his Uzi machine pistol out of the way and pulled out his S&W scattergun, racking the shotgun for immediate action. The Uzi threw a lot of lead, but bats were small and fast, often carrying rabies or the black cough. The only cure for that was a bullet from a friend.

Quickly passing Dean her candle, Mildred pulled out her flashlight and pumped the leverlike handle on the survival device a few times to charge the battery inside, then clicked the switch. A pale yellow beam came from the flashlight, but it was still stronger than the dancing flames of the tallow candles.

Playing the beam about, the woman saw the papers on the desks fluttering from the breeze coming through the smashed windows.

"Nothing," Mildred reported succinctly. "It's clear."

Accepting the recce, Ryan continued downward, but kept a watchful eye on the high ceiling above them for any suspicious movements. Bats and rats were a constant danger in any preDark ruin and... Fireblast, these weren't ruins! He had better remember that. This dead town was unique in his travels, and nothing Ryan had ever seen before had truly prepared him for this.

The stairs ended at the mezzanine level, but the door was locked. J.B. tricked the mechanism easily enough, but then the portal refused to open more than a few inches as something was blocking it on the other side. Holstering his weapons, Ryan put his shoulder to the door and shoved hard, digging in his heels until the portal finally moved enough to create a gap for them to squeeze past.

Stepping through, he found what had been in the way—more bodies. The carpeted floor was covered with corpses of every age and sex. Umbrellas and packages dotted the human morass, thin, dried arms with clawed fingers rising from the sprawled bodies like bare autumn trees, with jewelry and watches glittering in the candlelight.

Kicking the dead aside to make room, Ryan got the door fully open and the rest of the companions joined him in the hallway of death.

A soft glow could be seen from the end of the hallway, and Ryan proceeded with extra care. Some of the dead were so well preserved, he wouldn't have been surprised if they rose and attacked. No wonder everybody was twitchy.

"They died waiting for the elevator," Dean reasoned, feeling slightly rattled by the blank, eyeless, faces.

"Ghastly," Krysty said, her animated hair strangely still about her features.

"This is Dantain, nay, surreal," Doc rumbled, as he walked among the men, women and children. "It is like something from a nightmare!" Then he added in a small voice, "Or is this a nightmare, and I'm not really here?"

"Easy, Doc," Krysty cautioned in a soothing tone, taking his arm and squeezing to reaffirm the man's hold on reality. "Easy there. Everything is fine. They're long gone and we're alive."

"Are they, madam?" he asked in a hoarse whisper. "Are they indeed? Or is it perhaps that they are alive, and we're the ethereal ghosts?"

"Doc, watch that hallway!" Ryan barked, pointing at a random corridor. "Cover our flank!"

For a split second, it seemed as if the ploy wouldn't work. But then the confusion left the scholar's lined face, and he smoothly drew both the Webley he'd acquired at Rockpoint and the LeMat to stand guard.

"None shall pass here, old friend," Doc stated firmly, every trace of madness gone from his voice and stance.

Surreptitiously glancing at the two people, Mildred nodded in approval. Ryan returned the gesture and proceeded along the crowded passageway, swiveling to avoid the outstretched hands of the gnarled dead. No matter how muddled he ever got, Doc always came back if there was real trouble. His brain may be somewhat damaged, but his spirit was still strong as steel.

Reaching the balcony, Ryan went to the ornate railing and studied the main floor illuminated by the sunlight streaming in through the smashed front windows. Bodies were everywhere, on the curved steps leading to the main floor, propped against the walls, sitting on a sofa near the reception desk. A delivery man was cradling a large bouquet of dried flowers with a satin banner proclaiming Happy Birthday. A mail carrier was crumpled on the floor before the open honeycomb of mail slots, undelivered envelopes piled at his shoes. Assorted others lay on the floor, limbs mixed, briefcases scattered, their loose clothing fluttering from the breeze.

Maneuvering down the carpeted stairs proved to be impossible, and the companions had no choice but to walk on the dead, the husks crushing into crumbling dust under their weight. Reaching the marble floor, Ryan and the others stomped their boots to get rid of the clinging dust, the vibrations causing several of the nearby bodies to fall apart.

Zigzagging through the corpses, Jak went to check the guard's weapon in its holster. But the leather was stuck to the revolver, and the albino teen had to yank hard to get it loose. As the gun came free, the guard tumbled to the marble floor and broke apart into pieces, his head rolling along the floor to careen off other corpses until coming to a rest near the phone booths.

Inspecting the blaster, Jak pulled the trigger and the weapon stiffly clicked, nothing more. Cracking the cylinder, he frowned at the .38 shells eaten through by crystalline deposits.

"Dreck," the teenager declared, tossing the useless weapon onto the reception desk with a clatter.

"Any ammo exposed to the air would be dead from the salt corrosion," J.B. stated, tilting back his hat. "But if we find any ammo still wrapped in plastic, I'm willing to bet that would be as good as ever."

"Like the gunpowder in our ammo in the re-doubts," Dean said confidently.

"Actually, no," J.B. said. "Gunpowder loses its ginger over the years. Especially crude stuff like the black powder that Doc uses."

"Nonsense!" Doc snorted, patting his LeMat. "Black powder is infinitely superior, sir!"

J.B. gave a snort. "Most of the weapons we find in the redoubts use cordite. Not the nitro-cellulose mix in the twentieth-century blasters."

"It's worse for the blasters," Ryan added, glad for the break from the endless dead. "That's why we have to clean so much, but the stuff really lasts."

"The modern propellant for guns was cleaner," J.B. continued. "But only lasted ten, twenty years on the shelf. However, cordite, under the right conditions, lasts a hundred. Sometimes more."

Reaching out with his ebony stick, Doc shoved the weapon off the desk. "Anybody seeing that would know somebody had been here recently," the scholar explained. "If the Core is not here yet, they soon will be."

"Take no chances with them," Krysty ordered,

blowing out her candle and tucking it away. "I've seen what they can do in your mind. Shoot them on sight, and ignore anything standing behind them. It'll be an illusion."

"Not prob," Jak stated, sliding the Winchester off his back and working the lever. The greater range meant better protection from the mind muties.

Just then, an explosion occurred far away, closely followed by the shattering of glass. Even though she knew better, Mildred half expected the sound to herald police sirens and the wail of an ambulance. But there was only the thick oppressing silence. With a shiver, the woman finally came to understood the term "graveyard quiet." This wasn't a city; it was a cemetery.

Going to the empty frame of a window, Ryan surveyed the area outside. Lines of cars were jammed end to end, trucks parked atop smaller vehicles, a motorcycle lying tangled with a baby carriage, the adult and infant grinning corpses.

"Nothing sight," Jak announced from the window across the lobby, the lever-action Winchester rifle held ready at waist level.

"Mebbe another fuel truck," Mildred guessed. "Or a car near the first one caught fire and set off its fuel tank."

A warm breeze blew through the broken windows, and Krysty sniffed a few times. "That fire is close," she warned. "Couple of blocks."

"Nuking salt has dried everything like tinder," Ryan said scowling deeply, glancing at the lobby of the building. "This whole city could ignite if the wind is right."

Suddenly, Jak gave a sharp whistle and raised a hand, clenching it into a fist. Instantly, the companions stopped talking and assumed a more aggressive stance, blasters raised.

The teen stood motionless against the marble wall, looking intently into the street full of cars and trucks. Black smoke wafted through the air, making it difficult to see very far. Then they heard a noise of metal on metal, and the smoke thinned for a moment for Jak to see something metallic moving among the preDark vehicles. A shiny dome with rotating red disks.

Holding his breath, Jak watched with a pounding heart while the machine pushed a crashed truck out of its way and turned a corner to vanish from sight.

"Dark night, a sec hunter droid," J.B. exhaled in a whisper, standing behind the teenager.

"And this one is in perfect working condition," Ryan growled, "unlike that wreck we found at the redoubt last week."

"Just great." Mildred sighed, glancing up at the ceiling and the world beyond. "We're trapped in a burning city, with a sec hunter, and Gaza and the Core in the desert above."

"Looting the city is no longer an option," Ryan stated as a fact. Nobody disagreed, so he continued.

"First we score some water, and then get some heavy iron. We're going to need more than blasters to handle a sec hunter."

"Then how get out pit?" Jak asked, still watching from the empty window frame. "No building near enough to top for us to try jump."

"We'll figure that out after we're armed better," Ryan said, then turned.

"Okay, Dean, what should we do first?"

Knowing he was being tested, the boy scrunched his face in concentration before answering. The rest of the companions waited patiently while he chewed the inside of a lip.

"Water coolers in office buildings like this are always useless," Dean started. "They drip and are always dry. Luxury hotels are good, they have those little minifrigs locked in the better rooms. Always some bottled water there."

Stone faced, Ryan said nothing, so the boy continued, feeling the pressure to come up with the correct answer fast.

"Got it!" He grinned. "Hot pipe, I'm a feeb. A supermarket! Normally, we don't bother with supermarkets since they were always looted during the rioting after skydark."

"But this city was never looted," Ryan finished. "Good call."

"Occam's razor," Doc rumbled, reaching out to

tousle the boy's hair. "Always try the simplest answer first. It is often correct."

Dean shifted away from the praise, then smiled back.

"Okay, I'm on point," Ryan ordered, serious once more. "J.B., cover the rear with your Uzi. Krysty, keep that .475 ready for the droid if it appears."

"Done," the redhead said, pulling back both of the curved hammers on the massive double-barreled elephant rifle. "Only a couple of rounds left."

"Then make them count, lover," Ryan told her. "Without implo grens or something equally big, a sec hunter could chew us apart like an MRE snack bar. We shoot and run for high ground. They don't go very fast on stairs and that gives us an edge."

"Be nice if Gaza arrives and we could trick him into fighting the droid for us," Mildred said, checking her Remington longblaster. The bayonet at the end glistening like a polished mirror, and she suddenly went cold realizing that could easily give away their position.

"Hold a sec," she said, setting the stock on the floor, and pulling out a butane lighter. Lighting a candle, she played the flame along the edge of the blade until it was a dull black. Satisfied, she tucked away the other items into her satchel and shouldered the weapon.

"Ready," Mildred announced.

Nodding in reply, Ryan slipped out the broken window on the opposite side of the office building from where the sec hunter had been seen. He had been going to mention that to the healer, but it was better that she caught it herself. When they first found Mildred, she had been useless aside from her medical skills. She'd been born and raised in a world where the biggest danger was overeating and boredom. But she had learned fast.

As they walked along the sidewalk, the friends could see salt dust everywhere, coating vehicles and corpses like snow. The tallest buildings blocked the sun, casting deep shadows across the rest of the city, brilliant slashes of light showing between the high rises. Ryan could guess that it would be pitch-black at the base of the cliff until high noon. That would be a good place to hide during the afternoon, and he filed that thought away. Right now, he had to stay razor.

The streets were empty of traffic in the middle of the blocks, but packed solid at every intersection. The inhabitants of the city were everywhere, sitting hunched behind the steering wheels, sprawled on the sidewalk holding packages and briefcases. Ryan saw that some poor bastard was lying on top of an awning covering a greengrocer stand, the vegetables long turned into shriveled, inedible lumps.

"Must have fallen from a window," Krysty guessed, hitching her heavy blaster.

"Makes sense," Dean agreed, stringing his crossbow as he walked. The silent weapon might catch a droid by surprise, and the cold iron quarrel in his quiver would pack a lot more penetration punch than a soft lead 9 mm slug.

As the group passed through a collection of crashed vehicles, Mildred gave a soft cry as she spotted an ambulance. Rushing to the rear doors, she found them locked, then cursed in remembrance that they were always locked to keep thieves from looting the medical supplies. Rushing around, she checked the driver's-side door and then the passenger's, but the ambulance was sealed tight, the EMTs inside still wearing their seat belts and grinning at her from across the ages.

"Good locks," J.B. said, testing one briefly. "Sorry, Millie, we'd need to blow them open, and that would give away our position to the droid."

The physician peered through the salted windows at the equipment cabinets in the rear; the supplies in there were priceless, irreplaceable! To be denied the tools of her trade by the thickness of a sheet of glass was intolerable! But Mildred turned her back to the treasure trove of healing supplies and strode away, trying not to cry from sheer frustration.

Stopping at a phone booth, Ryan picked up the telephone book, but it crumbled into dust at his touch. He had expected that, but hoped it might last long enough to give them the address of a supermarket, or a mall.

A hissing sounded from an alleyway and the companions spun about with their blasters ready. Then they saw a limousine slowly tilting as its hundred-year-old tires finally expired under the onslaught of fresh air.

"No rats, no muties, no looters," Krysty said. "If it wasn't for the Core hot for our blood, I'd say we take the place as a home. It would be very hard for anybody to invade from the cliff."

"We could make a hell of a ville wall with all these dead cars," J.B. said, pushing back his fedora. "Remember the ville defenses at Zero City?"

"Not really," Dean said stiffly.

Cradling the Winchester in his good hand, Jak bumped the boy with a hip. "Think not," the Cajun snorted. "Near dead whole time."

Dean shrugged. He had survived; that was what mattered.

Just then, the call of a bird echoing among the tall buildings made the companions glance upward with weapons at the ready. But there was nothing in sight. Then a puff of smoke appeared over a concrete parking garage.

"With the salt dome covering the sky last time, the fires ran out of oxygen and died quickly," Mildred said grumpily. "That's why there's anything here at all."

"Not happen this time," Jak said. "Burn all."

Ryan halted at a corner of a bank, the dead teller leaning against the bulletproof glass and staring down at them. Using a plastic mirror from a pocket, he

checked the next street to make sure it was clear, then
swept around to continue the recce. This road was
wider than the rest, more a boulevard, and every store
seemed to have a colorful awning and huge windows,
the powdery salt mixed with the glistening glass
shards.

Shuffling his boots to keep from stepping on the
glass and shattering a piece with every step, Ryan
swept the store with his eye, then paused and gave a
low whistle, imitating the bird they had heard earlier.

The companions hurried into view and saw the man
going across the traffic-filled street to a dark supermarket, its windowless front gaping wide. Spreading
out to avoid giving any hidden watchers a group target, the companions converged on the store and
slipped inside, with Doc and Jak staying at the front
as a rear guard.

Inside, the dead were everywhere, lying in disor-
ganized lines at the registers, sprawled on top of
gnarled fruit filling a bin, supine before an ATM with
slips of paper and cash clutched in their gnarled fists.

"Clear," Ryan announced, checking his rad
counter. "Only background rads. The place was never
hot nuked. Must have been a neutron bomb."

Dean remembered hearing about those. Some sort
of fancy nuke that only chilled people, but not buildings.

"I hope they were all slain instantly," Doc said
from the doorway. "Otherwise, any survivors would

have been buried alive in perpetual darkness, sans air and hope.''

Sadly, Krysty shook her head. "Such a waste.''

Going to an endcap display of fruit juice, Krysty inspected the top can only to replace it with a disgusted expression.

"Rusted through,'' she complained, wiping a hand clean on her thigh.

"Don't take anything with any rusty spots,'' Mildred warned. "The salt would eat through the galvanized tin easily. Stick with glass and plastic if possible.''

Spreading out in a standard search pattern, the companions walked along the deathly silent aisles, stepping over the desiccated bodies when they could. Which wasn't often. Soon, their boots were coated with a gray dust and the air began to have a strangely appetizing aroma that was almost meaty.

"Odd, it's sorta like beef jerky,'' J.B. said puzzled, then contorted his features. "Son of a bitch, we're breathing longpig!''

Krysty recoiled at that. Longpig, the cannie term for human flesh.

"Just deaders rotting,'' Ryan stated, prodding a display of plastic bags with the barrel of his blaster.

"Better put on your masks,'' Mildred ordered brusquely, pulling out a handkerchief. "There could be microbes in this dust that'll make us ill.''

The unspoken word of plague seemed to thunder in

their midst, and the companions quickly tied the clothes over their faces. At the sight, Mildred felt her mood oddly brighten as she thought about how the security guards from a hundred years ago would have had a heart attack at so many heavily armed people wearing masks invading their store.

"Something funny?" J.B. asked, cocking an eyebrow.

"Tell you later, John," she promised, smiling with her eyes. The earlier depression was gone. The past was past, and she was still alive. Mildred had true friends and a man who deeply loved her. There really wasn't anything more important in life than that.

Playing her flashlight on the ceiling signs, Mildred found the soda pop aisle and led the rest that way. It was dim between the tall racks, but the candles helped and she could read the colorful labels of assorted soft drinks. The names brought memories of ridiculous television commercials, and the physician found herself humming jingles that hadn't been played for a century.

"This brand seems to be the best," Ryan said, lifting a shiny container that audibly sloshed. "Glass bottles, good and tight."

It was only half full, but the fluid inside was crystal clear with no clouding to mark contamination. He cracked the plastic film around the cap with a simple twist but sniffed the water first, then poured some into a palm before touching it with his tongue.

"Nuking hell, that's good." He sighed thankfully, then took a long drink and ended finishing off the entire container.

"Fireblast, I needed that," he said, then placed the empty back on the shelf. "Everybody, fill your canteens, drink your fill and then put a dozen into your backpacks."

"We could load up a truck from outside," Dean suggested, placing a case of beef stew on the floor. "Take everything we can."

"Those wags are aced," J.B. explained, pouring a bottle of water over his head, then paused as it seeped into his dusty clothing. "This isn't a mil base or a redoubt. Nothing out there has a nuke battery or condensed fuel. The power is gone, the tanks are dry and the engine is seized tight from the grease dried solid as iron over the years."

Leaving the others to their work, Mildred proceeded deeper into the market, the reflected shine of her flashlight moving about here and there. After a few minutes, she returned, her satchel bag bulging with items.

"There was a pharmacy!" Mildred called in triumph. "Alcohol, white thread for sutures, powdered sulfur for wounds, bandages, aspirins, antibiotics! I found a thousand things we need!"

"Can you carry a thousand things?" Dean asked calmly, stuffing bottles into the bag.

As the beam started to wane, Mildred pumped the

handle of her flashlight to recharge the weakening batteries.

"No, Dean, I can't," she admitted honestly. "But even these few items will help us stay alive. My next batch of jump juice may actually do the trick."

"If we can get out of this pit alive," Ryan said, pouring a full bottle of water over his head and brushing back his soaked hair. It had been several weeks since they found a redoubt with a working shower, and he could almost taste the stink of his clothing.

Fully loaded, the group took a detour through the canned-goods aisle and found a dozen cans of soup and beef stew in acceptable condition. Privately, they each knew there was probably a lot of beef jerky in the snack aisle, but by unspoken agreement, they didn't go there. The meaty smell in the air of the store had killed any appetite for that staple for a long time.

Going to the front of the store, Ryan sent Doc and Jak back to fill up with water, but Mildred stopped the teenager.

"First I fix that arm properly," she stated firmly and dragged Jak over to sit down on a cardboard box of dog food. "Off with the shirt."

Removing his heavy jacket, Jak nodded in acceptance, and eased off his bloody shirt, the material sticking to him in several spots. In spite of her earlier work, Mildred was unhappy with the condition of the wound. The teenager had been using the arm, and the stitching had come loose. Fresh blood was seeping into the sandy bandages, and the wound was slightly red from infection. Damnation, and the dirty air of the store was only going to make that worse!

Quickly she checked his upper arms for any striation indicating blood poisoning, but thankfully there was none. Satisfied, she cleaned the wound with sterile water sold for contact lenses, then sewed it shut with actual sutures and washed it clean with pure alcohol. Drinking a bottle of mineral water, the teenager flinched at the contact but never said a word. Packing the wound with greasy antibiotics, Mildred tied off a military-style field dressing and hung it over his neck once more. The antibiotics would be incredibly weak, if there was any life in them at all, but it was the best she had.

"Hey, not itch," Jak said, flexing the arm and bunching the muscles. "Feels good."

"I used some hydrocortisone," the physician explained, packing the satchel again.

"Good stuff," Jak said in frank appreciation. "Got more?"

"Two full tubes."

Suddenly, a light fixture dropped from the ceiling to hit the terrazzo floor in a loud crash. As the companions turned, another object fell from a hole in the roof and hit with a metallic clang.

"Droid!" Ryan shouted, firing his blaster.

Smashing aside a display rack, the sec hunter droid came charging out of the darkness with spinning buzz saws attached to the ends of both ferruled arms.

Chapter Eight

Holding on to his spear, Alar ran with an easy grace along the crumbling edge of the huge sinkhole, the air thick with the smell of salt. A white fog was moving among the sand dunes, almost too heavy for the winds to shift. His eyes stung from the proximity, his throat constricted, and Alar constantly took a sip from the *jinkaja* bag hanging at his side.

At a restful distance behind the man was every warrior in the Core, their coverings rattling with knives and sickles. There had been no denying them on this holy vendetta. Kalr had been correct about the ancient ways, and he had been wrong. So terribly wrong. Death was the only way to protect the Core from the hated norms with their sterile minds. Alar had spared them out of the hope that the redheaded female would join the Core, and feed its line with the strength of her new blood. Her mind was great but undisciplined, chaotic, and useless as a weapon. But her children could have been giants, mindkillers of the old legends. It was his desire to improve the Core that had led to this disaster. No, it had been pride, foolish pride that he could control a bestial norm. The ultimate foolishness.

Stretching to his left were the endless buildings of the Source, the homeland where the Core had been born. Or created. Or awoken. The legends were vague on several details, and he knew in his heart that much was fantasy, word illusions to inspire the children of each generation. The truth was in the fact that the Core existed, and ruled the beasts by the power of their superior minds.

When the Core had first arrived, Ryan and the others were already in the heart of the holy land and then fired their longblasters, chilling a young warrior named Ghlat. Now every male and female of the Core had a smear of his blood on the face rags so that the outlanders would see it as they died screaming for mercy.

With a rumbling crash, another small section of the dome broke away from the edge of the cliff, and Alar halted to furiously watch the destruction. Tumbling end over end, the chunk of crystalline material fell onto a building and exploded into dust, shattering that area of the structure.

The Core had found several trails that led down the cliff. However, most didn't reach halfway, and several had crumbled under the weight of a single person, sending the Core member tumbling into the abyss. They sang a death song at the passings, and ran onward, fueled into a battle frenzy by the sheer grandeur of their blessed mission of revenge. Ryan and the others had to be killed. It was an edict from the gods of the sand. Spill the blood of the outlanders, or be damned forever.

A plaintive caw from above made Alar glance skyward, and he frowned deeply at the sight of a dozen huge black birds circling above the holy land. Already the buzzards had arrived, gathering their courage to swoop down and start feasting on the ancient ones. Their cries would attract others: cougars, stickies, other muties, and then the greatest destroyers of all, norms. Perhaps even too many norms for his people to stop. Their powers were great, but required the warriors of the Core to be very close together. Like wooden sticks bundled into a war club, each was strong, but together they were a deadly weapon.

Alar stopped at a sloping piece of stone, the desert sands trickling along the inclined plane like blood from a wound. The angled stone descended sharply, and seemed to end at a ledge fifty feet down. But after that there was nothing but a drop of countless feet onto a jagged pile of broken rubble, great metal beams rising like spears from the smashed stones coated white from the salt.

The leader of the Core slumped his shoulders, for the first time feeling despair. Perhaps the journey was impossible. The sinkhole was so huge! Larger than any seen before, and the sides were as sheer as a knife blade, sharp and smooth. But the warriors were still grimly determined to find a way down. They had to! A series of cracks that could be used as a ladder, a ravine they could crawl through, even a deep pool of hated water that could be jumped into from a height. Anything would do, but they had to enter the holy city and ace the outlanders.

It was beyond a necessity; it was a primal urge, fed by their will of the warriors and forged by sheer hatred.

FULL OF GRUBS and red ants, the tiny lizard was lying on the flat rock and showing its belly to the hot sun in total contentment. Then the ground began to shake, and the sky darkened as something radiating waves of heat blocked out the sky. Caught by surprise, panic seized the creature and it froze as the darkness rumbled overhead. Scrambling to its clawed feet, the mutie opened all three eyes and fiercely spit at the towering enemy. Anything larger was always considered an enemy. The acid spray hit with a sizzling hiss that usually marked the demise of the target, and its pea-sized brain reveled at the thought of all the additional food the kill of such a giant would yield.

Never even slowing, the huge studded tire rolled over the Gila monster, crushing it flat, pulsating intestines and blood spraying out on either side as the LAV 25 rolled on through the wide Texas desert. The splotch of deadly acid barely caused a minor discoloration in the resilient material of the preDark tires already marred by Drinker thorns, bits of glass, shattered bones, the broken wooden shafts of a dozen arrows and a swarm of small-caliber bullets.

Crushing scorpions, rocks and anything else that got in the way, the heavy military tires of the APC flattened every obstacle in the irregular surface of the shifting sands, leaving behind a trail of compacted debris that stretched out of sight for miles. The LAV 25 wasn't designed to be a stealth vehicle, but a battlefield juggernaut, heavily armed and armored, proof to toxic chems, radiation and most virus vectors, with pinpoint scanners, worldwide communication equipment, radar, radio scramblers, and yet big enough to carry six troopers and still be fast enough to escape anything larger that might prove to be a viable threat to the sleek U.S. Army leviathan.

Nowadays, much of the electronics, radio and comps and other fancy tech were gone, ripped out to make room for additional fuel, water and food. There had even been a set of rudders and propellers as if the damn APC was a boat of some kind! Pure madness to think steel could float. Just more deadweight, Gaza thought, to haul around and waste precious fuel. However, he had kept the winch and 40 mm smoke makers, even though he had no chems for those.

Stripped to the bare essentials of might and flight, the imposing war machine still ruled the wastelands. Thick canvas sheets draped the machine to offer protection from the deadly noon sun, the heavy material soaked with a tacky glue made from boiled bones and then sprinkled with sand to create an effective mask to hide its shape and armament, which were considerable. Where the canvas yawned, there could be seen the original mottle of tans and creams similar to those of an Appaloosa horse, near perfect camou for the desert surroundings.

The ventilated barrel of a .50-cal thrust out of the forward blaster port of the prow so the driver could fire and steer at the same time, and from the turret there dominated the imposing barrel of a 25 mm cannon that could traverse horizontally and vertically to track in every direction to find its prey.

Inside the war wag, the air was warm, reeking of diesel fumes and machine oil, the dangling belts of linked ammo jingling musically as the APC rolled over the warming desert. Crouched in the driver's seat, Baron Gaza grinned in pleasure at the sound of the dangling ammo. The jury-rigging to mount the cannon to the pintel mounting had been a bitch, but now the 25 mm cannon worked perfectly. Hawk had done a good job of cleaning and oiling the big blaster. Now the APC was a proper war wag, armed to the eyeballs, and more than a match for the armed trucks of the Trader.

Moving to the motion of the machine as if they were on a ship at sea, the five women in the rear wall seats leaned toward the small air vents, savoring every breeze that blew in from underneath the canvas sheeting. To endure the oppressing heat, the baron's wives had stripped down to the bare essentials, their wealth of bare skin shiny with sweat that dripped off their bodies to fall onto the corrugated steel deck. However, strips of cloth were tied around every wrist to keep their hands dry and ready to use the blasters holstered on their bare hips, and the loaded rapid-fires lying across their open thighs.

Sticking a cig into his mouth, Gaza kept one hand on the steering yoke while he lit the smoke and pulled the rich, dark smoke deep into his lungs. The damn things were as addictive as jolt, but smoking helped him stay razor. They were deep in Core territory now, and whatever that white nuke cloud had been, the baron was triple damn sure the Core would also be going there to do a recce. Fucking mutie bastards.

Shifting in his sticky chair, the baron stretched out his sore leg and in the gunner's chair, Kathleen moved out of the way to give him some more space. Gaza grunted at the act of kindness. His bad leg was starting to ache from being in the cramped position for so long, but that was a lot better than being crucified by the rebelling civies of his own ville for lying to them for so many years. Stupid feebs didn't understand that sacrifices needed to be made in war. They should have been honored that he choose Rockpoint ville as his base to strike at the Trader, and then use his stockpile of preDark weapons to build an empire in the Deathlands. To create a New America that would purge the world of muties and freaks. A world of norms! It was to have been—no, would be—a war of purification. And the blood of the dead would nourish the sand until it would grow crops, and America would be green once more. Alive and safe. With Emperor Gaza as the absolute ruler.

A world of norms, ruled by a mutie.

At the thought, Gaza stole a glance at the ragged scar on his left hand. His unknown mark of shame. The man told others the mark was from a cougar attack, but that was a lie. The scar was a memory, a secret from childhood when Edgar Gaza had been born with an extra finger on that hand. His wise mother had brutally chopped it off while he was still attached to her or else his father would never have allowed the dirty mutie to live and suckle at those gene-pure breasts.

A mutie who ruled norms. Yes, that would be his payback for every creature killed or tortured because it was born different. Once, a freak show came to Rockpoint, the zoo master displaying weird muties in cages for the people to stone for their amusement. In the cover of darkness, Gaza himself had hidden a blaster in the man's wag, then publicly accused him of being a thief and whipped him to death right there in the street before the temple of the Scorpion God. Behind their iron bars, the trapped muties blessed Gaza with their misshapen eyes as the hated master was slowly reduced to a bloody carcass under the bull-whip. Unfortunately, afterward Gaza had no choice but to ace the poor creatures. But it was done with blasters, as painlessly as possible. Revenge could only be carried so far, and only an idiot allowed personal feelings to get in the way of survival.

Stealing a look into a cracked mirror set in the corner of the sloped roof, Gaza could see his wives were chatting among themselves using the hand language they had created. He had tried in vain to learn their silent speech, and harbored a nervous belief that they had altered the lessons to exclude him from their private conversations.

As if sensing his disquieting thought, Allison reached into a duffel bag hanging on the armored wall and offered her husband a honeyed bread, a personal favorite.

"Sticky hands while I'm driving?" Gaza snarled, puffing away on the cig. "Are you insane?"

Bowing her head in apology, Allison popped the morsel into her mouth and chewed contentedly while looking ahead of the rolling war wag at the endless vista of the shimmering sands, lost in her own thoughts.

The hours passed slowly, and as the APC crested a dune, blinding sunlight exploded through the ob ports. Shielding his face with a hand, Gaza fumbled to find a pair of sunglasses tucked into a pouch clipped under the chair. As he slid them on, the polarized lenses automatically darkened in response to the illumination and he could see clearly again, although everything was tinted blue now. Then the APC slowed as Gaza stared in disbelief at the huge hole spreading wide across the landscape. Down below were dozens of preDark buildings rising upward to almost the level of the desert floor. What the nuking hell was this? Some sort of a sunken ville, its buildings below the desert? But why hadn't the wind filled the hole with sand over the long years?

The answer came in a flash. Because the pit was newly formed, no, uncovered! A salt dome! Blind norad, that was what he had seen in the distance! The blast cloud of a crashing salt dome that had covered over a preDark city.

Jerking upright in her chair, Allison grunted frantically and pointed to the right. Tracking in that direction, Gaza snarled as he saw the ragged figures of the Core running along the crumbling edge of the cliff about a half mile away. So they were trying to find a way down, eh? Perfect.

Thankfully, the wind was blowing in the wrong direction, hiding the smell and sound of the engines from the hated muties. This was the best chance he would ever have to end their foul race.

"Load 'em up!" Gaza shouted, throwing the war wag into a higher gear. "We're going in hot and hard!"

Allison strapped herself into the gunner's chair, and then released the ropes holding the .50-cal out of the way of the two people at the front of the vehicle. Expertly, she checked the linked ammo, making sure there were no kinks to tangle and jam the blaster, then she worked the arming bolt and took a few practice swings of the heavy blaster, testing its speed. The woman could feel the waves of rage from the Core, the pictures in their minds a visual tapestry hanging just below the subconscious level. The desert warriors were almost insane with anger and that was good. It would make them foolhardy, prone to taking unnecessary risks. An angry enemy was a weak enemy.

In the rear, Della awkwardly climbed the half step into the turret and prepared the 25 mm cannon.

"Short bursts only at group targets!" Gaza shouted at her, looking in the corner mirror. "That's all the shells we got, and we're going to need every damn one to face the Trader!"

The tall brunette thumped the metal chassis with a fist to let her husband know she understood the gravity of the situation, then she pulled out a .45 Ruger Blackhawk revolver from her holster and tucked it in the front of her belt for a faster draw.

All of the others were doing the same with their rapid-fires, stuffing spare ammo clips into belts, and working the arming bolts on their Kalashnikovs, M-16s and MAC-10 machine pistols.

The engine of the LAV 25 sounded deafening to Gaza as he tried to force the war wag to greater speed, but it got within a hundred yards of the Core before the last person in the group spun and shouted the alarm.

Instantly, Allison racked the group with the fifty, bodies tumbling in every direction from the brutal hammering of the heavy combat rounds. Now the rapid-fires began spitting flame from both sides of the APC, and a full dozen of the Core died from the barrage before the rest even realized what was happening.

Spinning with a snarl, Alar simply stood in the open ground, holding his spear. As Gaza headed straight for the male, he suddenly felt dizzy then cried out as a giant millipede appeared from behind a sand dune, the black insect larger than a preDark tank!

The baron cried out in terror and threw the steering hard to the left to escape the slavering jaws of the colossal beast. Releasing the fifty, Allison touched his temples and the vision faded away to show nothing before the APC but empty desert, and the rapidly approaching edge of the cliff.

It had been a damn illusion! Dangerously close to the edge, the preDark city rising into view, Gaza slammed on the brakes and threw the transmission into reverse, the gears grinding loudly as the machine fought its own momentum. The loose sand under the tires slithered away, and the APC continued forward toward the yawning abyss. Trying to regain control, Gaza stomped on the gas, and the big Detroit diesel roared with full power. Only fifty feet away from the edge, Gaza engaged the emergency brake and banked even harder, throwing his weight onto the yoke until he thought it might break. With half the wheels jammed motionless, the LAV 25 went sideways and continued sliding toward certain doom. Then Gaza released the brakes, the rear tires caught traction and the vehicle lurched ahead a few yards. Yes! Fighting for every foot of the way, the baron alternately worked the yoke and brakes and gas, finally bringing the war wag onto the desert proper.

"Chill 'em all!" he screamed, spittle hitting the controls.

Instantly, every weapon in the APC cut loose, hot lead chewing up the dunes as the Core rallied behind Alar. What the hell? Why would they give a group target to the rapid-fires? Then the leader of the Core vanished from sight as a duplicate APC came around a dune to barrel straight for Gaza on a collision course and a fire-breathing millipede rose from under the sand to their left.

Ignoring the mind tricks, the baron spun the LAV 25 hard and headed for the empty stretch of desert. He remembered a dune being there a moment ago, which was probably where the damn muties were going to escape his blasters.

"Della, shoot the sky!" he yelled as spears hit the APC from nowhere, the points shattering as they came through the air vents, throwing razor-sharp slivers of steel everywhere like shrapnel.

Dropping her AK-47, Victoria cried out and fell to

the deck with a length of steel completely piercing her throat, blood squirting out from the severed arteries.

Exhaling a guttural scream, Della cut loose the 25 mm cannon and turned in a full circle. The sand exploded everywhere, and swaddled bodies fell from the clear sky to land in gory pieces on the hot sand.

Suddenly, the rest of the Core became visible once more as they ran from the edge of the cliff where the heavy APC dared not go again. As Gaza leaned forward to urge the machine onto greater speed, he and Alar locked eyes for a long heartbeat as the leader of the Core fumbled to pull a gren from within his cloth rags. The APC hit the man, and he folded completely over the prow before flying. He was still airborne when the gren detonated in a blinding flash, a searing fireball expanding above the city, waves of flame stabbing outward from the miniature sun violently brought into creation.

His heart pounding, Gaza watched as the fireball thinned away on the wind of its detonation. That had been a thermite gren! The mil antitank charge would have blanketed the APC in chem flames hotter than a thousand Molotovs and roasted them alive. Alar had to have been saving that just for Gaza, but he used it one split second too late.

Unexpectedly, more spears hit the war wag, and as the rear women shot wildly, Allison frowned in concentration and then swept the nearby sand with the forward fifty to expose the underground members of the Core with bloody geysers as each round found living flesh. Literally torn to pieces, the broken bodies rolled along the desert, leaving a crimson trail as they went straight over the cliff and joined their aced leader on the last train west.

Braking to a halt, Gaza panted behind the steering yoke, glancing about in every direction, trying to find new targets. But the desert seemed to be empty.

"Another trick?" he demanded, looking to his right.

Allison shook her head and waved a hand in a slicing motion, explaining that everybody was chilled.

"Let's just make sure," Gaza growled, turning off the engine and grabbing a rapid-fire before exiting the vehicle.

The sand swirled around his hand-tooled leather boots as the man did a recce outside the LAV 25, checking the bodies of the slain. Most of the Core were obviously chilled, with limbs gone, or steaming holes in their chests from an explosive 25 mm shell. Resting the stock of his blaster on a hip, Gaza sneered at the sight. He was preparing to conquer the world, and a bunch of sand muties thought they could challenge him? The feebs deserved to die twice for such arrogance.

Joining him on the churned sand, his wives proceeded to loot the bodies of the fallen, finding a few blasters and another gren. Also several bags of *jinkaja*. Those they tossed away in disgust, and wiped their hands clean afterward as if the addictive juice were rank sewage.

Watching them work, Gaza was pleased. His wives knew their jobs well. He should have cut out the tongues of every slut in the ville and had an army of women. By the nukestorm, there was a good idea. A female army with him the only stud!

Chuckling at the notion, the baron went to the front of the APC and inspected the gory streaks left behind from the Core leader. The bloody rags partially hid the scorch marks received from blasting out of Rockpoint. Pity the ville no longer existed. He would have dearly loved to return and level the hellhole until rivers of blood flowed. But it wasn't to be. Pity.

A low boom of an explosion echoed from the nearby preDark city, and Gaza walked to the very edge of the cliff to look down upon the buildings with conflicting expressions. This would be his new home. Canned food for the rest of their lives, preDark liquor, machines and more blasters than could be counted. An empire to challenge the preDark days. Nobody could stand before him then, not the Trader or Ryan. Now his death should be something special. Hawk had known many things, and the baron learned the important tricks before killing the man. There was a way to torture a victim for weeks, without blood loss, and keeping him or her conscious without even the sweet release of fainting. Eventually the victim would go insane, but that was half the fun.

A low moan came on the breeze, and Gaza spun with his blaster leveled. The silence lay thick on the battlefield, with only the ticking of the hot APC engine cooling to disturb the peace.

"One of them is faking," the baron said loudly. "Find him and let's get some answers!"

Quickly, his wives searched the bodies, using knives to stab any corpse not blown to pieces. Then one small body drenched in blood and entrails jerked at the touch of the blade and the women descended in force, pinning the Core mutie and tying his hands across his back and looping a second rope around his neck. Any attempt to get loose would only cause the prisoner to strangle himself.

Walking over to the masked being, Gaza kicked it hard in the belly, and the desert warrior doubled over, heaving for breath. The prisoner was small in height and build, certainly no older than a teenager. Not that it mattered for very long. Alar had died much too soon. This mutie wouldn't share his good luck.

Pulling a stiletto from his boots, Gaza turned the blade about in the bright sunlight, the needletip gleaming evilly. The sand mutie jerked his head forward, to stare at him with blazing violet eyes. Cold fear filled the man's belly for a moment, but when nothing happened Gaza broke into laughter and the captive slumped with defeat.

"Can't send mind monsters alone, eh?" Gaza sneered and the captive slumped in resignation.

"Trapped, alone and helpless. But you have spirit. I respect that. Tell me about the underground city and your death will be swift and painless."

The prisoner continued to stare at the sand and said nothing.

Furiously, Gaza backhanded the being across the face, sending him sprawling. As the captive tried to rise, the ropes tightened and started choking him to death. Moving quickly, Allison and Kathleen grabbed the prisoner and hauled him upright where he gasped for breath wheezing from the effort.

"Is there any way down to the city?" Gaza demanded, walking around the being.

After a long pause, the Core soldier shook his head.

"Still stubborn. You must be kin to your baron."

The masked being remained mute, tilting his head slightly, but the violet eyes were full of confusion.

"The child of your leader, Alar," the baron explained impatiently.

Dumbly, the captive nodded and the front bandages became damp below the strange eyes.

Tears? Gaza was shocked at that. Nothing on earth cried but norms. "Remove the bandages!" the baron commanded, yanking off his sunglasses. "I want to see his face!"

The captive fought hard, but Allison got him in a hammerlock and pinned helpless as the others roughly used knives to cut away the layers of bandages, uncaring of any damage inflicted. Victoria lay dead in the APC from the spears of the savages, and the other wives no longer considered the captive a living being. It was merely a thing to be handle in any manner their husband decreed.

A small nose came first, then ears, and full lips, then oval eyes of deep violet and finally long blond hair the color of the moon. Gaza was delighted at the sight of the female. All the better for revenge. Reaching down, he rubbed her chest and felt the presence of breasts, large and soft.

"All of it," the baron said excitedly, feeling his lust rise. "Strip her to the skin."

The girl struggled, but the women had assisted in such things before and soon the captive was stark naked before the baron, cringing in shame as she tried to hide herself with one arm across her full breasts, the other between her legs. Her skin was bluish in color, and the man thought she might be a mutie after all, but then he realized it was just from the total lack of sun ever reaching her flesh for a lifetime.

"Magnificent." Gaza chuckled as he walked around the young female. "And human in every way."

"P-please," a new voice said.

Gaza spun at that to see the girl shivering. Ah, she was freezing in the desert heat. Her body was unable to handle the lack of bandages.

"What is your name?" he demanded, taking her by the jaw.

"Sh-shala," she stammered, and had to say the name several times before he comprehended.

"Shala. Such a pretty name," the baron purred, running a hand through her blond hair, then grabbed a fistful and forced her to face him directly. Her eyes were beautiful and filled with sorrow. It was a devastating combination, and her fate was sealed on the spot.

"You belong to me now, girl," Gaza snarled. "Understand?"

Fighting back more tears, she nodded, prepared to try to die with honor as a warrior of the Core.

Releasing her hair, Gaza slapped her face hard, then cupped both breasts, the delicious weight filling his palms and sending warmth to his groin.

"Prepare my new bride," Gaza snapped, releasing the teenager and starting to remove his own clothing. "I can think of no better place for a honeymoon than the field where her race died. We'll talk tomorrow about how to reach the city below."

Crying out in terror, Shala tried to get away as the women converged on her with ropes. But soon she was bound helpless. Then she started to scream when they brought out pliers and a straight razor, the wives of the baron grinning to display their lack of a tongue.

The horrible noises mounted until they echoed among the concrete canyons of the preserved metropolis, then suddenly and horribly were cut short.

Chapter Nine

"Are you sure the mushroom cloud was in this direction?" the Trader asked, scanning the horizon with a pair of preDark binocs.

Her battered Stetson was tilted back to accommodate the longeyes, its single eagle feather fluttering in the breeze. A bandolier of grens stretched across the swell of her breasts, and a boxy 9 mm Ingram machine pistol hung at her side, with an ammo belt of spare clips around a trim waist. Riding on her left hip was a hand comm unit, turned off at the moment. But ever since Hellsgate she always traveled with the radio link.

"Yes, this is it," Roberto said gruffly, checking the cracked compass in his right hand. "North by northeast. I marked the dial just to be sure."

"Doesn't look like any nuke damage that way," the Trader said, resting a boot on a large rock and leaning forward.

Closing the lid on the compass, the man snorted. "Never said it was a nuke, just a nuke-shaped cloud."

The Trader gave no reply as she continued to scan the horizon. The rad counters were reading clean, but she sure as shit wasn't taking her convoy into a possible hot zone without doing a recce first. Any triple-large explosion formed a mushroom cloud; she had learned that long ago. However, any blast that size always meant local fighting and to just roll on in could get all of them chilled and triple quick.

The blond woman stood tall to the others in her group, especially in these lean days with so many starving. Her clothing was simple, just denims and a heavy white shirt, the shirt worn more to impress folks than anything else, since clean clothing was only a legend in most parts of the Deathlands these days.

Turning her head to scan the horizon, the tanned skin tightened on her neck to expose a thin scar that went almost completely around her throat, a memento from where a rogue coldheart tried to ace her from behind, and failed. One of the fingers on her right hand was oddly bent, a bone break that never healed properly, and on the back of her left wrist was a large puckered area where a stickie had grabbed her with a sucker. Caught reloading, Kate dropped her empty blaster and used a knife to gut the mutie, slicing it open from belly to chin while the creature was still attached to her wrist. The sucker came off as the stickie died, but the skin was permanently damaged. But that was a trade she would make any damn day— a life for some skin.

There were more scars, some badges of honor saving a friend, others dark memories of when she was a slave. Whip marks and brands that only her bed partners saw for a brief moment before the candles were extinguished.

"Looks clear," Kate said, lowering the binocs to tuck a loose strand of hair behind an ear. The woman wore her pale hair tied off in a ponytail with a piece of rawhide to keep it out of her face. She wore no jewelry of any kind, although there was a junk box full of the stuff in War Wag One, items for trade at the various villes they encountered. The pretty baubles were sure to catch the eye of a baron's woman.

"But that don't mean shit this close to the Core," Roberto stated, checking the load in the sawed-off shotgun that he used as a handcannon.

Clicking the breech shut, he slipped the blaster into the low holster strapped to his thigh. At that height, his right hand hung exactly alongside the grip of the deadly blaster. Fat, greasy shells filled the loops of his wide belt, and a long curved knife was tucked into a sheath at the small of his back. Among his many jobs in the convoy, the first and most important was to watch the Trader's back. Some feebs thought he loved the woman, but it was much more than that, more than friendship, a deeper emotion based on respect. Recruiting him from a brutal ville, the woman had given him back a measure of self-pride, and that meant more to the man than any fleeting tug of the heart or sweaty roll in the hay. Twice so far he had stepped in the way of lead flying her way, and would do so again without hesitation. The day she crossed the dark river, he would follow her into hell to help plan the escape.

Placing the binocs aside, the frowning Trader pulled out the hand comm and thumbed the transmit switch. "Jake, it's me," she said. "Anything on radar?"

"All clear, Chief," a man answered over the comm, his voice oddly free of the usual distortion.

"Roger," she replied in old mil lingo. The woman knew that this kind of clear reception was only possible within a hundred feet of War Wag One; after that it got worse with every step taken. But with all of the crap still in the atmosphere from the nukecaust, even the most powerful radio could only broadcast for a few miles in ideal conditions. The military handheld radio the Trader carried had a shorter range than a mile, but still gave her a vital link to every wag at the same time in a firefight. The radios helped turn five wags into a single unit, which closed like a fist around an enemy to crush them with a coordinated strike.

War Wag One had started life as a big rig, but over the years had been built up with armored sides, another engine, machine-gun blisters, sleeping bunks, a kitchen, additional fuel tanks, more wheels, missile launchers, flamethrower and even a working comp to control everything on board the big complex machine.

She stole War Wag Two from a warlord, and it was roughly the same size as One, but without a comp and it carried more armor than blasters, making it a place to fall back to in case of deep shit. Although now six big Harley motorcycles were strapped to the sides as sort of additional armor. The big bikes were loot taken from the Blue Devils. Kate used the motorcycles for recce missions and flank attacks. They were sturdy and fast, able to outrun even the big cats that infested the western plains. But the machines took a lot of time to learn to ride properly, and were as noisy as a bar fight, absolutely useless for a night creep.

Only Roberto rode one constantly, rolling ahead of War Wag One as it crossed the burning desert, testing the ground for boobies and salt domes. Once they blew a tire hitting a big dome—bastard thing was almost a yard deep—but the domes were more annoying than dangerous. Still, it never hurt to have a pointman riding as an outrider in unfamiliar territory.

Behind the two armored transports were the cargo vans, trucks with only minimal armor and a few rapid-fires. Those carried the spare tires, machine parts, ammo, food and such, along with the trade goods: barrels of shine, dried sausages, planting seeds of gene-pure plants and such. There were even some lux items salvaged from the ruins: toothbrushes, jewelry, shoes, dinnerware and books. Lots of books. Those the Trader gave away as a gift after each successful barter with the peaceful baron. The more people knew about rotating crops, fixing plumbing, fixing wags and such, the more prosperous the ville became, yielding an even greater profit on the return trip. More food, better shine for the lanterns and bikes, and with fewer graves filled each year.

There were other traders, of course, mostly small-timers who did more smuggling of fuel and blasters through coldheart country than did any bartering. If they were honest, and didn't sell nuke water that glowed to fools who couldn't tell the difference, or deal in slaves, or jolt, then Kate would cut a treaty with them, and sell them a few blasters, and always toss in a book or two.

"Hold on," Jake said, and there was a moment of softly crackling static from the comm. "Okay, we have a report of blasterfire to the north of here. One mile, mebbe less."

"Explosions or handcannons?" Kate demanded, looking through the binocs again.

"Blasterfire, that's all Eric can confirm over the mike."

Rubbing a hand across his unshaved jaw, Roberto glanced over a shoulder at the parabolic dish on top of War Wag One. In reality it was merely a large ceramic soup bowl with a microphone positioned in the exact center. But the dish collected sounds too faint for people to hear and concentrated them on the mike for Eric to hear at his station inside One. The crippled tech had found the directions to build it from a children's book of fun science, and more than once the fellow had foxed an ambush by muties or a night creep with the contraption. Yet it was no more than a child's toy for the preDark whitecoats.

That thought always made Roberto uneasy. There were tales of preDark war machines still functioning in distant lands, randomly chilling folks as if all life was their sworn enemy. War machines that hovered above the ground in legs of wind, and were armed with L-guns even better than War Wag One possessed. Perhaps just tall tales for drunks in a tavern, or creepies told to scare little kids. But the chief gunner for the Trader had a gut feeling that some part of those stories might be true.

"North is toward Rockpoint," Roberto stated, looking first in one direction, then the other. "But the nuke cloud was east of here. Mebbe just a coincidence, but then again, mebbe the Core and Gaza have declared war on each other."

"All the better," Kate said with a hard smile. "That would just make it easier for us to chill them both."

"Unless they know we're coming," Roberto added slowly, as if thinking out each word before speaking, "and are staging a fake fight to lure us into an ambush."

Gaza and the Core combined—there was a grim thought. With his firepower and their mind demons, the two would be unstoppable and could seize control of the whole of Texas, forging an empire of death across a thousand square miles.

There were always outlanders and coldhearts who

didn't want peace, folks who thrived on chaos. She chilled them at every opportunity, and left them hanging naked with their cock and balls cut off, and her brand burned into their flesh—a lightning bolt crossing a star. The sign of the Trader.

Once, just once, she caught another trader pretending to be her and using the symbol. She gutted the man on the spot and rammed his heart down his throat right there in the ville bar. Sometimes, she'd hear the story repeated a thousand miles away, always with a lot of new details and embellishments. Good. It put fear into people, and reduced the number she had to ace to stay alive. Chilling was just a task, something she did when necessary. Kate had already seen more death in her life than any dozen people.

"Hopefully not. But either way, we're ready," Kate said firmly. "We'll head for the blasterfire. The nuke ain't going anywhere."

"Sooner started, sooner done," Roberto said, brushing back his hair. "I'll ride point and take Horta and Jennings along with me for flankers."

Frowning in thought, the Trader turned and started for the war wag. A curved section of the chassis was swung out, displaying steps to climb inside the elevated vehicle. A guard stood near the opening with an M-16 assault rifle resting in his hands.

"Not this time," she ordered. "I want everybody behind steel with fingers on triggers, and Eric running the L-gun in case it is the Core. That's the only defense we have against their tricks.''

''Only have two more charges for it,'' Roberto said, glancing at the rear of the armored wag. There was nothing to be seen up there, the delicate laser stored safely inside the transport to protect its focusing lens. A lot of hard work had gone into fixing the weapon and keeping it operational. But when it worked, there was nothing that could stand in its way. When it worked.

''Two charges is more than enough,'' Kate stated, nodding to the guard as she climbed into the machine.

Her boots clanging on the corrugated floor, Kate maneuvered past the ammo bins and boxes of MRE packs of the dimly illuminated interior of War Wag One, heading straight to the big command chair in the center of the control room, while Roberto took an empty chair near the port machine-gun blister.

As the door guard closed the hatch with a muffled clang, the crew at the control boards got busy cranking the huge tandem diesels of the rig, casting a rainbow of colors across their faces. As the engines started with a muffled roar, the nuke batteries disengaged and the generators came on-line. Flickering into life, vid screens began to show external views from around the vehicle, and specifically underneath, while the radio crackled the conversations of the drivers of the other vehicles.

At the aft of the big rig, a motionless man behind

a tinted Plexiglas blister silently watched Kate settle into the chair and store her rapid-fire in a holster bolted to the armrest. Glancing over a shoulder, she nodded at the long figure ensconced inside a nest of wires running in every direction.

There was only one small door to the blister, and it was mined with antipers C-4 charges inside and out. Nobody was going through without the express authorization of the man in the bubble.

Casting about a trained glance, Kate checked the power levels, fuel supplies, thermos and hydraulics. Everything was in the green, except for a slight drop in pressure on the rear lifts.

"Hasn't Anders replaced that busted hose yet?" the Trader snapped irritably.

Jake reached out to tap the pressure gauge with a finger. The needle flickered but didn't rise.

"Sure as shit doesn't seem like it, Chief," he said. "We're still operational, but not by much more than a pecker full of pressure."

Kate hid her anger. Damn the man! Just because he was the best longblaster shot in the convoy he thought that made him immune to work details! Time for the lazy bastard to learn some the hard truth. "Fine him all candy bars for a week," she commanded. "He works an extra shift and log the offense. This is the third screwup. One more and he's gone."

Every member of the crew scowled at that pronouncement. The road. That was usually a death sentence for anybody cast out of the convoy, unless they could find a friendly baron who wanted a sec man desperately enough to accept a known slacker. Few did.

"My fault, Chief," Jessica stated, turning away from the radar console. The luminous green arm steadily swept the blank screen, only registering small reflections from the other war wags and nothing more.

"It's his prob," Kate corrected, cutting off the tech. "I know you're bed partners, but every member of the crew hauls their own weight, or pays the price."

"How about I go tell Anders right now," Roberto said, rising from his chair. "We can have a private chat."

Removing her Stetson, Kate hung it on a nearby bolt jutting from the wall. "Just don't damage him so much that he can't fix the hose," she growled.

Roberto nodded in agreement and strode from the control room to head down the central access corridor to the rear of the wag.

"Let's move," the Trader ordered, reclining in her chair. "North by northwest, and watch the sand for traps."

With a gentle lurch, the armored wag rolled into motion and started down the inclined embankment, the other vehicles close behind. Reaching the plains, War Wag One took the point, with the cargo vans clustering close behind, and War Wag Two taking the rear guard. The ground had seemed hard underfoot, but the wheels of the transport sank inches into the gritty material from the tremendous weight of the transports. A tech flipped some switches, and the belly of the wag rose an additional foot.

"Lock it tight, Blackjack," Kate ordered. "We don't want to drag belly going over a dune and blow a power line."

Already doing the job, the man didn't bother to respond.

Taking a beer from a small fridge, Kate checked the bank of vid cameras and saw armed men and women standing guard at blaster ports along the huge vehicle. So many people depending on her decisions, and so many ways for her to geek things up and ace them all. Sometimes, Kate felt the pressure and had a fleeting urge to be alone again, just an outlander on the run with nobody to discipline and no friends to bury. But this was civilization, the completeness of her world. She was like a baron of a ville, or the captain of a ship at sea, with high, low and middle justice.

Watching the landscape moving outside the Plexiglas of the main window, Kate took another sip of the home brew. Damn her, but this was good beer. They would have to trade with those folks in New Mex more often. The farmers drove a hard bargain, but the brew was worth the price.

After a while, Roberto returned to the control room, the knuckles of his right hand bloody. Kate exchanged looks with the man as he took his chair and used an oily rag to clean his fingers. The skin wasn't broken anywhere, which meant the blood was Anders's. Hopefully, the hunter had finally learned his lesson this time. There would be no more chances. He was good, possibly the best, but nobody was irreplaceable. Not even her.

Swaying to the gentle motion of the wag, Kate finished the beer and tucked the bottle away for a wash and refill later. The drive crew was forbidden to drink anything potent on shift, but they made up for that lack when off duty. Only one time had she found a gunner doing jolt, and while on a shift. She shot out both knees and left him helpless on the ground, then took pity and drove over the fool, smashing him into pulp under the wide studded tires of the big wag.

The radar beeped suddenly, making everybody jump, and Kate studied their location on the map on the ceiling. Yeah, somewhere near here the town of Lubbock used to be. The radar was picking up the shattered ruins. But that was mutie land now, with nothing to find but death. The things in the ruins were unlike any other creature in the Deathlands. Twisted monstrosities that couldn't leave the Great Salt any more than green plants could live in a glass lake. Born in the ancient rad storms, they now had to live in the rad pit and couldn't leave. Which was so much the better for norms. From what she had heard…

"What the fuck is that?" Jake demanded, leaning into the controls. The purr of the tandem engines eased as the pneumatic brakes slowed the rig to a mere crawl.

"Trouble?" Kate demanded, glancing about. There was nothing in sight but some dark sand ahead. The glowing ruins of Lubbock were a long way in the distance.

"Get the missiles hot," Roberto directed, racking the bolt on his .50-cal. "Anything comes our way, launch on sight."

As the techs got busy, Kate didn't want to contradict the man, even though she doubted the weapons would be necessary, but it was always better to be armed than not.

"What do ya see?" a tech asked, craning his neck to look out the windows.

"On our right," Jake replied, angling the wag to roll alongside the dark line in the sand.

Then the woman looked again at flowing material and realized it wasn't moving to the motion of the wind, but against it.

"Vid!" Kate barked, and an external camera swung that way and zoomed in for a tight view. As the screen cleared, Kate could tell the moving line wasn't sand, or salt, but mud. A dirty stream of wet sand!

"It stretches for miles," Jessica said in a shocked voice. "A stream of water."

A burly man barked a disbelieving laugh. "In the middle of the Great Salt? Impossible."

"The hell it is," Kate muttered, unable to tear her eyes away from the incredible sight.

"Full halt," she ordered, scowling as war wag crested a low dune. Now before them was a muddy flatland stretching to the horizon.

Swiveling in his chair, Roberto said, "This was desert only a couple of months ago. Now, I've seen acid rain turn grassland into desert, but never the reverse. Where the nuking hell did this much water come from?"

"We can follow the stream," Kate started to say, when the ceiling speaker cracked into life.

"Eric here, Chief," a voice said. "I have blasterfire to the portside, and coming in fast." He paused. "And something else, another sound, I can't really tell what it is for sure. Mebbe rain, or a lot of folks bleeding bad, or—"

"Splashing," Kate said. "It's goddamn splashing, isn't it?"

"Could be," Eric said hesitantly. "But that can't be right. We're in the middle of the Deathlands! Ain't no water for hundreds of miles!"

"There is now," the Trader said, rising from her chair and going to the periscope near a blaster rack. Raising the Navy device to its full height, Kate pressed her face to the cracked eyepiece and slowly turned for a full sweep.

"Found 'em," she announced, staying hunched

over, hands on the guide posts. "Ten, twelve men on foot to the east. Two hundred yards."

Kate stood and lowered the periscope into the floor. "Get razor, people! They got a swarm of millipedes on their ass!"

"How many?" Jake asked.

"Too many!"

"Lock and load!" Roberto commanded, spinning in his chair and racking the bolt. "Close all ports! We go on canned air, right now!"

A series of hard slams sounded throughout the entire length of the vehicle, as the war wag sealed every opening with sheet steel, then the ceiling lights and control boards dimmed for a moment as the air conditioners kicked on and a cool breeze started blowing from the ceiling vents.

Then every blaster turned toward the strangers from the east, and the horde of slavering muties close behind them.

Chapter Ten

"Son of a bitch!" J.B. cursed, putting a long spray from the Uzi into the face of the sec droid hunter. The 9 mm rounds ricocheted off the machine flying in every direction, hitting cans on the shelves and the corpses lying on the floor.

"Outside!" Ryan shouted, firing his Steyr SSG-70 as fast as he could work the bolt.

Firing every step of the way, the companions backed out of the supermarket when Krysty cut loose with the H&H Nitro Express. A lance of flame extended from the twin barrels, the discharge deafeningly loud even in the open air. The first .475 round glanced off the droid, denting the alloy rod of its torso, the ricochet whining away into the distance. The second hit the joint of the left arm, ripping away the cover plating. Instantly, Ryan concentrated his longblaster there, the 7.62 mm rounds slamming into the exposed gears until the array from the soft lead froze the arm in position. But the spinning buzz saw at the end of the ferruled arm never slowed.

As the machine came through the smashed windows of the preDark building, Doc held the LeMat in a two-handed grip, waiting an insanely long moment before firing. The handcannon boomed like thunder as the .44 miniball slammed into the machine with triphammer force. The left eye lens shattered from the impact, and the droid started for the scholar as he fired a fast four times, trying for the other eye but missing.

Moving among the dead cars, the companions tripped several times on the dried corpses on the black pavement. This was the worst place to hold a fight.

Working the bolt on her Remington longblaster, Mildred fired twice at a car near the droid, the sporting rounds punching neat holes through the hood of the vehicle, but failing to ignite the engine. The gas tanks were as dry as dust.

Leaving the sidewalk, the droid bumped into a car and the desiccated corpse behind the steering wheel fell over. In blinding speed, the droid rammed its buzz saw through the glass to behead the dead woman and the passenger beyond.

Swinging the lever on his Winchester, Jak hit the good eye twice, with no result except for making the machine slow its advance slightly.

"Any grens?" the albino teen demanded, thumbing fresh rounds into the side port of the Winchester.

"Nothing!" J.B. replied, giving it another long burst from the Uzi. "Lost the last implo gren escaping from the ville!"

Slinging the Steyr, Ryan drew the SIG-Sauer and started firing steadily, hitting the sec droid every time.

Dean launched a quarrel from his heavy crossbow that glanced off the droid's body. Stepping behind a luxury car as protection, Doc holstered the LeMat and drew the Webley to fire a fast six times, hitting the droid only on the left side. The sheer force of the booming hardball ammo cut nicks into the shiny chrome rod body, making it spin once, momentarily out of control.

As it faced the wrong direction, Krysty fired the H&H Nitro, hoping the rear armor might be thinner than the front. The massive .475 nitro round put a dent in its domed head the size of a fist, but nothing more.

"How many more?" Ryan demanded, over the booming SIG-Sauer.

"Last round!" she replied, shoving in a single fat .475 round into the breech of the elephant rifle.

"Save it!" he ordered.

Walking backward onto the curb, the woman nodded and drew her S&W .38 to fire twice at the droid.

Holding a breath to steady his aim, Dean launched another iron quarrel. But this time, the bolt smacked into the ruin of the broken lenses and went halfway into the dome. The machine frozen motionless for a long pause, and the companions took the opportunity to run for more distance.

Sparks cracking along the conductive shaft of the arrow, the machine removed the quarrel from its head with a set of pinchers, then made loud clicking noises before starting after the escaping companions. The hole was now covered with steel leaves.

Fireblast, it was self-repairing! Grimacing in rage, Ryan tried for the opening anyway, but the machine was now keeping its weak point turned away from them.

"Sign!" Mildred shouted, firing skyward.

The rest of the companions copied her angle and threw a hail of lead at a large hanging neon sign. Under the brutal pounding, the corroded supports ripped free from the brick building, and it plummeted straight down onto the sidewalk in a strident crash of glass and steel that missed the droid by mere inches. Going around the obstruction, the droid continued relentlessly after its prey, its buzz saws whining loudly as the telescoping arms extended for a kill.

"Get thee back, Geryon!" Doc snarled, lowering the spent Webley to pull out the LeMat and shoot twice, the Civil War piece blowing flame and thick smoke along the sidewalk. The first round punched a hole in a fireplug with no result whatsoever, and the second struck the gas tank of a police motorcycle, making the corpse fall off the bike. The droid attacked the movement in mindless fury.

Then stepping around a corner, the old man switched weapons again, breaking open the top-loading Webley. The action made all of the spent cartridges jump out and he quickly shoved in live cartridges.

Ryan and J.B. maintained a steady fusillade as they backed into view past the corner, then Mildred, Jak and Krysty gave cover fire so the two men could reload their blasters.

"This isn't accomplishing shit!" Mildred growled, firing the Remington and working the bolt to eject the spent brass. "We need a bazooka!"

Abandoning the heavy crossbow and quiver for speed, Dean glanced at a fire station across the crowded street. From here, he could see the formidable axes hanging in the wall, the adamantine alloy blades designed to cut through lesser metals. The idea appealed to him for only a moment, when he realized that using the ax would put him within the reach of the buzz saw. Then the boy caught a whiff of smoke in the air. They had to be near the burning fuel truck. But try as he might, Dean couldn't think of a way that might be useful in this fight.

Snapping off shots from the SIG-Sauer, Ryan glanced in every direction to try to find something useful in the preDark city. Then he spied the fire station. Yeah, that might just work. In a flash, the man started sprinting through the maze of vehicles and disappeared inside the station.

"Here it comes!" J.B. shouted, firing a short burst at the machine. A jam caught in the ejector port, and the Armorer feverishly worked the arming bolt to clear the bent brass to start shooting again.

The rest of the companions maintained their fire while retreating from the machine. Unlike its brethren found inside certain redoubts, this one was in perfect working condition, and if it had been armed with any kind of a distance weapon, they would all have been chilled by now. But most droids had been designed more as a terror weapon, built to deter people from entering top secret facilities like the redoubts rather than to commit wholesale slaughter.

Moving into the street again, the companions shot at the droid and threw the occasional round into the fuel tanks of the better condition cars, hoping for an explosion, but it never happened.

Shoving a pizza van aside, the sec hunter droid charged for the companions, and they turned and ran. But as they passed the fire truck parked before the station, there came the sound of running boots, and Ryan appeared on top of the cab with a shining ax in one hand and a cloth bundle in the other. At the noise, the droid turned and Ryan spun out the fireproof blanket to cover the machine. As it raised both buzz saws to cut away the heavy material, Ryan jumped from the top of the cab, swinging the ax with all of his strength. The ax struck the right buzz saw, shattering the spinning blade with a ringing crash. Instantly, the shrapnel sprayed out in every direction, and for a split second, the one-eyed man saw his own distorted reflection in a flying chunk of steel as it passed his head.

"Now!" Ryan shouted, diving aside.

As the droid removed the blanket, Krysty, standing only a few yards away, fired, the muzzle-flash from the H&H almost touching the machine as the remaining red lens shattered into a million pieces. Recoiling to ride the force of the blow, the sec hunter droid rallied within seconds, blindly thrusting out its remaining blade to hit cars, walls and lampposts.

Now the companions hammered the damaged machine with blasterfire as slim burnished rods rose from within the armored body. Bending and flexing, the antennae probed the air and then once more the hunter started forward.

"LISTEN UP, Gordon," Kate said into a microphone. "Pull back to the dry sand and keep Two to cover the cargo vans! Those bugs could eat the tires off the rims in a heartbeat! Form a break with you at the center, and use the flamethrower if they get close."

Even as they watched on the monitors, a man tripped in the wet sand and fell. The rest of the people kept going, leaving him behind. Slipping and sliding in the muck, the man finally got to his feet only to scream as he saw a millipede crawling across his chest. Rearing its head, the insect buried its pincers into his flesh and started sawing off a piece. His screams became shrieks as he grabbed the bug and tried to pull it loose, its hundreds of legs ripping the skin off his fingers. Than another bug bit him in the leg and he dropped, wailing in agony.

The port-side .50-cal banged once, and the man dropped lifeless into the bloody water. The bugs converged on the twitching corpse and starting a feeding frenzy.

"Roger that, Chief," the bald man said, his picture on a vid monitor slightly out of sync with his words. "We'll keep the hull cold in case you folks have to get on board."

"Fuck that," she growled. "You get hot and stay that way! Pump as much electricity through the chassis as the busbars. can carry. If the bugs get inside Two, you'll be SPAM in a can for their dinner. Now move!"

Unhappy at the orders, Gordon just nodded. His picture began to shake as War Wag Two started pulling back, with the cargo vans already pushing ahead.

Rolling the big wags into the muddy water, Trader could see the people splashing frantically toward the machine. Friend or foe, it made no difference when millipedes were on your tail. Close behind them the muddy water seemed to boil in a black shiny patch twenty feet wide and about as long. That was a nuking lot of bugs. On a side monitor a camera had zoomed in for a close shot of the muties. The bodies were segmented, the rear pincers arched like a scorpion about to strike, and the front pincers were snapping with the sound of crumpling paper there were so many.

"Missiles armed," Jessica said, her hands poised above the fire-control panel.

"Too late," Kate replied, grabbing her Ingram and

arming the blaster. "At this range the blast would chill the people, and they got kids."

"So what do we do?" Jake asked, staring out the front window. "Light our flamethrower? Use the grens?"

"Wait for it," Kate ordered, standing behind the man, her hands on a ceiling stanchion. "Wait for it…now! Charge!"

The huge machine rolled forward, its headlights flaring and the air horns sounding like the clarion call of doomsday. The terrified people darted away from the vehicle as it continued onward until reaching the bugs. Suddenly, the cameras showed the fat insects everywhere, and a skittering noise came from the sides and roof.

"Zap 'em," Kate shouted. "Quarter power!"

"Quarter? But that's not enough to… Right!" the man said in understanding, and dialed down the voltage to barely enough to stun a human and flipped the switch. The monitors went crazy, scrambling and strobing as the raw current pulsed through the armored hull. From every direction there came high-pitched keens, and a score of the insects splashed into the water stunned or dead.

As the monitors cleared, Kate saw the people still moving, the low voltage dissipated through the yards of water not enough to slow them. But those bugs in direct contact with the metal hull were fried. Not all, but enough.

"Hit 'em again!" Kate commanded, watching the screens. The surviving bugs were concentrating on the killer thing in their midst, the splashing meat momentarily forgotten.

"Again!" she ordered, watching the reserve-power gauges drop quickly. "Again!"

"Almost there..." Roberto announced from the periscope. "Just another sec. Okay, they're on dry sand!"

The Trader bared her teeth in a feral grin. "About goddamn time. Now give me full power! Everything we got!"

The lights and monitors went out as the nuke batteries put every volt through the defense grid welded onto the outer hull. Keening screams sounded in every direction, and several of the insects on the Plexiglas windshield burst into flames, blue sparks crawling over their dripping wet bodies. The crackling continued for several minutes, the water around the war wag starting to steam until the reserve banks were exhausted.

As Jake released the switch, the engines started once more and everything came back online. Then a monitor winked out as a fuse blew, a curl of smoke rising from under the control board. The bald man rushed to fix the matter, while the others took stock of their own equipment, flipping switches and checking meters.

"No damage, Chief," Jake reported, spinning in his chair.

"That we know of," Roberto muttered, trying to see the muddy ground below the wag. But the angle was wrong. Then suddenly an alarm sounded and a red light flashed on the damage board.

"Nuking hell, we got a fire in the kitchen," Jessica reported, working the controls. A monitor came to life and showed swirling smoke, laced with fiery orange. "There must have been some arcing through the shutters."

"You, you and you, go handle it," Kate commanded, pointing to the gunners. "Foam only, no water, until you're sure it was an arc and not a live short circuit."

Grabbing preDark pressurized cans from wall mounts, the men rushed down the corridor and out of sight.

"Kill that alarm," Kate said, and the wag went quiet. Going to the transponder, she took a hand mike from a rack and pressed the transmit switch. "Gordon, you copy?"

"We're here, Chief," he replied over the ceiling speakers. "There's smoke coming out your ass, port side."

"We got a team on it already," Kate replied succinctly. "What about the bugs?"

There was a crackle of static. "I think you got them all. Can't see any movement on this side."

Which didn't mean shit, since the muties were notoriously hard to ace. Even the ones lying under the water might still be alive, just unconscious for a while. They could have found a chink in the armor and were burrowing into the wag as she tried to decide what to do. Seconds counted now.

"We're going to have to do a hard recce," the Trader said, taking the Stetson off the wall and patting it into place. "Gordon, get ready to burn us in case of trouble."

There was a brief pause. "Confirm, Chief," the second in command of War Wag Two said reluctantly. "Will do."

"Get hard," Roberto ordered, and everybody grabbed a blaster from the wall rack or pulled a weapon from beneath the seats. For a moment, the room was filled with metallic snaps and clicks as the blasters were primed for action.

"Harry, get the door," Kate directed, leveling the Ingram.

Before obeying, the guard checked the ammo clip in his M-16 and the 40 mm gren in the stubby launcher attached under the main barrel. Now ready, the man threw the bolts and opened the door. The curved section of hull swung down on well-greased hinges and hit the inch-deep water with a rippling splash.

Her Ingram chattered as a millipede fell onto the ramp from above and started inside the wag. Little bastard had to have been sitting on the weather strip used to make the door airtight.

Firing from the hip, she hosed the steps and sparks

flew as the 9 mm rounds ricocheted around the yard-long bug. Then it reared to strike, pincers wildly snapping and Roberto fired his shotgun. The sawed-off double-barrel blew a hellstorm of soft lead through the doorway, and the millipede exploded into pieces, pink blood gushing from the tattered remains.

Jumping outside into the wet sand, Kate spun fast and cursed as she saw more of the millipedes alive and moving. Another dozen had survived by being on the rubber tires!

Unable to shoot without blowing the tires, the woman kicked the nearest bug hard with her boot. Hissing loudly, it dropped off the wheel and started for her, wiggling through the mud when the guard cut loose with his M-16, the preDark hardball ammo chewing the bug to pieces.

But the scent of blood seemed to drive the others mad, and now millipedes dropped off the wag in a dozen places, hitting with little splashes and then starting after the Trader, some submerged and others in plain view.

Firing a line before the insects to hold them back, the guard emptied another clip into the muties as Roberto hit the water and thundered flame at the creatures. Then the rest of the control-room crew came out the doorway and splashed into the fight, hammering the bugs in a cacophony of firepower.

Jessica cried out and fell backward into the salt mud, a millipede clinging to her boot, the pincers sawing away. Kate slashed out with her bowie knife and cut off a dozen of the creature's legs. Hissing in pain, it stopped attacking Jessica and turned to snap at the Trader. Shoving her blaster into its mouth, she squeezed off a burst and the bug erupted from within, guts flying everywhere.

As the fighting slowed, the people turned to inspect the transport, firing a round here and there, extracting millipedes from inside the barrels of the 40 mm gren launchers, an exhaust pipe and an unmanned machine-gun blister. As a bug hit the water, the nearest person would stomp on it with a boot in the middle of the body where the pincers couldn't reach, and somebody else would blow off its head. Once the tactic was worked out, the slaughter continued relentlessly until there were no more of the monsters to find.

"That should be the last of them," Kate said, removing a spent clip from her blaster and pocketing the empty to slide in a fresh clip. "Anybody hurt?"

A few folks had gotten bitten, or scorched from a muzzle-flash of a friendly blaster held just a touch too close to unprotected skin. But the damage was minor, and when Jinx came out of the war wag carrying a bag of medicine, he seemed pleased.

"With all that firepower going off, I expected a lot more damage than these scratches," the healer said, walking among the crew. "Nothing important here. All right, everybody get inside. I'll want good light to clean those bites."

As the people sloshed back into the vehicle, Kate stayed in the mud, with the hot barrel of her rapid-fire resting on a gore-splattered shoulder.

"Okay, Roberto, let's get some dry land underfoot," she directed. "Roll her out, nice and slow. We're still checking for passengers."

The big man nodded and climbed inside. Soon the engine rumbled into life and the wag started forward at a stately crawl. Walking alongside the transport, the Trader watched the machine and the waters underneath just to make sure they had cleaned off every last mutie. For a moment, she thought one had escaped detection, but it was only a hollow body, the guts blown out by a large-caliber round. Good enough. As the war wag drove onto the dry sand, the woman relaxed and joined the group of soaked people panting in a huddle.

"Are you…" a man asked reverently, clutching a bundle to his chest, "are you the Trader?"

Nearby, a young woman kept a skinny arm around a small boy who alternated between looking at the bald man and the bloody woman with the blaster. There was some fear in his young face, but also a trace of defiance. These were ville people, not runaway slaves. Too bad. She always gave slaves preferential treatment.

"I'm the Trader," Kate stated, looking over the motley group. "Where the hell are you folks from? There's nothing closer than Rockpoint that I know about."

"That is our ville, my lady. Or rather, it was," the bald man said. He quickly added, "Thank you for saving us."

Kate waved a hand to cut that short. "Just call me Trader."

"Of course."

"And tell me about this water," Kate said, jerking a thumb at the muddy field. "Was there an earthquake? Some sort of river washing in from the mountains, or what?"

"No, my…Trader. There was an outlander," the man said hurriedly, rushing the words. "A man called Ryan Cawdor. He and some coldhearts snuck into our ville and started a riot. Chilled everybody they could and stole a bunch of horses."

According to the ancient laws of Texas, that was a hanging offense. Horses were infinitely more valuable than wags. They ate wild grass and reproduced themselves. No wag had ever learned that trick.

"Ryan Cawdor," Roberto said in a flat, emotionless voice from the open doorway of the wag. "The name is familiar. And you say he has turned into a coldheart."

The bald man nodded vigorously. "Yes! He—"

"That's a triple-damn lie!" a new voice shouted angrily.

Lifting the blaster off her shoulder, Kate watched as this new person shoved his way through the other people. He was heavily muscled, missing a couple of fingers on the left hand, and his left eye was marled white, with a long scar going from his forehead, across the dead orb and down to his dimpled chin.

"No, it is not!" the bald man retorted, starting to reach under his clothing.

Moving with astonishing speed, the newcomer punched the first man straight in the face. Teeth went flying, and the bald man staggered from the blow, but came back in a crouch and whipped out a blaster. But it was aimed at Kate, not the one-eyed man!

"Look out!" the mother cried, shoving the boy behind her for safety.

That was when the sky seemed to shatter as a dozen .50-cals from the war wags and cargo vans all spoke at once, the combined rounds almost blowing the man to pieces. As he spun wildly, his blaster discharged, the slug smacking into the sand between Kate's boots. The tattered body was shaking as the woman lowered her rapid-fire and put a single round into the back of the dying man's head. He twitched as it hit, then went still, the sands slowly turning red around his ravaged face.

"Thanks for the warning," Kate said, cradling the smoking blaster in both hands. "You were fast. I like that. We're shorthanded after some business down south. Want to join? We got space."

"Really?" she asked, hope brightening her careworn face, then her features went blank again. "No, please, I don't do that anymore."

Kate understood, and her hatred of Gaza increased. "We got no gaudy sluts here," the Trader stated gently. "If you ride, then you'll work, just like everybody else. But not on your back. My word. That good enough for you?"

Hesitantly, the woman nodded in agreement.

"Can you cook?"

"Some," she admitted. "And bake a little, too."

"Even better." The Trader smiled, then whistled sharply and lifted a hand.

From the doorway of War Wag One, Roberto tossed over a holster containing a revolver. Kate made the catch and handed it to the young mother, whose eyes went wider at each passing moment of comprehension.

"Mine?" she asked in a whisper.

"Everybody goes armed in my convoy," Kate said firmly. "Now, get your ass to the kitchen and start on dinner." She left the sentence hanging.

"Matilda," the young woman said, buckling the gun belt around her waist. "And this Avarm."

The boy peeked out from behind his mother, then hid again.

"Welcome to the convoy," Kate said, then gestured at the war wag with her chin. "Get on board. The kitchen is in the rear. Help yourself to anything you want. The cooks always eat first, or else they eat everything. Right?"

Matilda almost smiled. "You've done it yourself. I can tell."

"Yeah, but not for a long time," Kate agreed.

"Roberto, they're now in your charge. Find them bunks and some shoes for Avarm."

"Check," he said, and led the new recruits into the war wag and out of sight down the central corridor.

Noticing the bloodstains on the big rig, Kate pulled out the hand comm and hit the switch. "It's me," she said.

"Roger, Chief," Eric replied with only a faint crackle. "I'm way ahead of you. Got the ears turned up to max. Any more bugs come our way, you'll know it before they do."

"Good man," she said, and tucked the unit away.

Now the rest of the crowd was staring at her with expressions of awe. To most of them, a radio was only a legend.

"Could we get some food, too, Trader?" another man in the group asked, shuffling in the dust and salt. "It's been days since we last ate. Even longer since we had fresh water."

Glancing at the acres of muddy land, Kate frowned at that, then remembered the water was flowing over salted sand. Even if it started fresh, that stuff wouldn't be fit for a mutie to drink after ten yards.

"You didn't say or do shit when he tried to get the drop on the Trader," the guard announced from the doorway. "Now zip it, and speak when you are spoken to, outlander."

The words hit harder than the presence of the deadly

NO POSTAGE
NECESSARY
IF MAILED
IN THE
UNITED STATES

BUSINESS REPLY MAIL
FIRST-CLASS MAIL   PERMIT NO. 717-003   BUFFALO, NY

POSTAGE WILL BE PAID BY ADDRESSEE

GOLD EAGLE READER SERVICE
3010 WALDEN AVE
PO BOX 1867
BUFFALO NY 14240-9952

Get FREE BOOKS and a FREE GIFT when you play the...

LAS VEGAS
GAME

Just scratch off the gold box with a coin. Then check below to see the gifts you get!

YES! I have scratched off the gold Box. Please send me my **2 FREE BOOKS** and **gift for which I qualify**. I understand that I am under no obligation to purchase any books as explained on the back of this card.

366 ADL DRSL

166 ADL DRSK
(MB-03/03)

FIRST NAME

LAST NAME

ADDRESS

APT.#

CITY

STATE/PROV.

ZIP/POSTAL CODE

7	7	7	Worth TWO FREE BOOKS plus a BONUS Mystery Gift!	
🍒	🍒	🍒	Worth TWO FREE BOOKS!	Offer limited to one per household and not valid to current Gold Eagle® subscribers. All orders subject to approval.
🔔	🔔	♣	TRY AGAIN!	

blaster. Outlanders. They were now wanderers, people without a ville. Outcasts were the natural prey of any coldheart with a blaster.

"Everybody will get a meal," Kate said, releasing the bolt on her Ingram to ease their apprehensions some. "But nothing is free. I barter for a living."

"What do you want?" the big one-eyed man asked bluntly.

"Information," she said, crossing her arms. "That was a good punch. Why did you throw it?"

"He was a stinking priest!"

"Priest?"

"High priest, actually."

Kate gestured for more. The man was eager to talk, his rage almost palpable, radiating like heat from a foundry.

"The name's Red Jack," he said, thumping his chest with a hard fist. "Used to be the bartender at the ville tavern. Ryan and some folks came into town— that much the priest said was true. Anyway, Gaza jacked one of Ryan's people as a sacrifice to the Scorpion God."

"And Ryan got him back," Kate said. It wasn't a question.

Red Jack grinned, displaying a gold tooth. "Damn straight he did, that's a bullet in your blaster for sure. Blew the temple to hell, releasing this river of water. Son of a bitch Gaza had an ocean hidden away while telling folks he was squeezing it out by the drop. Made us obey or die, plain and simple. Used to say that blood made the water flow faster.''

Awkwardly, the bartender hid the mutilated hand behind his back. "If you broke his rules, sometimes, the payment was flesh,'' he added with a grimace.

"So Gaza is aced?" Kate asked.

"Hell no. He escaped in a wag of some kind. Big thing, eight wheels, loaded with blasters and grens.''

Eight wheels, could be a LAV 25. "Any rockets?''

He frowned. "Nope. But Hawk stole the ville 25 mm, along with a shitload of shells.''

Kate frowned at the choice of words. Shells, not rounds or bullets. Damn, that was real trouble. The armor plating on the war wags was as thick as they could make it without slowing the vehicles and eating excess fuel. They were tough, but not indestructible. A functioning 25 mm cannon could tear open the war wags like a rusty tin can.

"Now, Gaza has the big wag, but Hawk has the twenty-five, is that it?'' she demanded. "You sure?''

"Ya got my word,'' Red Jack stated.

The Trader had half expected that, and had to accept his oath. If you give your word, it was meaningless unless you also accepted the word of others. At least, to a point.

"Any chance they could join forces?''

"No way!'' an old man in the crowd snarled. "Just before leaving, Gaza shot Hawk, and that sorta made Hawk mad.''

"Damn well think so," Roberto said from the doorway. "Okay, food is coming. Line up by the other wag and you'll each get a meal and canteen of water."

"After that," the first man asked hopefully.

"After that," Kate repeated, "you leave."

As the hungry people tramped over to get an MRE pack and hot water from a steaming kettle, Trader kept turning the news over and over in her head. Hawk, Gaza and Ryan in Core country. What a shitstorm this was becoming.

"Imagine Gaza with that 25 mm cannon," Roberto drawled, walking closer, then standing alongside the woman. "Shitfire, Chief, that would change everything. Mebbe we should leave. There's nothing holding us here. No treaties, or blood kin at risk."

"You want to go?" Kate asked.

The big man barked a laugh. "Fuck no. I say we take Gaza down once and forever. End it here and now."

"Agreed," Kate said, removing the Stetson to brush back her hair and then replacing the wide-brim hat. "Okay, after they're fed, we'll head out."

"Which way? Toward Rockpoint?"

"Straight for the nuke cloud," she said grimly, watching the sunlight play on the rippling salt water lake. "If they're anywhere out there, that is where we will find them."

"The only good point was that Gaza and Hawk would never join forces."

"Yeah, thank God for that."

Chapter Eleven

With its antennae quivering in battle frenzy, the sec hunter droid paused in the middle of the littered street, battered and damaged, but nowhere near chilled.

"Head to the left!" Ryan shouted, waving toward the right with his handcannon.

Trying to be as quiet as possible, the companions obeyed, and the machine started going in the other direction, then stopped and spun fast. But by then, the companions had gained valuable yards of safety.

Moving carefully over the corpses on the sidewalk, Ryan noted the actions of the droid in grim satisfaction. Blind, but not deaf, eh? The man thought as much. Okay, he could use that.

Using hand signals, Ryan had Jak throw a knife and smash the windshield of a distant car. As the machine rushed over to the noise, the companions crept through the windowless front of a large liquor store. Ryan would have preferred a paint store, or gas station, but this was the only useful place in sight.

Soon discovering the trick, the sec hunter returned to exactly the same spot it had been standing with machine precision, then started doing a circular recce pattern through the vehicles. As the droid swung past the store, Ryan fired once, hitting it from behind. Immediately, the machine rushed inside with its remaining buzz saw slashing the air.

Firing again, Ryan busted a magnum of champagne on the counter, the popping cork and gush of bubbling wine masking their movements in the store. Then Ryan and J.B. both threw a case of whiskey at the droid. But it heard the clinking bottles coming its way and slashed the box open in midair, shattering the contents and drenching itself completely.

Now the rest started bombarding the machine with bottle after bottle of pungent alcohol. Going behind the counter, Mildred and Dean toppled over a tall display rack to crash a hundred bottles of vodka and rum onto the confused droid. Deafened by the noise, the machine attacked wildly, only managing to shatter more bottles and increase the volume of booze on the floor.

As the machine went berserk trying to find its prey, the companions used the shattering glass to cover their retreat to the rear door. While J.B. oiled the bolt and hinges, the companions kept cover with their blasters as Ryan took a mop from an empty bucket and dabbed it into the liquor covering the floor, then used his butane lighter to set the stringy head of the mop on fire.

The droid paused at the sound of the crackling flames, and Ryan threw the burning mop like a spear across the store. It landed near the front door with a clatter, and the droid attacked as blue flames rose from the igniting alcohol and began to quickly spread, soon covering the droid in flames. As it spun about mindlessly, more bottles began to explode from the spreading conflagration.

Easing out the back door, the companions raced away for several blocks, before climbing the ladder of a fire escape to reach the top of a motel. Then they hurried across the salty roof to jump to the next structure, and then did it again. Several blocks away, the friends finally paused to catch their breath and frantically reload weapons.

"Mother always did say that alcohol was bad for your health," Doc muttered, starting the laborious reloading process of the LeMat. It took about five minutes for the man to properly purge all chambers in the cylinder, then compress black powder, ball and wad using the attached hand-press.

"No sign of the machine," J.B. announced, lowering the Navy longeyes and compacting the tube. He tucked it into his munitions bag and began reloading a clip for the Uzi from a box of spare rounds.

"Thank Gaia that worked." Krysty sighed, then suddenly realized she was still carrying the Holland & Holland. With virtually no chance of ever finding more ammo for the elephant rifle, she placed it gently on the roof and checked the load in her .38 S&W revolver.

"This just bought us some time, nothing more,"

Ryan growled, thumbing fresh single rounds into a spent clip. Tucking the clip away, he started on the next. "You know these machines are triple tough to chill and never stop hunting their prey. If the machine comes after us again," Ryan went on, working the slide on the SIG-Sauer to chamber a round, "aim for the other blade. Once that's busted, we'll have a better chance to escape."

"Escape, not chill," Jak said with a frown.

"We're going to need something other than blasters to stop this droid," Ryan stated bluntly.

"I can make us some Molotovs," J.B. suggested, removing his glasses to clean them on a pocket rag. "But those only confuse and don't do any real damage."

"Pipe bombs?" Dean suggested.

The Armorer replaced the glasses. "Unless we find a National Guard armory, I'd say that was our best bet."

"A sec hunter in a civilian city," Doc said thoughtfully in his deep bass, holstering his piece. "There must be something here of military value."

Furrowing his brow, Jak got the idea. "Means mil blasters."

"Unless it was for a missile silo outside the city," Krysty suggested pragmatically. "Or an escort for some big gov type riding through."

"True enough, dear lady."

Somewhere distant there came the sound of cannons, or mebbe only a series of fast explosions.

"Trapped in a burning city, with no way out, and a sec hunter on our ass," Mildred grumbled. "Plus, the Core and Gaza waiting above."

"Mebbe not waiting," Ryan said, studying the edge of the cliff rising above the city. "We're going to do this by the numbers. First we get more ammo, then we try for the big stuff."

Moving with a purpose, the companions hit the streets. Finding a bank with unbreakable Plexiglas windows, they located a phone book not eaten by the salt and got the address for a sports store, since there didn't seem to be a military base or National Guard armory in town. A police station was useless, as cops never kept their extra ammo sealed to make it easier to use in case of trouble. Which meant the dead air would have corroded every round. But sport stores usually kept their stock of ammo sealed in plastic wrapped boxes to prevent pilferage. Moving fast and silently, they reached the store without incident and found a wealth of ammo under the counter, securely behind a steel lattice. J.B. easily unlocked that and everybody filled their pockets, taking a few spare boxes of a size used by some mil blasters, just to be sure. In the camping department, they found some MRE packs in acceptable condition, a lot of dehydrated food completely inedible, plus some underwater flares and other items that J.B. happily tucked away into his munitions bag.

"Plumbing store is next," he said. "Then we need someplace secure to hide for the night. I need time to make the explos."

"Already found the perfect spot," Mildred said, patting a pocket now holding a local street map. "Thick walls, heavy doors, small windows."

"Jail or library," Ryan asked, tucking a few candles into a pocket.

"Museum."

"That'll do."

Leaving the store, Dean glanced at the modern lightweight crossbows and fiberglass arrows, started to leave, then doubled back and took one plus a double quiver of razor-tipped hunting arrows. The crossbow and quiver combined weighed less than just the home-made crossbow from the ville.

There were several hardware stores in town, and the companions needed to scavenge three before getting every item on the list. However, as they started to leave the building, a sec hunter droid came around the corner, its scissor-tipped arms snapping steadily in a mechanical beat. The droid was undamaged, not even scratched. After a moment, it was gone.

"Fireblast, it's another one," Ryan cursed softly. "We hit that museum right fucking now. I don't want to face another of those things without some heavy iron on our side."

Heading away from the second droid, the companions moved from building to building, watching the darkening shadows carefully, their weapons leveled and ready.

The smell of smoke was getting stronger in the air, the growing fires illuminating the center of the city, casting eerie lights onto the rising black plume. High overhead, the chem clouds rumbled with thunder, and lightning crashed down to strike at the city as if offended by its presence.

The group ceased any further explorations for supplies and headed straight for their bolt-hole. Reaching the museum, Krysty noted a swarm of scorpions scuttling along the courtyard of the stately building, each carrying a grisly piece of the past—a finger, an ear.

"Didn't take them long to get here." Ryan scowled, watching the scavengers scurry away into the sewer gratings. One arm was full of plumbing supplies, mostly short pipes about a foot long and threaded at both ends, but his gun hand was free and lightly resting on the checkered grip of the SIG-Sauer.

"The smell of this much food is going to attract everything in the desert," Mildred agreed, fighting a shiver of repulsion. "Buzzards, cougars, stickies, everything."

"Millipedes," Dean said with a frown, shifting his load of cleaning supplies. The chems had a lot of uses.

Her hair flexing, Krysty advised, "Let them have the dead. The Great Salt can't support that much life, and mebbe the scorpions and bugs would have wiped each other out by morning.''

''At least this might mask our presence from the sec hunter,'' J.B. said, working on the lock to the steel grille covering the entrance to the museum.

''No,'' Ryan said grimly, ''it won't.''

As the grille came aside, they stepped in and J.B. closed the gate, expertly locking it again. Anything that wanted to get to them this way would make a hell of a racket and give them more than enough warning. The wooden front door oddly proved a greater challenge, and J.B. thought he might have to blast for a moment when the corroded lock yielded and the thick portal swung wide.

A rank wind came billowing out like the last breath of a corpse, and the group covered their faces to wait for the building to be flushed with clean air before entering.

Once inside, J.B. bolted the door tight, and the companions spread out to do a quick recce. However, the feeble light of their candles barely touched the vastness of the main room. Then with a cry, Dean turned and fired, the muzzle-flash illuminating a snarling mutie coming straight for them!

But the creature didn't react to being shot, and as Mildred shone the yellow light of her handflash onto the creature, everybody could see its shoulder was blown wide open, with fat tufts of some sort of gray foam coming out.

"Oh, hell, it's a museum of natural history," Mildred said, pumping her flashlight to try to brighten the beam. The sign outside had been too badly corroded to read, and the store map had simply listed it as a museum.

"A what?" Jak asked, raising his candle to the other exhibits. More creatures stared at him with dead glass eyes, forever frozen in a tableau of mock ferocity.

"Sort of a trophy room," the physician attempted to explain. "For folks to see the creatures that once roamed Earth."

"All aced?" the albino teen asked curiously.

"Time itself did that," Doc replied haughtily. "For once, the hands of humanity were clean of the crime of slaughtering living things for pleasure."

"No hunt fun," Jak corrected. "Hunt food."

The scholar smiled benignly. "Ah, my dear Mr. Lauren, your wisdom is boundless."

As the group moved through the display of dinosaur skeletons and dioramas of Neolithic life, they came upon a Tyrannosaurus rex rising high above the terrazzo floor, standing dramatically on a raised platform, with velvet ropes holding back the visitors to protect the creature from them.

"This real?" Dean asked, poking at a leg bigger than a wag.

"Real, but long dead," Mildred explained. "Most of the creatures lived and died millions of years ago."

"Millions?" Jak asked, scowling.

"A century of centuries of centuries," Doc espoused, walking around the Jurassic behemoth. "The preDark world, of the preDark world, in a manner of speaking."

"Come on, the offices are what we want," Ryan commanded, and headed that way, leaving behind the killers from the past.

After finding a secure room, the companions dug in for the night, buttressing the doors with marble benches. Once settled in, dinner was cooked over a small fire built in a metal waste can and fed pamphlets and brochures from the tourist shop. When those were gone, they moved on to paper from the desks and then the desks.

"At least we don't have to burn the oil paintings in the executive office," Doc rumbled, contentedly picking his teeth with a paper clip. "It was an unwelcome experience to dine on hundred-year-old military stew warmed by the million-dollar fire of a stack of burning masterpieces."

"We saved the Gauguin and Edward Hopper," Mildred added around her toothbrush. Then she rinsed with mineral water and spit into a trash can. "But we should have done the Jackson Pollocks. Never did like the abstract expressionists."

"Agreed, madam." Doc smiled, displaying his oddly perfect teeth. "But the fumes from his depressing works would have only made the food sour."

Mopping his mess kit clean with a piece of bread from the MRE pack, Ryan idly listened to the old-timers chat and really could make no sense of it. Some of the artwork had been beautiful stuff, pastoral scenes of flowers. The rest were just splotches on canvas.

After dinner, Ryan and Krysty took the first shift of walking a patrol of the building while J.B. showed the others how to make pipe bombs from the plumbing supplies, mixed with items from a paint store and a garage. If there had been the time, the Armorer could have made much more powerful guncotton from the treasure in most banks. A big stack of money, a sack of silver quarters, a high-school chemistry lab and in less than a week he was producing fulminating gun-cotton at a tremendous rate. The stuff was ten times more powerful than dynamite, yet much easier to make. He and Ryan had tried reloading bullets with the stuff once and even with a half charge mixed with common dirt, the blaster was blown apart. Since then, he never tried again, using the reloads found in the redoubts. They were infinitely safer.

One at a time, each section of pipe was filled with a batch of cooked chems poured from a coffeepot, then the end cap screwed on tight and gently laid aside. While they cooled, the bombs were sensitive to shocks, but once cold, you could toss one down a flight of stairs and nothing would happen. Unless the fuse was lit, and then they detonated with staggering force, throwing out a deadly halo of shrapnel from the lead pipe.

Doc, Jak and Dean took over the production of the explos, as Mildred and J.B. walked a patrol. Ryan and Krysty found the private office of the curator with a comfortable sofa for sleeping and settled in for the rest of the night. Their next tour wasn't until just before dawn.

Chapter Twelve

The stars disappeared and the sky brightened as dawn rose in the east, but the preDark buildings stood in shadows until the sun crept over the rim of the crater and shone upon the burning city.

Sleeping on a blanket near the dwindling campfire, Baron Gaza awoke at the infusion of light. The air was chilly, his breath fogging slightly, and the waves of heat from the crackling fire felt good on his face. Dimly, the man could sense something was wrong, but nothing about the area seemed awry. Food was cooking, although there were no frying pans in sight lying amid the burning wood. Kathleen was sitting in the open rear doors of the APC, a rapid-fire across her lap. Della was inside the war wag, wrapped in blankets, and the others were lying nearby, naked limbs intertwined from the previous night's orgy of debauchery.

With streaks of dried blood on her cheek, Shala lay curled into a ball, still trembling under the blankets. Gaza smiled briefly at the memory of the rape. He had been her first, in so many ways, so after his lust was slacked, the baron wasted time giving her pleasure. And his wives had done a superb job removing her tongue, the cauterized stump barely bleeding at all it had been done so quickly. The combination of mutilation, pain and pleasure did the trick as always. She now silently worshiped him like his other wives, although he would have the rest keep a close watch on her for a while. Sometimes there were slips, and he always hated having to slit a throat on the honeymoon.

Rising from his nest of sweat-and-sex-stained blankets, Gaza rose and stretched, luxuriating in the warm morning breeze. Limping over to the edge of the cliff, the man openly relieved himself while Allison stood close by with a longblaster cradled in her arms. She grunted as he finished, then waved a hand at the city below.

The view was murky, and Gaza tried to force the sleep from his sight when cold adrenaline coursed through his powerful body and the man violently cursed. That wasn't the fog of sleep; it was smoke, billowing clouds of thick smoke, with flickers of writhing flames deep within. He tried to wish it away as a bad dream, but as his eyes became adjusted to the growing light he saw the ruins of some smaller buildings on the south side, charred timbers mixed with priceless debris, the perfect wags in the street reduced to smoldering wrecks.

"Blood of my fathers," the baron growled, taking a step toward the metropolis, "it's burning. All of it is burning!"

Fearful for his safety, Allison grabbed his shoulder

in a strong grip, and he shook her off, then backhanded her to the ground.

"It's burning!" he screamed, spraying spittle into her startled face. "My empire is on fire and you let me sleep? You feeb slut."

Tears running down her face, Allison used both hands to try to explain she had only discovered the destruction moments before her husband. Watching the hand gestures, Gaza couldn't follow what she was saying and turned away before he struck the ignorant bitch again. The city was burning, the wealth of the preDark world vanishing before their very eyes. There was no time for recriminations or beatings. Every moment counted now.

"Everybody up!" Gaza shouted, striding across the campsite to reclaim his clothing draped over the front prow of the APC. "Put everything back into the wag! We're going in to loot the ruins for blasters."

As he climbed into his clothes, his wives began to hurry about the area, picking up loose items and herding Shala into the vehicle. Shuffling over the uneven ground, the girl dropped her blanket, exposing her pale skin and pert breasts. Yanking on boots, Gaza paid no attention to the battered female, with more important matters on his mind. Who the nuke was this Ryan Cawdor to come out of the Deathlands like some whirlwind of destruction? First, Rockpoint was destroyed by water, and now this nameless treasure trove by fire. It was like something from the fragging preDark Bible. What in hell was coming next, a plague of mutie locust?

As if in response, the fiery clouds in the sky rumbled ominously, making Gaza almost drop his gun belt. Trying to hide the fear in his stomach, the man forced trembling hands to buckle the holster around his waist, and he cleared his mind of foolish worries with the comforting routine of checking the big blasters. His personal handcannons had been bought from that bitch Trader before she decided he was stockpiling too many blasters. As if there was such a thing as too many weapons. She just wanted to keep him weak, unable to leave the desert and expand his domain. But that was changing now, and soon he would have that blond bitch under the knife. Not to make her a wife, oh, no, this time it would be just for the sheer pleasure of bloody revenge.

Going to the rear of the vehicle, Gaza checked the clutch and electric motor for the heavy winch. Designed to pull the wag from swampy ground, the cable was thick and strong. When Gaza had first obtained the vehicle, he had walked out the cable to its full length to learn exactly how long it was. He had used a knife to scratch the framework for every ten paces, and now counted ten such marks. Roughly a hundred feet. The sinkhole was about that deep. Which meant there was no way he could anchor the cable and have the APC lower itself to the ground below. Damn. But he could lower down a couple of his wives to raid the ancient structures before the whole place was leveled by the flames.

"Damn you Ryan!" he screamed at the buildings showing below the cliff. "Damn you to hell!" Strangely, the words echoed among the windowless concrete hives, as if carrying onward forever.

CLOSING THE DOOR to the museum, J.B. locked it with a click and stood to join the others on the front steps. Washed, fed and well rested, the other companions were spread out in a defensive arc with their backs to the museum and blasters held ready. Just for a moment, J.B. thought he heard somebody calling a name, and then it was gone, carried away on the breeze.

The plaza of the building was alive with scavengers, insects of every kind and flocks of rustling birds, mostly black buzzards. They had arrived during the night, hundreds of them, along with some vultures. Normally bitter enemies constantly fighting over every scrap of food, now the birds roosted side by side, stuffing themselves on the dried human flesh that lay sprawled in the streets in such abundance.

Trying to hide it, Doc was repulsed by the sounds. The noise of the feasting was horrible, the ripping of cloth followed by the stabbing of sharp beaks and then the ripping of skin and cartilage. It reminded him of pigs at the trough, and he forced away the madness that welled at that dark memory.

Away from the bloodless carnage, a smoky pall

hung over the city, thick clouds swirling along the streets, distant reddish lights showing new buildings burning out of control, mingling with the occasional crash of falling masonry and splintering wood.

"Ryan," Mildred said, licking her lips.

The big man turned. "Yeah?"

"You know how I'm always pushing for us to recce just a little more, and try to salvage more technology, medicine, whatever?" She frowned. "Well, not this time. We're standing in the middle of the powder keg, and we can't leave fast enough."

"I second that," Dean added grimly, adjusting his grip on the lightweight crossbow.

Krysty glanced around at the other buildings and stores near the museum. Her hair was strangely still, its lack of motion showing her deep concern.

"The question still remains," she muttered. "How do we get out of here? A hundred feet straight up is a hell of a climb."

"We've done it before," J.B. stated, tilting back his hat to survey the sprawling metropolis. "But only as a last resort."

Every building seemed to be crawling with birds and other scavengers. More winged creatures were circling the exposed city, some of them soaring between the buildings and roosting amid the gargoyles and spires of a cathedral. The stained-glass windows were about the only glass remaining intact.

"Hell of a climb," Ryan agreed, "so we best try

and find something else before we go grabbing bastard rock.''

Walking along the steps, his presence caused a stir among the birds and he worked the bolt action on the Steyr without conscious thought. As if understanding the action, the buzzards moved away from the man to feed on other corpses. Only the vultures stayed, arching their snakelike necks in annoyance as they gobbled down ragged pieces of dried flesh.

The companions were closest to the northern side of the cliff, the smoke thin enough to see the vertical rock wall of the sinkhole. There were a lot of cracks, and even a few ravines, but nothing that would offer a route to the surface. The sinkhole made a hell of a trap and once inside, there was no easy way out. They were like rats in a garbage can, with the open sky directly above, but no way to reach it.

''Buried alive,'' Mildred said softly, her words carrying on the morning breeze much farther than she had expected.

Just then, a soft, familiar hooting sounded from the burning city, and the companions turned together, fingers tightening on triggers. A few blocks away, a humanoid figure was clinging to the side of a luxury hotel, holding on to the stonework with one arm while the other was batting at the birds swooping close to feed on the helpless prey. But as one vulture got too near, the humanoid grabbed a flapping wing. As the vulture frantically tried to get free, the manlike being released its grip of the wall but stayed oddly secure to the flat stonework with just bare feet as it tore the screaming vulture apart in an explosion of bloody feathers. Screaming their rage, the other vultures flapped away.

"Stickies." Krysty cursed, frowning. "Mother Gaia, protect us. Everything in the desert must be heading this way."

"When the dust dome cracked, it must have been visible for dozens of miles," Doc stated, both hands resting on the silver head of his ebony stick.

"Hundreds of miles," Ryan corrected, "We need to recce the rockface, and the top of a building would give the best view. Just need some place the fire hasn't reached yet."

"Or stickies," Jak said, checking the clinking bag at his side. The museum had been full of useful items, and now they had eight Molotovs made from wine bottles, carpet stain cleaner, vodka and some odd chems. Since J.B. was hauling the majority of the lead pipe bombs, Jak had opted to carry the heavy Molotovs. Besides, he was a better aim at throwing things than the Armorer.

"Where we came in looks okay," Dean said, pointing in that direction.

As J.B. used his Navy scope to check the building, Ryan squinted at the structure. Sure enough, the central office building wasn't yet on fire, but the flames were close, reflecting on the sides of the structure.

"Too risky," his father declared. "Once we reached the top, the fire could jump and we'd be trapped for sure."

J.B. lowered the longeyes and compacted it before tucking it away. "Nothing else looks any better," he said ruefully. "What ain't on fire yet is blocked by the buildings that are."

"So we walk the skirt," Ryan stated firmly, settling the matter, and the man turned to head toward the section of cliff that was nearest. "It'll be awhile before the fire reaches the outskirts, so anything there we can use to recce, or as a ladder to climb out."

"You really think we're going to find something?" J.B. asked,

The one-eyed man shrugged. "You got a better idea, start talking."

J.B. merely grunted in reply and fell into step with his friend, the stubby barrel of the 9 mm Uzi regularly sweeping the street and sidewalks before them in a steady pattern.

Crossing the street, the companions put the feeding birds in their wake, and maneuvered through a morass of cars all jammed together in neat rows. The machines had to have been in gear, held in place purely by the pressure of the driver's foot on the brake when the world ended. As the corpses went limp, the vehicles surged ahead, but only for a few feet before slamming into one another and forming an orderly crash that stretched for blocks.

Halfway through the crumpled vehicles, Ryan heard a faint moan and walked closer to a black limo to touch the hood. The metal was vibrating slightly under his fingertips. How the hell could the horn still be operating a hundred years later? Unless the engine had a nuke battery for a power source. But that was for mil wags only, and not even every one of them got the unique devices.

Studying the driver and passengers, Ryan deduced it was some sort of a gov wag, loaded with the barons of their day. Oddly, there seemed to be movement amid the passengers, and he instinctively swung up his blaster as protection. A black millipede crawled into view from under the jacket of a corpse, then several more from the other corpses. The bugs were everywhere inside the limo, and Ryan could only guess that the things had been attracted by the mag field of the still working horn. For some reason, they were drawn to mag fields the way a shark was to blood in the water. Mildred had tried explaining it once, but the whitecoat jargon was out of his league. However, the fact remained that bugs liked mag fields.

Away from the traffic jam, a lifeless mob of people filled the sidewalk and street in front of a movie theater, and the companions had no choice but to walk on the dead, the desiccated bodies crunching under their boots like autumn leaves.

Heading for the cliff, Ryan turned a corner and stopped. The intersection was clear of traffic, the bodies of police lying before the side streets full of cars, and some sort of a mil convoy parked forever at a stoplight. Motorcycles flanked an unmarked armored truck, the driver and passenger both openly carrying shotguns. The local cops had been holding back civilian wags for the mil wags to get through.

"Must have been important folks," Krysty said, looking under the vehicle for any more millipedes.

"Or they were carrying something important," Dean suggested, checking the fallen motorcycles. "Prob just gold, or some other useless stuff."

The boy knew that far too many folks had wasted precious time and effort busting open armored wags only to find them stuffed with jack, jewelry or pieces of silver. Totally useless. The paper jack was too stiff to use for wiping your ass, and silver was too soft to make ammo.

Of course, J.B. knew how to make explosives from preDark money and silver coins. But he and Ryan were the only folks still alive who could do that. Dean knew most of the procedure, but it was damn tricky and one mistake put you on the last train west in a fuck lot of very small pieces.

"Gold okay," Jak replied, surveying the rooftops fort any signs of stickies. Many times, he had made reloads with gold bullion from a bank. The yellow stuff was just as good as gray lead for bullets, almost as if they were the same stuff, only different colors. Nothing wrong with finding a load of gold.

Going to the cab of the armored truck, J.B. tricked the lock and cracked the door a hair, allowing the century-old air to escape in a whispery sigh. Its passage made the two corpses slump forward slightly as if suddenly tired.

As the ancient death fumes cleared, the Armorer swung open the corroded door with a squeal of hinges and reached in to remove the keys from the ignition and toss them to Ryan. The other man made the catch and started for the rear to check inside.

Climbing onto the step of the front cab, J.B. carefully removed the shotguns from the crumbling hands of the dead men. Working the stiff pump to eject the shells, he got ten before the second shotgun gave a loud crack and jammed solid, the pump no longer able to move in either direction. Eight of the shells cracked apart into dried powder and shot when the Armorer gently squeezed the plastic housing, but the two remained firm and he lovingly tucked those into empty loops on his belt. Checking the seat, he found a box of ammo, but spilled coffee had splashed onto the cardboard and over the decades the brass base of the shells had crusted over, making them useless.

Rummaging under the front seat on the other side, Doc unearthed several road flares in good condition, the waxy cylinders fogged with age but still intact. However, whether they would ignite was problematic, at best.

"The proof of the pudding," Doc rumbled, tucking them away.

"Is in the eating," Mildred said as she located a first-aid kit in the glove compartment, and slipped it into her satchel with the other medical supplies. Most likely, everything it contained was useless, but even the plastic box itself would be good to keep her small supply of bandages dry and clean.

Without a qualm, Jak removed a cap from the driver and took the MP's sunglasses. Sliding them into place on his own face, the polarized lens darkened in response to the bright desert sunlight and the albino nodded.

Reaching the rear of the wag, Ryan stopped short at the sight of the single thick door twisted off its row of hinges, the steel battered and torn. But the metal was bent outward, not inward. Something had escaped from the military vehicle, and he could guess what it was.

"The sec hunters," Krysty guessed, standing alongside the scowling man.

Turning, Ryan frowned at the buildings, cars and stores nearby, searching for any sign of movement. But the area was quiet, with only a creaking sign swaying in the smoky breeze and the ghastly noise of the eating birds breaking the deathly still.

"Damn things must have been en route to somewhere when skydark hit," Ryan said, keeping a sure grip on his blaster. "Mebbe even the Grandee redoubt.

And they've been sitting here on their tin asses, warm with juice from the nuke batteries until the dome cracked.''

''They probably read that as an act of aggression and activated themselves to repel the invaders,'' Mildred added, working the bolt on her Remington longblaster. Only four rounds remained, but she planned on making every shot count. Her Czech ZKR pistol would be used for millipedes and stickies. The bigbore bone-shredders were reserved exclusively for the lethal military robots.

''You mean,'' Dean said, ''to repel us.''

Then without further comment, the boy took a stance toward the swinging sign and worked the arming lever of his new crossbow to nock a fiberglass arrow into place. The droids were smart and might decide to try to get close using the noise of the sign as cover.

In a swell of fatherly pride, Ryan noted the boy's actions, then returned to the van, knowing his back was secure. Inside were floor brackets about the size of the base of a sec hunter, power cables dangling impotently from the ceiling, a bank of meters and dark vid screens flanking the two spots. For Ryan, the number was deeply reassuringly. Just the two they had seen so far, then, no more.

There were also some skeletons at the front of the wag, strapped into seats, with steel briefcases chained to their wrists, the dusty uniforms hanging loosely off the wizened corpses of the officers. Holstered at their sides were a couple of plastic boxes like the remote control of a vid. Snapping loose a restraining strap, Ryan slid the device from its holster and it crumbled in his grasp, completely eaten through by the leaking acid of its own batteries. He tried again with the other and got the same results. Chilled by sheer time.

"These must have been the remotes to control the droids," Ryan guessed, tossing the fistful of circuits and chips aside.

"Anything else?" Doc asked, craning his neck to see the interior.

Glancing at the briefcases, Ryan saw a logo on the stainless-steel lock and knew better than to waste time trying to get inside those. Most likely it was the best the government at the time had. Even if they were successful, he knew it was possible that the cases were boobied.

"Nothing here for us," Ryan said, coming out. "We better move in case the machines return to check on their masters."

That was a sobering thought, and the companions quickly departed the area and didn't stop until they were a good two blocks away. From there, the cliff rose above the low buildings at the outskirts of the city, loose rubble from the salt dome lying in plain sight, some sections a dozen yards thick, others only broken into a million small crystals the size of a fist. Loose white salt covered the streets inches deep, a few mounds rising over fireplugs and bodies, making the area look like Alaska in the winter.

Crunching through the salt, they reached the base of the cliff and studied the rock face. It was as they had feared—the cliff was a sheer vertical rise, without ledges or cracks to use for climbing. Even worse, the plain of the city seemed to be larger than the cliff above, so that any climb would be partially inverted, the climbers hanging downward.

"Nobody here before us," Jak stated, only glancing momentarily at the pristine salt. Not a single footprint or spoor showed in the loose material.

"Not here anyway," Ryan said. Trying to gauge the slope of the cliff, it appeared that the rock was less angled inward to their right, toward the east.

"This way," he said. "Doc, use your coat."

As the companions started forward once more, Doc removed his frock coat and tied the arms around his waist. Now hanging on the ground, the material smoothed over their prints in the salt to disguise their passing. It wouldn't hide their presence from a human tracker, but might be good enough for the machines.

"Wish we had one working wag," Krysty added, sliding a backpack over her shoulder.

"Pity about those two-wheelers," Mildred said, looking at the display of racing bicycles inside a dark sporting goods store.

Bikes were good for doing a recce in a city, and able to go places no motorcycle could because of their weight. But while most of the frames in the front window were badly corroded from the salt air, the better titanium frames were in excellent condition. The problem was the tires. The majority were only tatters of rubber draped over the shiny rims. There might be some in the back storeroom, but finding enough of the right size to fit seven of the titanium bikes would take hours. Time better spent making distance.

"Need a lot of oil to get those moving again," J.B. commented, pausing to look into a crack of the salt before stepping over and across. "A hell of a lot more than I carry, and there's not a garage or hardware store in sight."

"Furniture store on the corner," Dean noted, gesturing with his crossbow. "Got a couple of lamps on display. See 'em? Just drain the lightweight oil on top, and there's enough heavy machine oil on the bottom to lube a hundred bikes. Good for blasters, too."

"An exemplary notion, my young friend!" Doc rumbled in good humor, clasping the boy on the shoulder. "Highly laudable! Is this your own idea?"

"Learned it at Brody's school," Dean answered.

"Head's up," Ryan said, coming to attention. "We found them. Ten o'clock high."

Facing in that direction, the others took a moment to study the preDark buildings, then scanned the top of the cliff. Barely visible against the light-colored sand of the desert was a dark shape traveling along the very rim of the sinkhole, a cloudy rain of loose stones and sand falling in its wake.

"Dark night, that's a LAV 25," J.B. said, peering through the Navy longeyes. "Got to be Gaza."

"Or Hawk," Ryan added, backtracking the sand cloud of the war wag's passage. It reached only a half mile or so. Good enough.

"Okay, if they're going left, then we go right," he stated, turning and proceeding quickly in the other direction. "Best to put more distance between us and hopefully cover ground they haven't yet. We've got to locate some way out before they find a way down."

"No prob," Jak stated confidently. "Need cracks to climb. Gaza need highway for big wag."

"The APC has a winch," Mildred reminded him, "and can easily support its own weight."

Walking along the soft salt, Ryan frowned. Fireblast, he hadn't considered that possibility before. Turning to ask J.B. a question, he stopped as something dropped from the bare rocks above to land near the companions. Incredibly, it was a humanoid figure with skin the color and texture of the rock. Male sexual organs dangled obscenely between its scrawny legs, the hands and feet covered with rippling suckers.

"Stickie!" Ryan cried, firing his blaster at point-blank range.

The creature recoiled, hooting in pain, thrashing its limbs wildly. Doc and Krysty frantically jerked out of the way to avoid touching the creature, and it fell to the salty ground, a gaping wound pulsating in its shoulder. A thin fluid trickled from the ragged opening, but then it started to close, and the stickie rose again, its naked legs already changing into the color of the powdery salt.

"It's a goddamn chameleon stickie!" Mildred cursed, pumping two rounds into the creature's face, going for the eyes. Both orbs exploded into a gelatinous mass from the arrival of the .38 slug, and the pure-white stickie fell to the ground.

Several more of the disguised creatures dropped into the middle of the group from the rocky overhang, and the companions suddenly found themselves attacked from every side.

lywed didn't run off during the scavenging. Which
meant the task was middle-wife work.

"I'm sending down Carol," Gaza announced, wrap-

Chapter Thirteen

The eight heavy wheels chewed the ground along the
edge of the cliff, sending a salty dust cloud across the
preDark city.

Baron Gaza didn't like it. To give away your position before a fight was bad tactics. But he hoped it
wouldn't be noticeable mixed in with the smoke from
the burning buildings. Besides, there was no other
choice. He needed to be this close to the rim of the
cliff to see the buildings below. The baron had small
hope of spotting the hated outlanders, but Allison was
standing in the aft turret, ready to unleash the 25 mm
cannon at the first sight of Ryan or the others.

The heat of the rising sun hadn't yet turned the desert into an oven, and the baron had the top hatch raised
to admit a pleasant breeze into the war wag. The smell
of hot metal, oil, diesel fumes and sweaty bodies had
been making the interior of the APC almost unbear-
able, and he now bitterly regretted ripping out the air
conditioner to save fuel. The baron had no idea how
the Trader could stand the reek of humanity for those
long treks across the nukescape.

In tumbling majesty, the dying city was spread out

to the left, the light of the fires fading in the sunlight, but during the night the sky had glowed from the reflected flames. Entire blocks had been reduced to blackened skeletons of twisted steel from the raging fires. Smaller structures were ablaze, filled with flames that occasionally exploded, throwing out a spray of burning debris.

Lines of cars were burning, like knots in a fuse, until the flames reached a preDark gas station and created new detonations, fireballs rising into the sky and fading away long before the sound of their creation echoed to the distant observers.

The sheer waste of the precious materials was a knife in his gut, but the man accepted the loss and concentrated on trying to steal what he could before the rest of the city was consumed by the growing conflagration.

Reaching for the water bag, the baron turned his head for a moment when a descending buzzard jerked his attention back to the metropolis below. What was it?

Slamming on the brakes, Gaza downshifted until the wag slowed to a shuddering halt. Almost immediately, the dust cloud in its wake washed over the vehicle, blocking out the world for a few moments.

Turning in the navigator seat, Kathleen silently asked her husband what was happening. Gaza ignored the woman and, grabbing hold of the overhead hatch, pulled himself from the driver's seat and climbed

down the angled hull of the APC to rush to the
bling edge of the cliff.

Partially blocked by the smoke, he saw a parking
lot

... about a block in filled with military vehicles—4X4 trucks, Hummers, a lone LAV 25 and several huge tanks. It was a convoy of some sort, stopped for lunch or fuel, and caught in the salt-fall to never move again. Until now. The machines looked in perfect condition from this distance, and Gaza could barely breathe at the idea of how much ammo and fuel had to be there just waiting to be taken. For a wild moment, he toyed with the notion of trying to get one of the tanks to the desert, then abandoned the idea as impossible. The steep sides of the sinkhole would be tough for even a strong man to climb. And so far he hadn't even found a trail that would handle the lumbering APC, much less a gigantic preDark tank. Those were made prisoners of the city from their own weight and size. But the contents could be scavenged, every drop of fuel and every live round of ammo.

"Wake up, my dears! Time to work!" the baron said, going to the external winch and releasing the cable.

With a bang, the rear doors of the APC slammed aside and two of his wives came running around the machine, with blasters in their hands. As the wife in charge, Allison would stay with the APC, and Della would keep a watch on Shala, to make sure the new-

ping a length of the greasy cable around an arm. "Latch the hook on to anything you can and we'll haul the stuff up here for sorting. Pay special attention for weapon lockers. Those will be large boxes resembling a green plastic coffin. If you find something big, I'll send down Kathleen."

Shifting the boxy Ingram rapid-fire to hang out of the way across her back, Carol nodded dumbly. The small brunette was on point for the recce. Understood.

With Allison watching from the turret atop the APC, Kathleen helped Carol loop the woven steel cable around her body, under the arms and between her legs for reliable support. It was a long fall onto hard rock.

Gaza stayed with the winch and kept a hand on the control box, taking his cue from Kathleen when to spool out some slack. Careful of her balance, Carol eased herself over the side until she was dangling freely. The loops shifted position as the metallic length fully supported her weight, and for a heart-stopping moment she thought they were coming off. But then the steel hook cinched firm and the cables tightened securely about her clothing.

Glancing up at Kathleen, Carol waved a hand to show that everything was okay. Turning toward the APC, Kathleen wiggled a finger at her husband, and Gaza began feed out the cable nice and slow. Long minutes passed as the woman descended into the city, and the main reel was getting low when Kathleen made a slowing gesture. He complied, and then after a few more yards she clenched a fist and the baron cut the power and set the brake.

Staying in the cable, Carol unlimbered her rapid-fire and looked over the area for any immediate dangers. Black birds were eating the ancient corpses, but no other creatures were in sight. However, she made a mental note to stay clear of the sewer grates and any dark shadows.

Releasing the catch on the heavy steel hook, Carol slithered out of the cable and loosely attached it to a piece of salt-corroded machinery sticking out of the ground. Whatever its original purpose, the thing would now function well as an anchor. Checking the spare clips in her belt, Carol glanced at the cliff and got a reassuring wave from Kathleen, her husband standing nearby with a longblaster held at his waist. Good enough.

Wary of her footing, Carol headed through the jumble of smashed concrete and sparkling salt crystals to reach the ruins and slipped past a collapsed piece of a building, ducking to avoid having a lamppost hit her head. Once on the street, the woman weaved through the posed corpses, marveling at the amount of metal they wore as ornaments. It was on their wrists, fingers, ears, and one female even seemed to have it in her tongue and nose. She had to have been very bad for her husband to torture her like that.

The corner was free of cars, and Carol paused at the entrance of the parking lot, listening hard, her rapid-fire balanced in both hands. On the other side of the fence, the mil wags were parked in a paved lot, and more corpses in fatigues lay on the hard ground, with blasters and clipboards scattered nearby.

The wisps of smoke moved eerily over the streets, the grinning bodies staring out through the closed windows with sightless faces. Carol shivered from the feeling that thousands of eyes were watching her every move. But her unease grew from the shadows of the tall buildings, most of them higher than anything she had imagined—five, six stories tall reaching toward the very stars. Carol fought the urge to say a prayer to the ancient ones and beg pardon for entering their lost world.

And the carrion birds were everywhere feeding on the dead. Although she knew the scavengers were terrible cowards alone, they were brave in a group, and might attack if provoked. The sooner another wife came down the better.

Swallowing hard, the woman squared her shoulders and started for the nearest truck in the convoy. The mil wag was huge, many times larger than the APC, and the rear doors had flopped open, spilling out the cargo. At first she thought they were food packs, those MRE things her husband spoke about so avidly.

Checking inside the vehicle, she found even more of the objects, hundreds upon hundreds of small green squares. Then Carol realized they were actually cubes. A big rig full of plastic cubes! Thousands of them! She had absolutely no idea what they could possibly be.

Listening to the moan of the wind, Carol lifted one and held the cold cube in her hand, half expecting it to vibrate or radiate warmth. But the cubes were as inert as the sec men guarding the convoy.

Reluctantly exiting the truck, Carol went past a couple of empty Hummers and started for the tank. A corpse lying across the top, halfway out of the hatch, showed how to gain entry. But she already knew how to get inside such a war wag, where the live shells would be stored and how to release the catches holding the ammo in place.

Then she slowed, realizing that it was pointless to raid the big machine. Each shell was almost too big to carry, and even if she got it to the APC, there was no way to shoot the ammo. Forgetting the heavy brass, Carol went to the rear of the tank and rapped on the spare fuel cans strapped to the side. She was rewarded with an answering slosh. Fuel to spare!

Dragging a can over to the cable, she attached the hook and watched as it was hauled upward and out of sight. As the empty cable started snaking downward once more, Carol got the next two fuel cans and sent them up together, the winch handling the load effortlessly. Good, this would save a lot of time. Choosing the next target, the woman headed directly for the APC sitting on top of a smashed Hummer, a pile of corpses wearing camou uniforms crushed beneath the war wag. Even from here, she could see the sealed plastic tubes of the LAW-givers amid the wreckage. Those were the best. PreDark rocket launchers that could destroy even the largest war wag. With only one of those her husband could ace the Trader from a safe distance. Those she had to have immediately.

Then she could do the LAV 25. Since it had a rapid-fire and a 25 mm cannon mounted on top, there should be lots of linked ammo stored inside. Mebbe even fresh chems for the smoke-generators. Her husband would be delighted over such a find. But this was more than she could carry. There was so much to take!

Turning toward the cliff, she fingered a message for Kathleen to come down. Standing dangerously close to the edge, the busty woman nodded and stepped out of sight. Returning, Kathleen slipped over the edge and the cable started extending with the woman dangling at the end.

As the woman landed, Carol helped her loose from the hook and they returned to the park. Kathleen went to explore the APC as Carol started straight the Hummer.

Passing the tank, Carol heard an odd sound, almost like empty ammo shells jingling in a pocket. Curiously, the woman turned to see a machine of some sort came out of the war wag and start toward her. Its body was composed of chrome rods, the domed head fronted by two enormous red crystal eyes and both of its weird flexible metal arms tipped with scissors. Was it some sort of device for farming, to harvest crops? Born and raised in the desert ville of Rockpoint, Carol had never seen anything vaguely similar before and couldn't even hazard a guess to its purpose. However, it was still working, so mebbe her husband would want it for parts.

As she approached, the machine suddenly reached out and she automatically jerked backward, the scissors snapping closed only a hair away from her throat. Carol had actually felt the passage of the metal on her skin.

Snarling a curse, the woman unlimbered the rapid-fire and hosed the preDark device with a stuttering stream of 9 mm rounds. At this range it was impossible to miss and almost every round hit the sec hunter droid but merely bounced off its armored body.

Now the droid charged again, the twin scissors closing with a loud crunch, and she saw that the barrel of her blaster was cut off at the magazine. Nuking hell, it was a guardian of some kind! Firing wildly, the panicked woman could barely control her weapon without the aid of the barrel and she hastily backed away, trying to shout for help, the impulse returning unbidden after so many years of being rendered mute.

Then her weapon jammed, and as the droid reached

for her face Carol turned and ran blindly into the street, bouncing off the dead cars and rattling the ancient occupants. Then cutting through a courtyard, she ran through a feeding flock of buzzards, hoping the birds might distract the machine. Screaming in outrage, the carrion-eaters erupted into flight, and while the urge to look was strong, Carol dared not risk a glance to see if the trick worked.

Pelting down the street, the woman zigzagged through the rubble and dashed under the crashed lamppost. Unable to hear anything but her own rushed breathing, she scrambled up the rubble, feeling a rush of relief that the cable was still hanging in place waiting for her return.

Rushing for the hook, Carol tripped and landed hard, losing her blaster and a hand went straight onto a cluster of salt crystals, the sharp prisms stabbing through the soft part of her palm like a glass daggers. Writhing in agony, she pulled her hand loose just as the jingling noise came again from behind. It was here!

Blasters started shooting suddenly from above, the rounds hitting everywhere nearby. Safe for the moment, the woman reclaimed her rapid-fire and savagely yanked the arming bolt of the boxy 9 mm Ingram SMG, finally freeing the bent casing caught in the ejector port. Firing as she turned, Carol saw only the brief flash of mirror-bright steel as the scissors stabbed into her chest.

Searing pain filled her world as she saw her own blood gush onto the machine, then the second scissors reached for her throat. Everything went chaotic as she went flying sideways to land on the ground, then rolled away until eternal blackness swallowed her whole.

Casting away the headless torso, the sec hunter droid swiveled its lenses skyward, easily finding the APC on the ledge. It waited a full minute for an order from the soldiers operating the U.S. Army vehicle, but when nothing was received on the proper channels, it immediately switched to defense mode. Cycling out a pair of secondary arms equipped with pliers, the droid grabbed on to the dangling hook and started to climb steadily arm over arm.

Now from above and below small-caliber rounds hit the droid, then a nearby section of the rock face exploded thunderously as a LAV rocket slammed into it. Shrapnel ricocheted off its primary hull in a hundred places, but nothing penetrated.

Then the damage around the smoking blast crater began to spread, the cracks yawning wide in every direction. Large pieces of the rock started to fall away, causing a minor avalanche. Then there came the roar of a diesel engine and the cable began to move as the APC departed the weakened section.

Gripping even harder, the droid continued to climb even as it bounced and slammed off the crumbling face of the cliff. More than once it was sent spinning away, sailing over the city, only to come crashing back against the rock with brutal force. An eye cracked, distorting its external view, and a secondary hydraulic system went off-line from the pounding, but the droid accepted the damage as minimal and continued toward the enemy.

The droid was only a few yards from the top of the cliff, when the APC stopped moving. Redoubling its ascent, the sec hunter clawed its way onto the desert floor and stood just as the 25 mm cannon atop the LAV 25 roared into life. The explosive rounds detonated on its hull in strident fury, smashing both primary and secondary systems. Forced backward from the sheer force of the continuous detonations, the sec hunter tried to get out of the way and it suddenly was falling.

Unacceptable. Reaching out for the blur of rock with every arm, the machine found the cliff was just outside its range, even with the longarms fully extended. Sending out a radio signal for immediate assistance, the machine emotionlessly tried to find a solution to the problem when it hit a pile of broken concrete with triphammer force and abruptly ceased to process information.

INSERTING A FRESH ammo clip into his AK-47 assault rifle, Baron Gaza snarled a guttural curse as the tumbling machine crashed into a million pieces, wires and gears flying wide and far. Then there came a crackling electrical explosion from within the wreckage, and an oily cloud of dark smoke rolled skyward.

"Try to chill me, will ya?" he shouted, firing a burst at the destroyed remains. The pieces jumped and danced from the incoming barrage of rounds, but no other result was achieved from the expenditure of ammo.

A grunt caught his attention, and Gaza turned to look at Allison still in the turret of the APC, an arm draped across the 25 mm cannon, its multiple barrels visibly radiating heat. He arched an eyebrow and she asked a silent question.

Shrugging in response, Gaza went back to looking at the city below, now searching for any sign of Kathleen. Studying the littered street, the man saw a movement in the shadows and started to swing the Kalashnikov that way when a breathless Kathleen raced into view, her arms cradling a LAW rocket launcher, the plastic tube fully extended for immediate firing.

Scanning the desert above, she looked quizzically at the baron, until he pointed downward and his wife tracked to where the droid lay smashed amid the salt and concrete. Exhaling deeply, Kathleen sadly shook her head over the incident, then started back toward the convoy in the parking lot.

There still was a lot of ammo and fuel to harvest before it would be time to sing the passing of her beloved sister. Business came first, then mourning and, eventually, sweet revenge.

Chapter Fourteen

Caught by surprise by the rain of muties, the companions were forced to withhold using their blaster out of fear of hitting one another at such close quarters.

Even as Ryan ducked and dodged out of the way, the hooting stickies charged. With his back to the rock wall, the one-eyed man fired the Steyr only inches from the face of a mutie, the muzzle-flash washing over the distorted features and seeming to drive it away more than the 9 mm round that punched through its head.

Rushed from both sides, Jak dropped the cumbersome Winchester and jerked both hands straight out. With hard thuds, knives slammed into the throats of the two stickies, cutting off their terrible cry. Then, grabbing the Winchester again, Jak raced between them, firing at another heading for Mildred from behind. At the noise, the woman turned and fired, the combined impacts to the head killing the creature.

Shoving the Webley into the belly of a rushing creature, Doc fired the big-bore handcannon, blasting open its abdomen. But as the mutie was thrown backward, the blaster went along, pulled from his grasp by even the brief contact to the gelatinous ooze of the dreaded stickie.

Firing his shotgun twice from the hip, J.B. blew two of the muties into each other. They fell in a tangle of limbs, then stood again without any problems, their damn secretions obviously not adhering to their own kind. Slicing out with the bayonet on the end of her Remington, Mildred tried to gut the monster, but the blade went in only so far before becoming bogged down inside the guts of the creature. As the sucker-covered hands went for her face, Mildred triggered the blaster as a distraction, then shoved the Remington as hard as she could, making the stickie stagger away as it took the weapon along, buying a few feet of precious distance.

Free for a moment, the companions unleashed a hellstorm of lead, peppering the hooting creatures in the head and driving them from the cliff. But even as the companions scrambled for some combat room, the surviving stickies started forward again, already altering their naked bodies to meld with the scenery. One male standing on the pavement and the salt was morphing into black asphalt on the left and sparkling crystals on the right. The effect was more than disconcerting. Standing amid the rubble of the ruins that circled the preDark city, the chameleonic muties were fragging difficult to track properly.

"Force them into the open street!" Ryan shouted, shouldering the Steyr and fanning the creatures with a hail of 9 mm rounds from the coughing SIG-Sauer. "Jak, light 'em up!"

While the others formed a ragged line to discharge volley after volley of rounds to drive off the creatures, Jak pulled out the Molotovs and started to throw them. The first hit the ground between the two groups to keep the muties at bay, but the next two bottles arced down directly onto the creatures, the glass shattering as it hit the ground, and splashing them with the fiery contents.

One stickie caught a Molotov in the chest and the bottle just stayed there, the burning rag fuse hanging impotently. Then Dean triggered his Browning, shattering the glass. Burning fuel engulfed the stickie, and it hooted wildly as it started running about blindly. Coming through the pool of fire, the creature headed for Krysty. The woman dodged frantically and it collided with a rusty mailbox, instantly trapped by its own resinous secretions. Even as it burned alive, the skin was turning bright orange and red to match the colors of the fire.

Incredibly, one more stickie fell from the cliff to land near the companions. Moving fast, Doc threw a fistful of salt into its face, and Ryan grabbed a bent curtain rod from a pile of junk and used the pole to beat the stickie into the growing pyre.

The stench coming from the frying muties was horrendous, their anguished hooting getting louder all the time, but the companions stood their ground with blasters at the ready until the thrashing creatures finally succumbed into quiet death.

"Mother Gaia! Hellhounds would be easier to ace than a stickie," Krysty said, cracking open her revolver and dumping the spent brass to quickly reload. The shells hit the hard ground and bounced away.

"Stay razor, people," J.B. growled, switching from the M-4000 scattergun to the Uzi machine pistol. "There could be more of them."

"Probably not," Mildred said, glancing into the rock shadows overhead and in the wreckage piled outside the city. "The food supply in the desert is too meager to support many of these creatures. Big as a human usually means a human-size appetite."

"Doesn't mean that for sure," Ryan countered grimly, slipping a fresh clip into the SIG-Sauer. "We best stay together. That'll reduce the chance of another mutie slipping in close."

"Camou stickies," J.B. muttered, working the arming bolt of the Uzi. "Thought I'd seen it all."

"There is a first time for everything, John Barrymore," Doc rumbled, purging and recharging the LeMat. The Webley would be sorely missed.

"At least once," Krysty agreed, her hair flexing and curling from her agitated state. Her steel blaster felt warm and familiar in her grip, but the woman drew no comfort from the weapon. This ancient city of the dead was quickly becoming a city of death. How many more battles would they have to survive before they could leave? But she already knew the answer to that question. Too damn many.

Thumbing fresh rounds into the side feed of the Winchester, Jak approached the grisly bonfire and frowned at the sight of his leaf-shaped throwing blades mired in the crackling corpses of the deceased muties.

"Damn, good knives," the albino teen muttered angrily, working the lever to prime the single-shot longblaster. "Hate lose."

"Blasters are better," J.B. said.

Masked by his sunglasses, Jak snorted. "No reload blade," he stated. "Silent, too."

"You're preaching to the choir," Doc rumbled, patting the bony swordstick thrust through his belt.

"I prefer distance," J.B. said, straightening his fedora. "And the farther away, the better."

"Talk with your boots," Ryan commanded, walking along the perimeter of the city. "Jawing and yapping ain't getting us any closer to the surface."

Staying alert for any suspicious movements, the companions trudged along the base of the cliff, climbing over piles of preDark rubble and around a couple of deep chasms in the ground. The footing was treacherous, the pieces of the fallen dome constantly slipping away underfoot, and often shattering at the first step. Soon the smoldering corpses of the stickies were left far behind, only a thin plume of smoke visible to mark the location for the circling vultures.

"Freeze," Doc whispered softly, going motionless. "Droid. Two o'clock."

Everybody stopped moving at the words, and only shifted their eyes to search along the stores lining the nearby street. Halfway down the block was the damaged sec hunter droid, its eyes gone and its chrome body covered with quivering antennae. But the racing machine wasn't coming toward the companions; it was charging along the street, crushing the corpses in its way until going out of sight.

"Dark night," J.B. said, rubbing the scar on his chin. "I wonder what the frag it's after?"

"Don't know, don't care," Ryan muttered, shifting his longblaster. "As long as it ain't us. Shift it into high gear, people. I want to be far from here when it returns."

The hours passed slowly as the day progressed, but the rising sun could do little to penetrate the thickening layer of turbulent clouds. Sheet lightning was crashing among the roiling orange-and-purple clouds with ever increasing ferocity. A major storm seemed to be brewing, a real Texas tempest, but at least the telltale smell of rotten eggs wasn't in the wind, forecasting the arrival of a deadly acid rain.

Walking carefully up the slope of a piece of the fallen dome, Ryan paused to scowl at something on the other side. Then the big man started forward, and as the rest crested the dome they could see a body sprawled on the ground, its bandage-wrapped limbs splayed at angles impossible for any living being.

"A member of the Core," Krysty said, squinting upward. There was no sign of any activity along the edge of the cliff, but the desert muties might be hiding like before.

"No sign of a wound," Mildred said, kneeling to inspect the crumpled body. "He must have simply fallen from the top."

"No, from that ledge," Dean stated excitedly, pointing.

Sure enough, only fifty feet above them was a rocky ledge in the cliff, an extension of a meandering crack that formed a kind of natural trail leading from the top.

"And there's our exit," Ryan said, cracking the knuckles on both hands. "No more than fifty feet max. We can do that easy."

"Yeah, but we're dead meat if stickies attack while we climb," J.B. said gruffly, surveying the area.

"Gotta take the chance," Ryan stated, sliding the pack off his shoulder. "Okay, drop your packs. The lighter we are, the easier the climb. J.B. and I will stay behind to give cover. Once the rest of you reach the ledge, hitch your belts together and haul up the backpacks. Then cover us while we climb."

The simple plan needed no discussion, so divesting themselves of the haversacks and assorted shoulder bags, the five companions started feeling the details of the rock with their fingers. Finding small purchases, the friends wiggled the toes of their combat boots into some cracks and pulled themselves off the ground. Then testing their positions, they reached high again to continue the endless process. Time was short, but they had to move slow. They might only get one chance at this, and a single mistake would be deadly. A fall of fifty feet onto concrete would chill as fast as a round to the head.

Taking a Molotov and a homemade pipe bomb from the bags for quick access, Ryan and J.B. readied their blasters and alternately watched the cliff and the burning preDark city as the others slowly began to ascend toward the ledge above, and freedom.

WATCHING THE SMOKE RISE ahead of the convoy through the front windows of the lead wag, the Trader suddenly jerked alert as the desert abruptly yawned wide before War Wag One. What in hell was that, a nuke crater? But then she saw dozens of burning buildings sprawling in the ground below. That was no skybomb crater, but a sinkhole with a preDark city inside!

"Stop!" Kate ordered, placing aside her cold can of soup, the spoon rattling loose.

"Bet your ass I'm stopping," Jake replied, as the massive vehicle rumbled to a slow halt. "Black dust, will ya look at that. Just look at it!"

That Kate was doing, and even as the Trader rose

from her chair, the woman found herself unsure of what to do next. The ruins were enormous! Dozens of blocks, with huge brick buildings rising almost level to the desert floor. From the billowing smoke, it appeared that most of the place was burning, but her people had done raids on crumbling preDark ruins before. Once while a mall was sinking into a swamp, and another while it was getting bombed during a sandstorm. Burning made it trickier, but not impossible. Nothing was impossible.

"Nuking hell," Jessica said, massaging a temple. "Just look at it!"

"Shitfire, mebbe it is a blast crater," Roberto muttered, hunching his shoulders as if braced for a blow. "Check the rads immediately!"

"Already did, and it's clear," Eric said over the ceiling speakers. "Whatever destroyed this place wasn't atomic."

"Not a hot zone, good," Kate said, running stiff fingers through her hair. "But this was the source of that mushroom cloud we saw before?"

"Dead on," Jake replied, both hands still on the steering wheel of the war wag. "Same lat and long."

"Mebbe it was white smoke, or a salt whirlwind forming in the hole," Jessica offered hesitantly. "Hell, I dunno. But look at all those buildings!"

"Just fucking think of it. A complete preDark ville!" the door guard started, rubbing the back of his free hand across his mouth, the other clutching the

M-16 with white fingers. "Fuel, ammo, food, clothing, meds…"

"Rads, tox chems, muties, bobbies, cave-ins, avalanche, Gaza, the Core," Kate added in a growl, hitching her gun belt. "The bigger the prize, the more ants there will be trying to carry pieces away."

"At the rate it's going," Roberto added, craning his neck for a better view out the front windshield, "there won't be anything left in a few days."

Which raised an interesting point for Kate. Two villes destroyed in the desert, one by water, now another by fire. Could this also be the work of the outlander called Ryan? Mebbe her info on the man was scragged like a comp disk. Could be he was a technophobe, and hated any kind of science or whitecoat. She had encountered such feebs before, but generally only as loonies running about in rags. Folks like that weren't really a threat to anybody but themselves. But this was another matter entirely.

"Okay, we're going to do a full recce," Kate decided, watching the buzzards circle in the sky about the sunken city. "Put the cargo vans behind those big dunes to the south, with War Wag Two as protection. I want hands on blasters and fingers on triggers."

Pulling his sawed-off from the holster, Roberto scowled, "We're going in alone?"

"Not quite," she replied, but then was interrupted by a shout of surprise from the tech at the radar screen.

"Chief, we have a bounce on the screen," he announced, working the controls. The luminous arms of the radar swept along the glowing screen, leaving ghostly blobs in its wake of varying sizes.

"Something from a skyscraper?" Roberto asked, studying the screen.

Glancing out the front windows, Kate scowled darkly. "No, the sig is too small and a good mile away. Must be on the far side of the crater, sinkhole, whatever this fragging thing is."

"Hard to tell for sure," Blackjack said, the tech caressing the controls to urge greater clarity from the old patched equipment. "There's so much fucking hash in the atmosphere! But it appears to be something large and metal on the far side on the crater."

A wag? Going to the periscope, Kate pulled it up and tried to get a look, but even with the max magnification the billowing smoke from the conflagration below masked most of the city, along with anything beyond.

"Is it moving?" she demanded, chewing the inside of a cheek.

The man didn't reply for a minute, then relaxed. "No, Trader, it appears to be standing still."

"Just some wreckage or ruins then," Roberto said confidently, but then added, "Although this part of the Great Salt is normally bare as a baron's heart."

True enough.

"Jake, move us farther away from the edge of the cliff. It doesn't look too bastard stable," Kate ordered.

"We're staying here as the anchor. Rob, send out some troops on the bikes for a recce. I want a complete circle of the pit."

"Looking for a way down?" Roberto asked, checking a canteen hanging from a metal peg on the wall before slinging it over an arm. "No way in hell we're ever finding a trail wide enough for the rigs. Much less secure enough to take the weight."

"Only nobody tries a descent without my permission," she commanded bluntly. "Gaza could have set fire to the ruins as a distraction to night creep us from behind."

"Eric, keep the ear going at full power."

"Done and done," the man replied over the speakers.

"Think Gaza is going to try and jack the whole convoy?" Roberto asked, adding a pair of binocs and an Uzi to his load. "Mighty ambitious for the baron."

"He jacked a ville once," she reminded him. "Why not a convoy?"

Stuffing some spare ammo clips into his pockets, Roberto took an Aussie digger hat hanging from the rear of his chair at the .50-cal.

"Fair enough," he rumbled, heading for the door. "Be back in a few."

"Stay razor," Trader directed as the armed guard lowered the curved section of the hull to the sandy ground outside. Instantly, a warm breeze blew into the control room of the rig. "Radio when you can."

"If we can, sure," he told her, descending the metal steps, wisps of smoke coming through the open hatchway carrying the smell of wood and some kind of meat. Whatever the frag that could possibly be she had no damn idea.

Watching the rear vid screens, Kate saw Roberto and five other troopers haul down the motorcycles from the side-mounted racks of War Wag Two and check the engines and fuel tanks.

"Prime the missiles in the main pod," the Trader commanded, "We may have to provide some cover for the riders."

"Already on it, Chief," Jessica replied, both hands throwing switches and turning dials. "We're loaded and ready."

"Not yet. Turn off the heat-seekers, or the damn rockets will just arch down after the fire."

"But we'll be shooting blind without them," Jake said, his hands playing over the controls like a musician. "Might ace our own people!"

Resuming her chair, Kate grunted at that possibility. "Lock the first one on the metal thing," she said.

"Alert, I have blasterfire," Eric reported over the ceiling speaker.

"Shitfire, gimme a location!" the Trader demanded, leaning toward the front window of the war wag.

"Inconclusive," he reported slowly. "Almost sounds like two different spots at the same time."

"Are they near each other?" Kate demanded. "We got some sort of a firefight going on down there?"

The ceiling speaker crackled for a few seconds. "Negative on that, Chief," Eric said at last. "The blasters are much too far apart to be shooting at each other."

"Probably just old ammo cooking off from the heat," Fat Pete said, chewing on a piece of jerky. The man had both hands on the grips of the port-side .50-cal, and was nervously shuffling his boots on the corrugated floor.

"Yeah?" Kate muttered angrily. "Mix 'probable' with 'always' and you get aced constantly."

The man had no response to that and lowered his head as if to block her from his sight.

"Stay loose," the Trader ordered in a softer tone. "Gaza is the one to be worried if he's here."

Fat Pete grunted in reply but took on a more normal stance.

"And what if it's Ryan?" Jessica asked.

"Ain't decided on him yet," Kate replied honestly.

Just then, the darkening clouds overhead rumbled with thunder, and the wind slightly increased, kicking up more loose salt and sand until it was almost a visible river of motion. As each bolt of lightning lit up the fiery clouds, there was a faint crackle of static from the speakers, and several of the meters flicked, the radar screen went out of focus and the compass spun wildly.

Pulling the half clip from her Ingram, Kate placed it aside for reloading later on, and inserted a full mag into the blaster, working the bolt to chamber a round and clicking off the safety.

A blaster fight, or old ammo? Gaza or Ryan, or something else entirely? There was no way of telling, but something down deep in her bones told the woman that, one way or the other, there was a hell of a storm coming.

ON THE FAR SIDE of the sinkhole, masked by the raging fires filling the city, the second sec hunter droid finally responded to the radio beacon of its smashed brother.

The damaged droid began to remove bits and pieces of the destroyed machine, replacing weapons, servo-mechanisms, solenoids, eyes and power packs. The work steadily progressed with the motions of the buzzards eating the dead almost perfectly duplicating the utilitarian mechanical salvaging.

Chapter Fifteen

"That's the last of it," Baron Gaza said, tossing aside the empty can. Tightening the vapor cap on the fuel tank of the LAV 25, he locked the protective shutter into place and patted the heavy metal shielding with an open palm.

What a find this city had been! Along with the weapons, MRE packs and ammo, he now had a full tank of fuel. Just incredible. The ground around the APC was littered with empty fuel cans, laboriously hauled up from the preDark convoy at the bottom of the cliff. But all the work had been worth it. Both the main and reserve tanks were full, and there were five more twenty-gallon containers stuffed inside the war wag.

And best of all, it wasn't reg fuel—that would have evaporated long ago—but that good mil stuff that Trader called condensed fuel. It didn't have a smell and didn't evaporate worth a damn even in direct sunlight, yet it fueled a gasoline engine or a diesel.

The ammo bins were jammed full of grens, linked belts of brass, even a couple of those fancy LAW rocket launcher things. Never having seen one before,

Gaza had no idea how to fire the damn things, until Allison read the directions on top of the plastic tube. After that, it was easy as knifing a blind man. With this kind of heavy iron, nothing could stop the baron now!

Going to the canteen hanging from a steel loop designed to attach equipment to the outside of the LAV 25, Gaza drank his fill, then poured some more on his face and slicked back his soaked hair, enjoying the feel of the drops trickling down the collar of his new khaki shirt. He didn't know what the colorful bar of decorations meant on the left side of the shirt, but since the clothing came from the leader of the convoy below, that meant they were important, which was good enough for him.

Standing halfway out of the APC turret, Allison frowned as she pulled back from the scope bolted on top of the big .50-cal machine gun. The longeyes couldn't be used when the .50-cal was firing, or else the brutal recoil would remove an eye, but on single-round firing, it turned the big gun into a longblaster of fantastic range, if only moderate accuracy. However, the scope served many functions aside from merely locating a target.

Rapping her knuckles loudly on the armored chassis of the war wag, Allison got her husband's attention and pointed urgently toward the southern desert.

"Trouble?" Gaza asked, scowling that way, the rivulets of water running down his face from the wet hair.

To the east was the burning city, mostly hidden by the billowing plumes of dark smoke. In every other direction lay only the Great Salt, utter desolation for a hundred miles.

The woman nodded urgently, and splayed both hands twice.

That many were approaching? Although, the man could see nothing, the doomie was rarely wrong on such matters. She only got rare glimpses of the future, but could smell an enemy over the horizon.

Going to the rear doors, Gaza accepted an AK-47 assault rifle from Kathleen, who had another in her hand and a LAW slung across her back. At the front of the wag, Della was starting to turn over the big diesels, while Shala was checking the huge steel box full of linked ammo for the 25 mm cannon. The former member of the Core was wearing norm clothing now, and although the girl seemed frightened by machines of any kind, she was much more terrified of Gaza and his horrible wives and would do anything she was told, just not willingly. Not yet, anyway.

Just then the sound of engines came on the wind, and was gone, only to return again stronger and louder. Machines of some sort. Could be strip-downs, cars reduced to bare frames to max their fuel, a favorite of the coldhearts who raided the villes beyond the desert. Grimly, Gaza worked the arming bolt on the rapidfire. These sounded more like motorcycles. As always, the baron went with his gut feeling on such matters.

Better to prepare for the worst than to have it happen to you.

"Bikes, coming our way!" the baron shouted, grabbing a few grens from the wall bins and dropping them into the pockets of his new tan jacket. "Let's close her tight!"

The diesel roared into life as the man headed for the front of the wag, Kathleen closing and locking the heavy rear doors. The baron knew the riders might only be the Blue Devils, not exactly allies, but mercies who ran a stretch of villes and brothels to the west of the Great Salt. Hard boys with a taste for pain, the group was tough and fast, with a secret source of shine to fuel their bikes and an unhealthy appetite for longpig. These were people Gaza could understand, and he wanted them as his new sec men. The first recruits for his conquering army.

Taking over the controls, Gaza moved the APC away from the cliff where the ground was weak and a single gren could send them hurtling over the side. Better to play it safe.

Charging out of the thick smoke blowing across the desert, the six bikes came into view, leaving eddies swirling in the dark fumes behind. At the sight of the APC, the riders' faces became shocked, and they all drew blasters, boxy rapid-fires, and one guy on front hauling out a sawed-off double-barrel.

There were no decorations of any kind on the two-wheelers, no human skulls, no flaps of scalped enemies, no necklaces of teeth. That was suspicious enough, but their clothing was in good shape, and they had extra ammo in the loops of their gun belts. Mebbe they jacked the bikes and blasters from the Devils, but nobody had clothing like that except for barons and that blond bitch. Baron Gaza had no fragging idea who these assholes were, but it sure as shit wasn't the Blue Devils.

"Outriders!" the baron cursed, in sudden understanding. "They're fucking sec men for the Trader! Take 'em down!"

As his wives started firing through the blasterports, the bikers gunned their engines and separated quickly, only taking a few wild shots at the APC in passing. But as they converged behind the LAV 25, the .50-cal in the turret exploded into action, the heavy rounds ripping through the riders and machines, throwing sparks and blood to the desert sands.

The two flank men dropped, their bikes toppling over to pin them helpless on the sand. Then another motorcycle detonated as its fuel tank was ruptured, the fireball engulfing two other riders. The screaming human torches continued riding their bikes blindly over the cliff and out of sight.

Revving the engine, Gaza started for the others when something hard bounced on top of the APC and then hit the ground, exploding with deafening force and throwing a hellstorm of sand and shrapnel against the armored side. The shrapnel from the antipers gren sounded like hard-driven hail for a long moment, and then was gone.

"Missed! That all you got?" Gaza sneered, throwing the transmission into high gear. "Aim for the bikes! I want one of those bastards for questioning!"

Sitting alongside the man, Kathleen nodded and started to fire short bursts from her new AK-47 out the blasterports.

More weapons boomed outside, closely followed by another gren bouncing loudly off the chassis. It landed in plain sight directly before the ob port of the driver, only inches from Gaza's face. The man locked the left four tires and gave full power to the right four. The APC heaved into a sharp turn, the gren tumbling away to detonate a split second later somewhere to the side. With a pounding heart, Gaza slammed the gas pedal to the floor, and the mammoth machine lurched forward, catching a man pinned under his crippled bike, his screams cut off almost before they started.

The fifty stuttered once more, and Kathleen let loose a long spray of lead when the roaring diesel of the APC suddenly cut off and interior light winked out.

Out of power, the war wag rolled on for a few yards, the bikers hammering it from every side. Throwing a switch, Gaza flooded the interior with emergency lights, and there by the rear doors stood Shala, still holding a fistful of wires as she fumbled with the lock.

"Fucking traitor!" Gaza screamed, clawing for his handcannon.

But Kathleen moved first. Firing from the hip, the slim redhead put a full burst into the busty teenager, stitching her from knees to neck, just as the doors opened and she fell outside.

"We got 'em!" a biker shouted, and started racing for the open rear of the APC, his sawed-off blowing thunder at the startled people trapped inside the dead war wag.

In War Wag One, the ceiling speakers crackled with static, then came back loud and clear.

"We found Gaza!" Blackjack cried. "His wag is busted, and we're going in…" His voice faded away.

"Get him back," Kate directed sternly, hunched forward in her chair.

"Working on it, Chief," Eric said, and suddenly the ceiling speakers rushed with a background hum of full power.

"…trap," Roberto coughed, his voice distorted from pain. "Repeat…fucking trap. He's got a 25…blew us to hell. Forget us… Use the—" Static took away the transmission of the hand comm, and there was only crackling silence.

"Shitfire, Gaza and Hawk have joined forces," Kate raged, slamming a fist onto the arm of her chair. "That APC armed with a 25 mm cannon would chew us to pieces!"

"Want to send a rescue team?" Jake asked, turning from the control board. "We can send Two east, and we go west, and catch him between us? Mebbe save our guys?''

''They're already chilled,'' Jessica stated. ''No sense wasting more lives to rescue deaders.''

Frowning at that, Trader started to speak when the radio crackled with power, mumbled words barely discernible over the atmospheric hash. Then the distortion lifted and the signal came in loud and clear.

''Hello, is anybody there?'' A new voice chuckled over the ceiling speakers.

The control room crew stopped moving, and Kate felt her skin crawl as memory flared at the sound of Baron Gaza's voice coming over one of their own hand comms.

''Your sec men are dead, bitch.'' Gaza laughed, then there came the sound of a blaster shot. ''Correction, now they're all dead. Let's end this today, slut. Right here and now. Come get me! I'm staying right fucking here!''

There was a crackle of static that blocked the next words, and Kate made a slashing motion. The techs cut off the speakers, but the Trader waited until the indicator lights of the transponder had gone dark before she spoke.

''Ready a missile!'' she ordered. ''If the radar can find that APC, then the missile should blow him to hell!''

''On it,'' Jake replied, both hands busy.

A few seconds later there grew a loud rustling from

above, and then thunder shook the war wag as flame raced by overhead, flying straight into the heart of the smoke above the preDark city. Long moments passed before the radar screen blossomed with a patch of white. Seconds later a low rumble rolled in from the distance.

"Got him!" Jessica cried, raising a fist.

"Well, we hit something at least," Red Jack muttered, watching the screen clear back to normal. Then he frowned. "Black dust, the goddamn APC is still there!"

Straining to see something through the rising smoke of the city, Jake scowled. "We missed?"

"Must have hit a sand dune," Kate gritted through clenched teeth. "The range is too far, especially with all this shit in the air blocking the warhead. We gotta get closer."

Then the radar screen gave a single loud beep, closely followed by another, and then a mounting series.

"Holy shit!" Red Jack shouted from the increasing noise. "We got incoming!"

Snapping her attention in that direction, Kate couldn't believe her eyes and ears for a moment. Was their own fucking missile now coming back for them? No, wait, the heat sig was wrong—too small a wash and way too fast. Gaza had to have launched a missile of his own and it was coming faster than jackshit right down their fragging throats!

"No time to dodge. Eric, fire all guns!' she commanded. "Bring it down!"

The lights dimmed as the comp drew unlimited power from the electrical system. Now the servomotors on the front .50-cals whined into life, the comp linking the weapons onto the signal of the radar screen and filling the air ahead of the rocket with hot lead.

The noise was deafening. This was why they had a comp and Eric to nurse it. To give them an edge like this. But was it enough? Would it work? There had never been a chance to try their missile defense system before, and now it was all or nothing. Aces or diamonds, as the river folks liked to say. Life or death.

Unexpectedly, the machine guns stopped firing, and in the ringing silence the beeping of the radar could still be heard, but different, slower and less urgent.

"The missile is starting to descend," Red Jack reported in disbelief. "Look at her drop! Nukeshit, the damn thing didn't have the range to reach us this far away! Must have just been a LAW or HAFLA or mebbe something he cobbled together."

Just a man-portable rocket, not a real missile like War Wag One was packing, Kate realized, easing the tension in her shoulders. Shitfire, she couldn't lock on to Gaza from this distance, and he couldn't reach her. Stalemate.

"We could use the L-Gun," Jake stated.

Kate cut him off. "Not with all this smoke," she

replied sternly. "That cuts its power by half. I wanna ace the bastard, not merely piss him off.

"Okay, we have no choice," she continued. "We go in as a group, the wags keep close and chill everything in sight. Send a runner to Two about not using the standard radio channels."

"Roger that, Chief!"

"Switch to channel four and use the scramblers," Eric said over the speakers. "No way the baron can hear us then."

She grunted at that. "Good. Red Jack, stay glued to that radar. You get a blip, don't waste the breath to tell me. Give the info straight to Eric. The closer we get, the less time we have to shoot down one of his rockets."

"Then we give him missiles up the ass," Jessica spit hatefully.

"Damn straight," Kate ordered. "We're going in nose to nose with that bastard, and end this now!"

The control room crew scrambled at their posts, sending messages throughout the wag over the phone lines while a runner hit the salty ground and started racing for the other wags.

As the tandem engines started revving to full power, the lights of the war wag brightened to full strength and the rig began to roll along, staying a good distance from the crumbling cliff.

"Here we come," Kate muttered softly, looking across the swirling smoke at their invisible enemy.

As Gaza and his wives fired another rocket into the billowing smoke clouds, left unnoticed on the ground Shala forced herself to painfully crawl for the safety of the nearby desert. She could see the wide open plains of salted ground only a dozen yards away. She was close, so very close....

But every motion brought racking pain to her chest, the salt stinging like acid in her terrible wounds, and Shala could see the blood dripping off her arms as she tried to claw another foot forward, just one more inch toward the blessed sands of time.

Rising from the shifting sands, the women of the Core started for their girl only to see her tremble and die, a single gory finger resting on the clean sand of the true desert outside the forbidden zone. A crimson trail of her blood marked a direct path backward to the machine and the top-walkers near the cliff. Raising a spear, a woman started forward but others held her back. There was no courage in dying. The spears and mindkillers of the men had sadly proved the superiority of the brutal norms.

Gathering the still child in holy strips of tan cloth, the women brought the little one deep into the heart of the earth where she would lie forever safe and warm. And lying on the ground at that spot was a large leather bag removed from the ruins to the north, the outlanders' water bag. But the polluted contents had been washed out and replaced with mineral water from a clean spring, then laced with enough undetectable *jinkaja* to cause instant madness, violent seizures and eventually agonizing death.

It was a hard truth that the Core couldn't match the mighty machines of the norms, but the desert always found a way to balance the scales of death.

Chapter Sixteen

A fiery dagger came out of the billowing plume of smoke and streaked past the APC to slam into the dune behind. The sandy hill heaved and blew apart, a roiling column of fire rising into the rumbling sky.

Kneeling over the exposed engine, Gaza still flinched as the concussion rumbled over the dead war wag. Okay, that bitch had the range, but not him. Not him! Feverishly, the baron worked on the diesel, trying to remove pieces of the dead comm system to replace the missing parts and getting nowhere. Damn that girl! The APC engine had been too often repaired and was far too easy to wreck. He had been a fool trying to recruit the girl. But when those rags came off and he saw the pale trembling figure, reason and logic had fled as blind lust took over. Now he was paying the price.

Standing in the open turret, Allison triggered a long sweeping blast from the 25 mm cannon, angling the barrel ever higher in wide circles. She knew the shells didn't have the true range to reach the Trader, but she would gain valuable distance by shooting high and allowing the shells to arc downward. However, there was no way to see through the smoke of the city, and she was guiding her shots purely on the feelings she was receiving of approaching death. That had to be the Trader. Who else could possibly challenge her husband?

Going to the rear doors, Kathleen extended a LAW tube and started to open the lock. Rushing close, Gaza slapped the weapon from her hand and it hit the metal floor in a clatter.

"Stop that! Save ammo!" the baron ordered brusquely, towering over the startled woman. "They're too far away for the rockets. Even the fifty can't reach them."

Against the wall, Kathleen raised two fingers and quickly brought them toward each other.

"Yes, I know that!" he raged, clenching both fists, the greasy wires from the engine still dangling impotently in his grip. "She's coming fast, and with everything they got on the trips."

Reaching out to touch the tangle of wires, the woman asked her husband an urgent question with her eyes.

"Useless!" Gaza cursed, throwing aside a fistful of assorted wires. "Without the proper parts, the same damn parts, we're not going anywhere in this tin box."

Stomping her boot, Allison got everyone's attention and pointed around at the LAV 25, then raised two fingers and pointed one into the fiery ruins.

The landscape shook once more as Gaza raked stiff

fingers through his hair, but was forced to agree. Their only hope of surviving was to be mobile, use the greater speed of the APC to outmaneuver the Trader's lumbering war wags and strike from the dunes. A night creep in broad daylight. Hit and git. Which left him no options at all. He would have to go after the wiring in the second APC below the cliff.

"Stop firing! Mebbe they'll think we've moved!" Gaza ordered, going to a rack and grabbing an M-16 recovered from the convoy in the park. He worked the bolt, chambering a round, and slung the blaster over a shoulder. "Kathleen, you're coming with me. Allison, prepare the land mines. Lay 'em out in a diamond pattern around the wag. That may buy us some time. Don't bother to bury them. The damn things may not work, but at least it'll scare the Trader into going slow if she sends more bikes."

Closing the top hatch of the war wag, the doomie waved both hands in a mime of driving a Harley to ask about the motorcycles outside.

"After you're done with the mines, try and find three that work," he decided, stuffing his pockets with spare clips and grens. "If I can't find what we need in the other APC, then we'll ride out of here and mine the war wag to blow."

Ducking under the empty framework of a radar unit long gone, the baron grabbed some canvas gloves with a box and tossed Kathleen a pair.

"Stay razor," Gaza ordered, stuffing the other set

of gloves into his gun belt. "Allison will be busy up here, so we'll be on our own down there."

Sliding on the gloves, the slim redhead nodded, and collapsed the tube on the LAW rocket, making the sights retract. Expertly, she hung it across her back and grabbed an AK-47 from the ville armory. It was her preferred blaster and most of the ammo was hand loaded by her, or the other wives. She considered homemade ammo much more dependable than the preDark stuff, no matter how well it was preserved inside sealed plastic boxes.

Stepping to the turret, Gaza grabbed his first wife by the scruff of the neck and pulled her close for a hard kiss.

"Don't you fucking die on me," he muttered softly. "Worse happens, set the ammo bins of the wag to blow and slide down the cable to join us below. This is far from being over."

Brushing some loose hair from his face, Allison nodded at her husband, then turned to do the same to her sister standing by the aft doors. The women shared a moment of understanding, wishing the other goodbye. In spite of what their beloved husband said, the chances of this working were virtually zero, but they would stand by him to the end.

Pushing past them both, Gaza threw open the rear door and stepped outside. The air was murky with smoke and the drifting dust from the missile hits. Hurrying among the sprawled forms of dead sec men and their bikes, Gaza reached the winch and checked the nuke batteries on the electric motor. He was relieved to find the machinery working perfectly. At least that much was going his way.

Kathleen joined him at the winch. Stuffing his hands into the stiff gloves, Gaza freed the cable and together they dragged it to the edge of the cliff and started to snake it down. When it reached the bottom, the baron locked the winch tight and Kathleen started over the edge of the cliff to grab the cable. She started to slide down, using her boots to brake the speed. The gloves grew uncomfortably hot in only a matter of yards, but the woman kept going and gratefully released the hot woven steel upon reaching the ground.

Gaza was already sliding down the cable and landed only a few seconds later. Sliding was a dangerous way to use the cable, but the fastest way to reach the city and time was against them right now. Every moment counted.

Anchoring the cable in case Allison had to follow, the man and woman readied their blasters and charged into the morass of rubble and wreckage that ringed the burning city, firing sporadically at anything that moved.

WITH THE SIG-Sauer leading the way, Ryan crawled out of the steep ravine and reached the top of the cliff. Pausing for a moment to recce the area, he studied the tattered bodies of the Core littering the sandy ground.

Large-caliber rounds had chewed them apart, along
with small explosions, mebbe that 25 mm cannon he
had heard about. But this was no recent fight. The ripe
smell of the corpses made it clear that the Core had
been chilled a while ago. Hours, mebbe a full day.
Odd thing, no buzzards were feasting on the meat, not
even the scorpions or the red ants. Mebbe even the
fragging insects knew how dangerous that *jinkaja*
dreck was that saturated their flesh.

Standing slowly, Ryan listened for a minute to the
wind blow and the crackling of the fire. If this was the
only way into the sinkhole, then it made sense for the
Core to be waiting for them to come out here.

Black hair whipping about his face, Ryan swept the
killing field with the muzzle of the deadly blaster,
ready for betrayal from the deaders, or the soil underneath. The airborne salt particles made it difficult to
see. But the area was clear. Could be Gaza got them
all.

Finally satisfied, Ryan whistled sharply twice
through his teeth and stepped out for the others to
ascend. Helping one another up the last few yards, the
rest of the companions gratefully reached the floor of
the desert and looked over the battlefield.

"Tire tracks," Jak said, pointing at what appeared
to be merely churned sand. "APC was here."

"A day, mebbe less," Ryan agreed.

Bending, Dean lifted the spent brass from a .50-cal

and inspected the bottom before sniffing the dirty inside.

"Homemade," he stated. "Not preDark loads."

Just then a tremendous explosion came from the west, but the drifting smoke and distance combined with the rolling sand dunes to hide the source of the detonation.

"Could be anything," Mildred said, glancing about nervously. Her arms ached from the hurried climb, and the woman felt vulnerable just standing there in plain sight.

A few seconds later another explosion came from within the city, the cornice of a skyscraper exploding into pieces, the entire roof breaking apart to slide off and plummet into the streets below.

Studying the fiery metropolis, J.B. slung the Uzi and dug out his longeyes to recce the cityscape.

"The angle of the blast is wrong for that to have come from this side," he said slowly, as the thick clouds thinned for a moment, moving to the force of the northern wind. "It came from across the city, say, about twenty degrees to the…"

The Armorer's voice faded away, then came back strong. "Dark night, there's a land tank over there! No, wait, there are two of 'em! Big as anything I've ever seen."

"Alone?" Ryan demanded pointedly.

"Some smaller wags, too. Couldn't get a good look."

"Is the war wag an APC?" Krysty asked, squinting to try to see past the conflagration.

"Converted trucks," J.B. said, lowering the long-eyes and compacting it before tucking it away into his bulging munitions bag. "Machine-gun blisters, rocket pods on the roof and what sure as shit looks like a radar dish."

"Just sitting there, or is it turning?" Ryan asked scowling.

"Turning steadily."

"That means it's probably working," Ryan muttered, a hard smile coming to his face. "That's gotta be the Trader. He and Abe escaped after all and reached a stockpile."

"Indeed, logic dictates it to be so," Doc rumbled.

Estimating the direction the rocket traveled across the preDark city, Ryan leveled the Steyr SSG-70 and swept the opposite desert cliff with the scope. He had only seen Baron Gaza once with the sun at his back hiding his features. But if there was anybody shouting orders while the others ran to obey, that would be him and Ryan would see if the 7.62 mm long cartridges of the sniper rifle could do what the missile couldn't.

For just a brief moment, Ryan saw an APC about a half mile away sitting on the edge of the cliff, and then it was gone behind the black smoke once more. The urge came to try anyway as he had before to chase off the Core, but the range finder on the scope told the brutal truth that it was too distant for an accurate shot.

"No good," Ryan muttered, lowering the long-blaster.

"Too bad about the Holland & Holland," Dean said, shifting the pack on his back to a more comfortable position. "You would have had the range with that."

"But not the accuracy needed," Mildred stated. "A sniper weapon is a hell of a lot different from a standard longblaster, or an assault rifle."

"Like a knife is to a scalpel, right?"

"Exactly."

Pulling out a plastic mirror from a pocket, Ryan debated trying to flash the Trader a message, but even if the man saw the reflected light, would he recognize the old codes or strike back instantly with a missile? Fireblast, he didn't even know if it was *his* Trader, or merely somebody new using the rep to do business. If that was the case, then a flashing light might be mistaken for blasterfire and bring down a shitstorm of lead their way. Best to stay low for the moment.

"Let's get moving," Ryan ordered brusquely. "We can go into the desert, use the dunes as cover. Last place we want to be is between any war wags during a rocket fight without some steel covering our ass."

Shuffling his boots in the sand, Dean frowned. "We just gonna leave?"

"We should take to the high ground," Doc suggested. "Reconnoiter the situation from the top of a dune."

"That's triple stupe," J.B. said bluntly. "Up high we'd be seen and catch a lot of lead. No, we stay low and leave. That's the smart thing. They are in wags and we're on foot. So let them fight it out, and we'll come back when the smoke clears and see who was the winner."

"If there are any survivors, much less winners," Krysty added grimly, looking skyward. "Check up there."

Craning his neck to follow her direction, Ryan saw the roiling storm clouds overhead were darker, more yellow than usual, and the ever present smell of acid rain was increasing. Nuking hell, a chem storm was coming and that changed everything. Down below the city was on fire, with a droid hunting them and muties everywhere. Up here were battling war wags and flat, open desert where the acid rain would easily catch them and strip them to bare bones in only a few screaming minutes. Damned if they tried to escape in any direction, that left only one choice.

"If we're going get chilled, it might as well be on our feet," Ryan said, hefting his longblaster. "Double time, let's go see who is in that APC and convince them we need a ride."

"And if Gaza?" Jak asked, massaging his aching left arm in its sling.

"Then we take it away from him. Let's go."

Chapter Seventeen

Scuttling from the smoky shadows along the preDark road, a fat lizard paused on top of the wizened corpse of a construction worker, its three eyes darting about in different directions searching for predators.

Wrapping a tentacle around his glass knife, Larry lashed out with the blade and the lizard's head was removed. Gushing blood, the body tumbled to the pavement, and a dozen other lizards charged from their hiding places to start tearing apart their fallen brother.

Now Larry pulled hard on the rope and a net erupted from underneath the snowy layer of salt, and the pile of lizards was hauled wiggling into the air caught in the crude net.

"Food!" Larry said in delight, rubbing his scaled stomach in delight. Carefully untying the net from the ropes, the mutant twirled it above his head several times and then brought it crashing down on the hood of a car, killing the lizards instantly.

"Food," he mumbled again. He pulled a large piece of window glass from a leather pouch and cut the reptiles apart and stuffed the bloody gobbets of raw flesh into his lopsided mouth.

"Good!" He chortled in happiness, then froze instantly at the sound of thunder.

Ramming the rest of a lizard into his mouth and stuffing the others into his pouch, Larry loped through an alleyway filled with huge sections of the salt dome and crouched in the ornamental wrought-iron fencing that edged a public library. When the sparkle-white ground fell, all things in the desert rushed in to see.

Much fighting, Larry remembered, and many things died. Larry and kin follow food into pit and hunting good. Until bad metal come. Two-legs try kill Larry with thunder sticks. Twice in the cold seasons he had been stung by black bees from booming sticks, much blood and pain. His mate died from black bee, child, too. And it been good child, Larry thought, no scales like parents, no claws. Two-legs would have thought it a norm aside from eyes. Norms had little eyes, not big like child, not see in darkness and know what animals think in head. Child had helped much in hunting, find big food Larry would kill with sharp glass across neck. Eat for week!

Then two-legs with bad metal come into stone forest, Larry remembered, kill everything. But Larry stay. He wait for two-legs to not have thunder stick, then cut across neck with glass, use claws on belly and face. Bad metal take little ones away. Someday he get them, drink redblood. Then mate and child sleep peacefully.

As the two-legs started his way, Larry retreated

quickly. Loping across the pavilion, the mutie disappeared into the sewer, his rubbery tentacles lashing about like wild snakes until he was through the grating and gone from sight.

ONLY MOMENTS LATER, moving through the jumbled ruins, Gaza led the way into the choking hot chaos. The smell of acid rain was a lot less noticeable down here, the thick smoke masking the smell of anything else in the atmosphere. Masked by the swirling black smoke were tall honeycombs of flame, burning buildings with fiery tongues lashing out every opening, a few structures reduced to only the twisted outline of the softening steel frames.

Glowing ash drifted past the two people like a snowstorm in hell, the red-hot residue floating on the thermal currents of the destruction, gray soot mixing with the sparkling cover of salt dust everywhere and turning the clean wintry appearance of the Texas city into filthy graveyard pallor. Softly in the background came the constant crashing of glass as window after window shattered from the pressure and heat, the shards and slivers raining down to smash onto the sidewalks and streets once more.

Many of the corpses in the street were reduced to bones and shoes, their clothing removed by the sharp beaks of the buzzards and vultures to reach the dried flesh and organs. But the scavengers were starting to leave, abandoning the wealth of food to fly away and take roost into the windowless stores of the city, to start anew on other bodies. Only the millipedes in the street stayed, the insects unconcerned with the growing heat and the smoke.

Staying well clear of the writhing bugs, Gaza and Kathleen kept in the open as much as possible and used their weapons freely. Time was pressing and ammo spent saved precious moments. A sudden flurry of movement at a sewer grating made the baron jerk back and fire a long burst from his M-16. The hardball ammo threw off sparks as it hit the corroded grating, but a few rounds passed through the small holes and something shrieked in the darkness. Echoing slightly, the cries faded as if retreating into the distance.

"We're in a goddamn mutie pit!" Baron Gaza roared, dropping the spent clip and slapping in a fresh one. "Shoot anything that moves and let's haul ass!"

Breaking into a stride, Kathleen braced the rapid-fire at her waist and sent a spray of lead into a flock of buzzards in their way. Several birds dropped to the ground in a fluttering of feathers and gore, while the rest rose hurriedly into the gray sky. With some measure of satisfaction, Gaza was chilling the millipedes, grinding their bleeding forms under his boots. A scrawny desert rat darted from underneath a car to grab a juicy morsel of an aced bird, and Gaza contemptuously kicked it aside with a crunch of bones. The rodent flew across the street to impact on the front counter inside a shadowy store, then fell limply to the floor, blood dribbling from its slack mouth and both hind feet still twitching as it tried to escape.

Brass arching in streams, the man and woman blasted a path through the feasting scavengers and reached the wire fence encircling the park only to find this section clear of anything living. It was as if they had crossed an invisible boundary that nothing was allowed to pass.

Or was afraid to pass, Baron Gaza realized grimly. But the sec hunter droid was destroyed; he had seen it crash and explode. There was nothing to harm them here. This was a safe zone in the middle of the hellish ruins. But no one ever got chilled by being too careful.

"Stand guard," he ordered brusquely, walking sideways toward the nearest APC. It was just beyond a crashed truck, set between a huge Army tank and two crashed Hummers. "I'll grab the wires and we leave."

Breathing deeply through her nose, Kathleen vigorously nodded in agreement as they proceeded past the tank. From the other side of the wire fence, hundreds of things seemed to be watching them, from the nooks and crevices of the city, as if hungrily waiting for the people to exit the park. Their hatred was palpable, like the beat of a powerful engine.

In a thunderous roar, a building down the street sagged inward and started to collapse, pieces of rubble slamming to the street and smashing cars while others hit lower structures like flaming meteor strikes.

Snapping her fingers for his attention, Kathleen twirled a single finger in the air, then made a fist.

"Bet your ass I'll hurry," Gaza grunted in reply, then gestured a direction with his rapid-fire. "Check the Hummer for any more of those rockets. We may need to blast our way out of here."

She nodded and started that way as he worked the latch of the heavy rear door and slipped into the APC. The interior was almost pitch-black, and he scratched a road flare to life, filling the wag with searing red light. A scorpion on the wall scuttled away, and Gaza thrust the flare at the creature, searing off its pincers and cracking open the shell. Thrashing wildly, the scorpion fell to the corrugated floor and started stinging itself in blind madness. Grimacing at the sight, Gaza deliberately stepped over the dying creature so that it would linger in agony as he proceeded deeper into the steel box.

Gaza found the access panel near the turret. Placing the flare on an empty seat, he managed to force open the panel with one hand, the other filled with the M-16 rapid-fire. Casting the lid aside with a loud clatter, he grabbed the flare and held it up, soon locating the needed wiring harness. Yes! Carefully as possible, he gently removed the connections and wrapped the harness in a clean piece of cloth before tucking it safely away inside a pocket. Okay, back in biz.

Suddenly, there was a frantic thumping on the metal side of the vehicle. Rushing to the exit, the baron paused for a moment listening for danger before joining his wife outside. He was losing spouses at an unprecedented rate, but it was still better them than him.

Kathleen now had another LAW slung over a shoulder and a pair of pressurized tanks strapped to her back, a vented blaster of some kind attached to the larger tank with a flexible metallic hose.

"Rad-blast my ass, a preDark flamethrower!" Baron Gaza gasped in shocked delight at the find. "Does it still work? Fuel okay?"

Hurriedly, Kathleen nodded, but also held a finger to her lips for silence. Gaza frowned at that until he heard a noise coming that chilled his blood. A weird combination of sounds unlike anything he had ever heard before, partially masked by the crackling of the flames and the crash of falling masonry. A sort of whirring mixed a horrible hooting. Stickies!

Then coming around a nearby corner was a mutie fighting a machine—the sec hunter droid from before, or another that looked exactly the same. Could there be two? More? Dripping gore, the preDark machine was battling a stickie, the rubbery mutie charging at the droid uncaring of the whirling blades and snippers. Mindlessly, the feral creature seemed to be fighting on a visceral level, without much common sense of fear.

The stickie was missing an arm, the blood running thickly down its side. Trying to move past the mutie, the droid charged with its buzz saw extending and the creature was sliced in two, the pieces dropping to the filthy street. But as the droid started forward, more stickies appeared, stepping out of a brick wall and the corroded side of a crashed bus.

Thunder and lightning crashed in the sky as the muties raced over the corpses, their bodies changing color and texture, blending into whatever they were near. A startled buzzard brushed a stickie, and the thing's arm became covered with black feathers. Another tripped in a pothole landing atop a desiccated corpse not yet eaten by the scavengers, and as it rose the stickie began to blend into the mummified norm.

Gaza couldn't believe what he was seeing, and Kathleen edged closer to the man for protection. Camou stickies. They had heard rumors from outlanders about such things but never really believed them until this moment.

As the stickies attacked, the sec hunter droid slashed out with its buzz saw and scissors at the same time, striking in the opposite direction. The closest two stickies died horribly, and the gore-splattered machine retreated again toward the convoy in the park. Sitting on the crumpled hood of a crashed car, a millipede hissed at the droid as it passed and was slashed apart by the flashing blades. Then more stickies attacked, slowing the machine by the sheer bulk of the bodies. One mutie got a good grip on a red lens and tried to pull it free, and the droid threw itself against a nearby truck, crushing the stickie's head. As the dead mutie released its hold on the droid, it fell to the street, its skin rippling in different colors and textures, the suckers moving like gasping mouths, until the humanoid went still and the skin become a dull pasty white like a drowned man long deceased.

Longblaster in hand, Gaza sneered at the sight. Muties always seemed irresistibly attracted to machinery, fires, diesel engines and the like, but this time the machines were fighting back and chilling them in droves. The armored chrome of the droid was dripping with blood, feathers, pincers and a few suckers adhering to its blades as grisly trophies of combat.

Making a guttural sound deep in her throat, Kathleen bumped him with a hip, urging the man to leave. Gaza agreed and eased around the APC, trying to keep its bulk between them and the approaching droid. Oddly, it didn't seem to be after the norms in particular. Mebbe it was merely returning to the tank where it had first been seen, like a guard on patrol. Suddenly, the baron had a strong urge to see what was inside the preDark war machine that needed such a high level of protection. Nukes? Nerve gas? But the danger of the droid was too great to risk a recce, and he followed his wife away from the imposing hulk of the huge preDark juggernaut, its titanic cannon resting against its armored prow and pointing uselessly at the ground. Or could it be the tank itself that needed guarding?

Dimly the man recalled a memory from childhood when a similar machine had been found in the ruins of West Virginia. The local baron had called it a

Ranger, and claimed it was a thinking war wag, as if a droid and an APC had been combined. The very idea of obtaining such a weapon made the baron slow his departure until shied onward by the urgings of Kathleen.

Careful not to trip over the corpses on the pavement, the man and woman crossed the intersection keeping low behind the lines of cars and trying to stay out of direct line of sight of the droid. But then the tentacles of the unseen thing in the sewer made another grab for their boots and got Kathleen around the ankle. As she swung her AK-47 down to blast it away, Gaza knocked the weapon aside and slashed with a knife. The flesh was spongy and severed easily. Gushing piss-yellow blood, the amputated tentacle slithered away, as an inhuman mewling and gurgling issued from the dark sewers. The baron had no idea what kind of a mutie was under the city, but was resolved not to be taken alive by the thing. There was something unclean about it that disturbed the man.

Keeping a finger on the trigger of his M-16, Gaza watched the sewer grating for any further movements as Kathleen got off the street by stepping through the smashed window of a store. He was right behind her, covering the rear.

Inside the building, the two glanced about at a line of chairs standing before a long mirror, the walls covered with pictures of people with strangely cut hair.

What the place could have been the baron had no idea whatsoever.

Only yards away, the fight in the street was growing; more and more millipedes were arriving to feast upon the dead and the dying. And apparently summoned by the death cries of their own kind, more of the camou stickies were dropping off the sides of buildings to land on top of the droid. Its blades tore them apart, but there were always a few suckers left behind on its hull, and the chrome ran thick with the mutie blood.

Shambling past the open window, a brick-colored stickie on the sidewalk turned to stare at the two norms, then lunged for them. Trapped, Kathleen fired a burst into its face, the impacts driving the mutie back against a car at the curb. But even as they watched, the bullet wounds in its chest began to close and the stickie started taking on the metallic sheen of the sleek preDark vehicle.

Seemingly bemused by the combat, the corpse behind the steering wheel was sporting tinted sunglasses and a white silk scarf draped around a shriveled brown throat.

As Kathleen fired again, Gaza lit another flare and shoved it into the stickie's left eye. Hooting in pain, the creature stumbled away, sucker-covered hands swatting at the flaming stick sizzling inside its distorted face.

Unfortunately, it had been too little, too late. The

droid had heard the blaster shots and was heading their way fast, the millipedes and other stickies ignored at the appearance of the armed humans.

"Aim for the eyes!" Gaza cried, slinging his M-16 over a shoulder and drawing his knife once more.

As Kathleen hammered the oncoming machine with the hardball ammo of her AK-47, Gaza used a knife to cut the strap off her shoulder and free the LAW. Pulling out the pin, he extended the tube to its full length. The sights popped up on the front and the firing button was uncovered.

"Watch the wash!" he warned, assuming a launching stance. Still shooting, Kathleen moved as far away from the man as she could.

Flame vomited out of the aft end of the launch tube, filling the hair salon with a strident volcano that blew everything loose across the store with hurricane force. Almost faster than they could follow, the antitank rocket streaked away from the front of the tube on a contrail of smoke and sparks, the propellant obviously weakened over the long years. It started straight for the droid, then unexpectedly veered slightly and went straight past the machine to slam into the side of a millinery shop. An explosion shook the entire building and it collapsed, a tidal wave of bricks and cinder blocks cascading outward to bury the droid. For several long moments, the man and woman waited, watching for any indication that the droid was still operational. But nothing stirred under the tonnage of assorted debris, and soon they lowered their weapons.

"Let's move," Gaza growled, "before another one of the damn things arrive."

Kathleen nodded her agreement, and the two slipped out the rear door of the shop, running down a smoky alley to reach the street once more and head back toward the cable at the cliff.

PUSHING THE THIRD motorcycle to lean against the side of the APC, Allison suddenly could feel the cold, clammy hand of death squeeze her heart, and the doomie knew that death was in the immediate vicinity. Her own or somebody else's, she wasn't sure, as the woman had never been able to read her own future and help guide it along.

Which was why she had joined with Gaza. He was ruthless and powerful, an excellent stud in bed, and she could foresee things for him that would only bring wealth and pleasure to herself. All of the other wives had been chosen with extreme care so that they would never be rivals for his affection, such as it was. Any slut who might replace her was killed on sight.

Folding her arms, she closed both eyes and tried to open herself to the whispers of the universe. Almost immediately, the doomie felt her mind swirl with the bizarre visions of some different place, perhaps a different world. The chaos seemed to last forever, and when the vision finally cleared Allison stumbled inside the war wag and took a knife to scratch a message into one of the hard plastic seats. The doomie wasn't sure exactly what it meant, or when the deeds would take place—this day or a hundred seasons from today. But she felt it would be soon, and was absolutely certain that this message would be her revenge, the only way Allison had of striking back at her killers after buying the farm.

Shaking off the disturbing mental images, the woman closed the rear doors of the LAV 25 and climbed into the turret, trying to find her husband in the madness below. Death came to everybody sooner or later, but the doomie had no intention of greeting the blackness with open arms. Allison planned on fighting for every second of life, every gasp of breath.

Chapter Eighteen

The companions ran along the salty desert, watching the streamers of smoke come over the top of the sand dunes when the bandaged figures rose from the sand directly in their path.

Ryan froze at the sight, his Steyr sweeping from one member of the Core to the next. His first impulse had been to chill them on sight, but none of them was carrying those weird spears like before.

"Krysty?" J.B. asked nervously, expertly cradling the Uzi machine pistol.

"They're not sending any mindkillers, if that's what you mean," the redhead replied slowly, her eyes narrowed in concentration. "At least, I don't think so. Can't really tell for sure."

As if stirred by those words, the mysterious beings now all pointed in unison to the left.

"What about the city?" Ryan demanded, stepping toward them. "Something there you want?"

Lowering their hands, the Core gave no reply, then turned away and descended into the loose sand to once more vanish from sight.

Scowling deeply, Doc glanced at the sand dune hiding whatever was on their left. "It's a trap," he declared. "It has to be. Enemies do not become friends without a reason."

"Gaza might be that reason," Ryan said thoughtfully. "This could be a simple matter of we're the enemy of their enemy."

"Mebbe want us chill Gaza," Jak said as a suggestion. "Then ace us, could be."

Shifting her grip on her Czech ZKR pistol, Mildred curled a lip at that idea. "Could be," she agreed. "Or maybe they're sending us somewhere safe from the coming storm."

She knew that the others weren't overly concerned about acid rain. They had been caught in many downpours before and were still alive. Plus, they each had plastic ponchos made from the shower curtains taken from the last redoubt they looted. The military material was very thick, and should protect them somewhat from ravages of the chem storm. Puddles were the real danger, finding themselves trapped in ever deepening pools of the sulfuric acid rain until it rose above their boots and started to irritate their legs.

With Ryan in the lead, the companions proceeded another twenty yards west before going around a dune. Jak could have been right about this being a trap. Besides, it never was a good idea to blindly follow the directions of anybody.

Staying low, Ryan paused as a trail of what seemed to be blood stretched from the desert toward the cliff.

Following it from a distance, the one-eyed man brought up his longblaster with a jerk at the sight of a corpse, its arms and legs blown off from some sort of explosion to the chest. J.B. prepared a pipe bomb and Jak got a Molotov ready while Ryan attached his pocket mirror to the end of the Steyr and took a recce around the slope of the dune. Now he could see more bodies scattered about, mixed with the remains of smashed motorcycles, along with a few unexploded land mines. Possibly duds, but there was no way of telling from this range. And parked in the middle of the destruction was a tan-colored LAV 25 with three motorcycles leaning against the armored chassis.

"Hell of a fight," J.B. stated. "Outriders from the Trader?"

"Then why the nuke hasn't Gaza left yet?" Ryan queried, angling the mirror to try to find any other vehicles. But the war wag was alone with the deaders and the broken machines. The only oddity was that the winch had a cable going over the edge of the cliff and down into the city below. Gaza was looting the ruins while the Trader came charging down his throat? That made no bastard sense at all.

"Unless it's busted," Ryan said aloud, finishing the thought. "Guess the Core really was helping us."

"No way the baron would leave the wag unprotected even if it was crippled," Krysty said slowly, straining to hear the sound of an engine, but the vehicle was deathly quiet. "Which means it's either boobied or has a guard."

Thumbing back the hammer on his LeMat, Doc rumbled, "Probably a guard, dear lady, to operate the cable and haul his worthless hide back up with whatever he deemed was of such protean value."

"Three bikes in sight," Mildred added, doing the same to her ZKR target revolver. "I would guess Gaza went down with a guard, and left the third person here to cover his escape."

"Makes sense," Dean agreed, craning his neck to try to see the top of the transport. "Hot pipe, the hatch is closed! There goes using a Molotov."

"No, a Molotov is just what we need," Ryan said, trying to keep the tension from his voice as lightning flashed overhead, the thunder following only seconds behind. The storm was coming closer. They had to do it right the first time. There might not be a second.

Wrapping the strap of the Steyr around his forearm to help steady the longblaster, Ryan leveled the weapon and placed his eye to the scope. "Jak, hit the front of the wag with a Molotov," he directed. "Then J.B., put a burst across the rear doors. The rest of you play dead."

"Not prob," the albino teenager said, lighting the rag tied around the neck of the glass bottle. "Tell when."

"On my mark," Ryan said calmly, placing the crosshairs a foot above the top of the turret. "Now."

Whipping his arm forward, the miscellaneous bits of metal and glass sewn into Jak's camou jacket jingled from the abrupt motion as the firebomb arced high and crashed directly on the nose of the APC. Instantly, J.B. stitched a short burst along the rear doors of the wag, the 9 mm rounds ricocheting harmlessly off the military armor.

A split second later, the top hatch flew open and a hand came out to grab the .50-cal and blindly fire the weapon in every direction. On cue, Krysty, Mildred and Dean screamed in pain from behind the dune as if mortally wounded.

At the sounds, a blond woman rose into sight from the hatch and grabbed the firing grip of the big-bore 25 mm cannon just as Ryan stroked the trigger of the Steyr. The rifle bucked once and a single 7.62 mm round smacked directly into her left temple, the right side of her head spraying out in a pink froth.

Even as she fell limp across the blaster, her convulsing hands triggered the cannon and a spray of 25 mm shells hit the ground in front of the companions, the cacophony of detonations throwing out a tempest of debris before coming to an abrupt stop.

While the salt and sand were still in the air, the companions raced across the open ground low and fast and hit the rear doors of the APC, pressing their bodies flat to the steel and ramming the barrels of their blasters through the louvered slats of the air vents.

"Surrender, or we shoot!" Ryan ordered loudly. "This is your only chance!"

But aside from the crackling flames of the Molotov, only silence answered the challenge. Which was a damn good thing, since the man had no intention of shooting into the APC. It could easily be packed full with fuel or ammo, and a single round might have obliterated the wag, along with the companions and the entire section of cliff they were standing on.

After a few more moments, Ryan motioned to Dean, and the boy removed a self-heat from his backpack and gently lobbed it up and into the open top hatch of the vehicle.

"Gren!" the boy called as it bounced off the corpse and dropped down inside.

But there was still no reaction from anyone inside. J.B. got busy tricking the door locks from the outside. As the bolt was disengaged, the door swung open and the companions got clear in case of outgoing rounds. But the interior of the APC was empty aside from the deader dangling from the turret.

Doc and Dean stayed at the doors as rear guards while the others climbed inside and did a quick recce for a boobie, but the wag was clean.

"Bunch folks were here, mostly women," Jak said, opening a handmade backpack and pulling out loose white gowns. "Not gaudy slut, either."

Krysty squinted at the clean clothing and the abundance of weapons lying openly in the boxes on the metal floor. "Gaza had five wives, right?"

"Four now," Ryan said, pulling the corpse down from the hatch. Her clothing matched that from the packs, and the handcannon tucked into the holster of her gun belt was clean, oiled and carrying six rounds.

"Baron's wife, all right," he stated.

Finding an Ingram machine pistol hanging on the wall, Dean yanked out the clip to make sure it was carrying the same 9 mm ammo he used in the Browning Hi-Power, then tucked the clip into a pocket to be emptied later.

"Found the engine," J.B. announced, kneeling to try to see into the darkness. "Millie, hit the lights, would you?"

Going to the control panel in the front, Mildred dodged the waves of heat coming off the dwindling fire on the armored prow outside and flipped a few switches to activate the emergency lights.

Now the war wag was brightly illuminated, and the companions were astonished by the display of armament lying about. Belted ammo for the fifty and the 25 mm, four LAW launchers, one in questionable condition and even a hand comm, which was strange since the radio transponder in the dashboard was no longer present, along with the radar and most other of the preDark equipment.

"Lightening the load to save fuel," Krysty muttered. "Idiot."

"What's wrong with the wag?" Ryan asked, joining his friend at the hole in the floor.

Tilting back his fedora, J.B. looked up from the exposed engine. "Primary ignition wire harness is gone," he stated. "Somebody ripped it out hard. Repairs have been tried and failed."

"Sounds internecine to me," Doc rumbled softly from the rear of the wag.

Checking over an AK-47 assault rifle, Mildred gave the silver-haired scholar a stern look, but said nothing in reply. The crazy old coot was right. This did seem like some sort of a rebellion in the ranks.

"I'd say Gaza is in the city," Ryan announced in sudden understanding. "He's down there trying to get parts to fix this wag."

"A bold move," Doc said in grudging respect. "What else this baron may be, he is no coward."

"That's just self-preservation," Mildred replied, slinging the Kalashnikov across her back. "Got nothing to do with bravery."

Retrieving the self-heat from under the seat where it had rolled, Jak tucked it safely away into his leather jacket. Ammo they had; food was short. "Release cable and let rot down there," he suggested, zipping the pocket shut.

"Leave it alone," J.B. countered harshly, looking up from the cramped engine compartment toward the turret with its two huge blasters. "That way Gaza comes to us, and as he steps into sight we can blow him off the cliff with his own blasters!''

Ryan nodded and started for the turret. ''Sounds good.''

But then the big man paused and scowled at a plastic seat bolted to the wall. There were some words scratched deep into the resilient material in big block letters. Stroking the surface with his fingertips, they came back flecked with tiny bits of plastic dust and curls. The writing was brand-new. Anybody sitting in the chair would have wiped it clean with their clothing.

''Mother Gaia,'' Krysty whispered, trying to control her pounding heart. ''Is that a message for Gaza or for us?'' Turning, the woman glanced at the dead blonde lying on the floor and had a flashback to their escape from Rockpoint ville when she had been looking at the keep and felt somebody look right back at her from behind a thick stone wall.

''This was written by her,'' Krysty said, staring at the corpse. ''The baron's first wife was a doomie.''

''What hell mean?'' Jak drawled, frowning was he read the words again. '''The seven will become six.' Bah, heat-crazy dreck.''

''There are seven of us,'' Ryan muttered, and oddly felt a shiver ran down his spine as if he had just pronounced the death sentence of somebody present.

''Just some mystic nonsense,'' Mildred said in false bravado. ''Besides, it doesn't say die. Maybe one of us leaves. If Doc was to find some to go way back home, that would be good news!''

"Indeed, it would, madam," Doc said, from the open doorway, his arms crossed and the massive LeMat resting on a shoulder. "But enemies rarely leave messages of gladful tidings for their rivals to discover."

She scowled. "You think it's psychological warfare? That's not really Gaza's style. He is more of a hammer-breaking-your-bones kind of guy."

True words, and Doc started to say more, when the sound of a broiling steak came to him riding on the desert wind. Feeling a touch of panic, the old man grew confused for a moment, thinking he was slipping into a delirium again, when the sound returned stronger and louder. No by gadfrey, not meat on a grill, but hard rain on dry ground!

"The acid rain is here!" Doc cried, hurriedly backing into the war wag, nearly tripping on the jamb.

Stretching across the desert, a faintly yellow wall was sweeping toward the APC like a curtain. Rushing to the rear doors, Ryan and J.B. pulled them shut and dogged the locks tight while the rest of the companions closed every blaster port, louvered ob port and hatch. The companions knew from reading some old documents found in the redoubts that the LAV 25 was an NBC-rated vehicle, designed to withstand nuclear, bacteriological and chemical attacks. But that was way back when it was new and fully operational, the seals firm and solid. Nobody had ever expected the bastard machine to still be in service a hundred years later.

Down came the rain in torrents, sounding like small-caliber rounds as it pelted the armored hull of the APC. In only moments, the sharp reek of sulfur was heavy inside the wag, and the companions quickly tied handkerchiefs across their faces.

"Leak!" Dean cursed as a rivulet of yellow water trickled across the corrugated metal floor from under a console.

Unsure of the source, the companions stepped on top of the ammo boxes to stay above the acid. But the stream flowed freely into the open engine compartment, and soon wisps of smoke rose from the organic components of the machinery being dissolved under the chemical onslaught.

Slowly the water level rose inside the compartment and upon reaching the top started to spread along the floor. As it touched the dead woman, the acid started to eat away at her flesh, and the stink of sulfur became mixed with a more foul-reek of copper.

Shifting to the wall seats, the companions watched for any other leaks in the hull when a tremendous explosion shook the APC from prow to stern, and a hellstorm of sand was blasted against the hull, temporarily making more noise than the rain. Only a second later, a whooshing roar passed by overhead, closely followed by another detonation.

"Dark night, that was a missile!" J.B. cursed,

clutching his munitions bag. "The Trader must be here and he fucking thinks we're Gaza!"

"Of course, we're in his APC!" Dean agreed, keeping a tight grip on a ceiling stanchion near the turret. "Dad, what can we do?"

Quickly, Ryan looked around for the hand comm he had seen earlier and spotted it floating in the acid rain, the plastic already reduced to a thinning goo leaving only a tangle of wires and transistors.

"No choice! Everybody outside!" Ryan ordered. "If they hit us inside this thing, we're chilled! Only chance we have is out in the open."

"In rain?" Jak demanded incredulously, stretching his neck forward as if to bring the other man into clearer focus. "Better stay here!"

"With missiles on the way? If we stay, we die. Now move!"

Pulling out the ponchos from their backpacks, the companions draped the plastic sheeting over their bodies and heads, pulling them tight with nylon cords. Some canvas gloves were found in a tool box, not quite enough for everybody, but they all got at least one for their blaster hand, the other stuffed deep inside their clothing for safekeeping.

"Better hope these shower curtains are tough enough," Mildred said, cinching another layer tight around her head in a crude bonnet. "But I better warn you that if anybody trips or falls face first in the water…"

"We do a mercy killing and shoot them in the back of the head," Doc rumbled from inside his white plastic cocoon. "Yes, we do understand, madam, and may God help us all."

Stepping down onto the flooded floor, Ryan braced himself for a rush of pain, but the tough U.S. Army combat boots resisted the pool of acid for the moment. How long they would was another matter entirely.

However, neither Krysty nor Doc wore the military garb, and precious seconds were spent while they lashed the last of the plastic curtains around their leather boots as additional protection. If the group hadn't taken spare curtains to make tents, they would be in a nuke load of trouble right now, even more so than they already were. He could carry Krysty, but who could have hauled the tall Doc Tanner around to keep him off the lethal ground?

"Everybody ready?" Ryan asked, going to the rear door and grabbing the latch. Just outside, he could hear the rain coming down in sheets now, wave after wave of death from the sky as every bit as deadly as the ancient nukes. "Okay, keep your head down and walk straight ahead! Let's move!"

As Ryan pushed open the door, the rain came howling in, smacking against the plastic wrappings in fat yellow drops. Suddenly, Ryan understood why the Core had been wrapped in thick bandages from head to foot. Clever bastards.

Using an M-16 to hold the door wide open, Ryan

stepped onto the soggy ground, his boots slipping about in the salty mud. Tucking away his blaster, he took Krysty by the hand, and then she did the same to Doc, and so on. Now supporting one another, the companions moved as a single unit across the killing field as another missile streaked by so close overhead their plastic coverings shook from the fiery wash.

Dragging their boots to keep from splashing in the downpour, the companions headed directly for the lee of the closest dune, the slope offering some minor degree of protection from the rain, and the elevated ground giving blessed relief from the deadly puddles. However, every breath was painful from the moisture in the air stinging their flesh and eyes. As they trundled through the rumbling hellstorm, they saw the aced riders of the smashed motorcycles dissolving, the dark matter runoff flowing over the edge of the cliff like ghastly sewage.

Nearing the dune, Ryan bent over to grab something from a portion of a bike not yet submerged when another streak of light split the rain and this time there sounded a metallic detonation, the concussion slamming them hard and threatening to tear away their plastic sheets.

Chapter Nineteen

Rushing toward the cliff, Gaza felt a wave of relief when the anchored cable came in sight, but scanning above he couldn't spot Allison on the cliff above. Where the nuking hell was the feeb slut? What were they supposed to do, climb the fucking hundred feet of greased steel using their hands?

Moments later, Kathleen arrived, panting from the exertion of carrying the heavy flamethrower. Quizzically, she tilted her head at the man and looked up the cliff.

Grabbing the cable, Gaza gave it a hard tug, waited and tugged again using even more strength, but there was no reply. Damn bitch! Doomie or not, he'd whip her for this unpardonable lapse!

Then there came the distant sound of sizzling, and both the man and woman reacted in horror. The desert dwellers knew that only one thing made that noise. But the rainy season was weeks away!

Gaza started to reach for the cable, then lowered his glove and turned. "Back into the ruins!" he ordered. "Now, woman!"

But Kathleen was already started for the nearest

building, a windowless ruin partially collapsed, but still several stories tall.

"Forget those!" the baron snapped, pulling her in a new direction. "We could get burned alive if the fires arrive. Back to the convoy!"

Nodding in compliance, the woman followed her husband through the maze of debris and back into the streets. As they headed for the APC, everywhere around them the birds were flying away frantically, seeking refuge inside the shadowy preDark structures. The millipedes were already gone from sight, but the noises from the storm sewers told of fresh fighting in the subterranean depths.

Running directly over the partially consumed deaders on the pavement, Gaza blew away a pair of vultures squabbling over a desiccated infant to clear a path to the park once more.

The area around the ancient mil wags was clear, and Kathleen felt a surge of hope. If the rear doors and top hatch of the APC could be tightly closed, they would be able to safely ride out the storm, and afterward there wouldn't be any stickies or millipedes left alive in the city. She only hoped that Allison would be okay left alone to face the Trader. But the first wife was extremely smart, and Kathleen had supreme confidence that the elder blonde would survive to rejoin them after the rains had gone.

Yanking open the rear door, Gaza cursed to see a stickie standing inside the wag, only its outline betraying the presence of the tan-colored mutie that perfectly matched the paint job on the inside of the LAV 25. Then the shadows on the walls moved, betraying the presence of more of the muties.

Slamming the door shut on a reaching hand, Gaza shoved his shoulder against the metal and the limb was severed. Strident hooting sounded from inside the wag as the hand dropped to the pavement, its suckers opening and closing like tiny mouths.

Unlimbering the flamethrower, Kathleen ignited the preburner, a tiny blue flame hissing steadily inside the vented main barrel. Then she assumed a stance directly before the doors, and Gaza yanked them open again, taking refuge behind the metal portal.

A roaring lance of flame shot out from the weapon to fill the wag completely, reddish tongues writhing out of the ports and vents. Covered with fire, the creatures inside shrieked and dashed madly about, hitting the walls in their death convulsions.

As Kathleen cut the flow of condensed fuel, Gaza backed away and pushed her toward the imposing bulk of the tank. They had escaped the stickies, but lost the APC in the process. Damn the luck! As he ran, Gaza found his shoulders were tense, braced for the first wet impact of an acid drop.

Reaching the titanic machine, the baron checked underneath but saw no danger. Placing a boot on the treads, Gaza boosted himself onto the huge vehicle, then gave his wife a hand upward. At the rear of the war wag, there was a gap in the armored skirt hanging around the chassis to protect the treads and wheels, almost as if it were specifically there to assist entry. And the treads themselves were odd, each individual piece coated with hard rubber, instead of the bar steel he would have expected. Protection to not damage the civie street? Possible.

Thunder and lightning crashed the turbulent sky as they headed for the turret, and as Gaza walked around the main cannon, a brick-colored stickie charged from the nearby ruins and grabbed the man by a boot, its body rippling to become a matching shiny black. Snarling in revulsion, Gaza tried to jerk free, but the mutie was firmly attached, so he lowered his M-16 and triggered a long stream of hardball ammo into its sex-less chest. Wildly, the stickie jerked about from the barrage of rounds, but didn't let go, and as the clip emptied, it weaved drunkenly, still on its feet and the puckered holes in its features already starting to close.

Squeezing past her husband, Kathleen pressed the vented barrel of flamethrower onto the hand of the thing, the blue flame of the preburner searing the glutinous flesh. Hooting in pain, the stickie released the man and Gaza gave it another burst, driving the mutie backward until it was far enough away. Now Kathleen triggered the pressurized fuel and unleashed a one-second spray into its misshapen face. Its head a ball of fire, the stickie stumbled away, waving both arms helplessly as the norms clambered on top of the turret to look down inside the open hatch of the great machine.

At the bottom of the short ladder, Gaza could see the interior of the tank was well lit, the dull red glow of ancient electric lights making the inside of the wag seem as if it were the belly of some great beast. Dropping the spent clip and reloading, Gaza entered the machine, watching the walls and floors for the slightest indication of movement.

The interior of the tank was like nothing Gaza had ever seen. The walls were painted a soothing white, and controls were everywhere, hanging in clusters, filling curved banks along the ceiling and three walls. The rear wall was a veined blast-door, sealing off the store of shells for the huge 120 mm cannon.

Yet in spite of its huge size, the war wag seemed to be built for only four people, a driver, a loader, a gunner and the boss. Those were the only chairs, with nothing more for sec men or passengers to use in transit.

As Kathleen joined him in the war wag, the blue flame of the preburner brightly lit the interior, and it was clear that they were alone.

"Save the juice," he ordered gruffly.

Uneasily, Kathleen cut the flame, the metal of the barrel immediately ticking as it started to cool.

Going to the turret, the baron swung down the hatch with a bang so loud it hurt his eardrums. Twisting the lock, he set it tight and dropped to the main floor.

There were no vents or ports in sight anywhere inside the tank, just a lot of thick pipes that he deduced were actually periscopes, six for the commander in the turret, and three for the driver, two for the gunner and nothing for the seat of the loader near the blast-proof door. Fair enough. His job was to move shells, not look outside and enjoy the view.

Sighing gratefully, Kathleen unbuckled the chest harness and slid the heavy fuel tanks off her back and placed them carefully on the rough metal floor. The surface wasn't corrugated like that in an APC, more like sand, and it gave a good footing.

Just then a patter of splats hit the hull of the tank, the noise softened by the dense triple armor. Then the rain arrived full force, sheets crashing over the machine, but even the mighty thunder was baffled down to a mere murmur.

Nervously, Gaza and Kathleen watched the floor and walls for any sign of a leak, but the interior of the war wag stayed dry, and there wasn't the slightest trace of the rotten-egg stink of the deadly rain. Then Gaza frowned as he realized that even the smell of the preburner fuel was gone. There had to be some sort of automatic venting.

Sitting in the commander's chair, Gaza ran his hands across the shiny console, thinking of what he could do with only one such machine and wishing with all of his might that the tank was still operational.

"Power," he whispered softly, thinking of the empire he could build with just one such machine.

"Order received," the flat voice said from nowhere. "Switching from standby status to primary power."

His chest pounding in fear, Gaza tried to breathe as the interior lights slowly grew in strength until giving a smooth white light. Then the baron laughed in delight. The nuking thing was still functioning, with some sort of preDark comp running the controls. Blind norad be praised, this was the find of a lifetime!

"Please, identify," a flat voice rumbled.

Fuck that, Gaza snorted angrily, he took orders from nobody, especially machines. "No, you identify!" he snapped. "And be quick about it!"

A blinding fan of thin green light came out of the console and played across the baron, stopping át the cluster of decorations pinned to the shirt taken from the deader in the first APC at the head of the convoy.

"Working," the voice intoned. "Acknowledged. Ident confirmed, Lieutenant Colonel Anderson. What are your orders, sir?"

Trying to hide his excitement, Gaza glanced at the colorful collection of rainbow-colored plastic squares in three neat rows. He had taken the stuff just because it looked pretty. But they had to have been symbols of some sort, the deader in the APC a chief sec man in his day. Now this dumb-ass machine thought Gaza was the long-gone person simply because of the clothing? Excellent.

"We're in the middle of a nuking chem storm," the baron started, then cursed himself for a feeb. He had to speak old talk.

"Correction," he said slowly. "There is an…NBC storm outside. Seal the fuc…seal every vent and make sure none of that dreck…poison gets inside."

There was a short pause.

"Acknowledged," the voice said, and suddenly from every direction there sounded slams and hisses. A moment later, clean-smelling dry air started blowing from the vents set under the control boards.

Approaching her husband, Kathleen tugged on his sleeve and made a gesture at the roof, urging him to leave. With a snarl, Gaza shoved her away and she fell to the floor. Tears on her face, the scared woman begged him to leave, but he just swiveled the chair away to face the winking array of controls spanning the incredibly complex instrument board.

"Tell me about yourself," Gaza ordered, reclining in the seat. "And start with the weapons."

OUTSIDE, THE DEADLY RAIN was starting to extinguish the rampaging fires. The exposed corpses on the sidewalks quickly began to dissolve under the deluge.

Louder than cannons, the thunder rumbled once more, lightning flashing down to strike a radio tower and starting a fresh fire that the rain soon drenched.

Across the metropolis, the muties sought cover from the storm, only to find countless small fires raging deep within the buildings where the rain could never reach. Bloody violence filled the city as the mindless creatures fought one another in bestial fury over the bodies, adding more corpses to the city of death. But that was only a harbinger of the slaughter to come.

IN WAR WAG ONE, windshield wipers worked steadily to keep the front glass clear of the rain. Humming and shaking, the patched air conditioner was working full power and the atmosphere inside the war wag was almost clear of the rotten-egg stink of the deadly downpour.

The burning wreckage of an APC sat blown apart before the rig, and all around the blast site bodies of the outriders eroded under the onslaught of the acid rain.

"Hit it again!" Kate ordered, brandishing a fist. "No prisoners!"

A few moments later, the rig shuddered as another missile was launched from the roof pod, and this time the APC was hit dead center. The crew in the control room cheered, as the radio crackled with static. Nobody paid attention to it, as the comm did that with every flash of lightning, but this time somebody started speaking.

"Anybody hear us on this?" a gruff man's voice demanded. "We got this hand comm from a bike that rain hadn't swamped yet."

Kate spun at that and stared hard at the speaker.

What the hell was going on here? That sure wasn't Duncan over in War Wag Two.

"You listening in the big rig?" the stranger continued. "The name is Ryan Cawdor, and I used to run with Trader back in the Darks. I'm here with J. B. Dix and some others."

"Weapons on full, shoot anything coming our way," Kate ordered, taking out her hand comm and extending the slim antenna until the telescoping silver almost reached the ceiling.

"Ryan, eh? The name is familiar to me," the woman said, pressing the transmit switch. "So where the hellblast are you?"

"Out here in the rain," the man said simply. "Look on your four."

"Bullshit," Blackjack growled in disbelief, checking the radar screen. "Ain't nothing out there but deaders and wreckage. It's some kinda trick."

"Incorrect," Eric said from above. "The ear is picking up their voices through the rain. They are exactly where they claim to be."

While the gunners in the machine-gun blisters swept their blasters across the soaked desert, Kate worried a knuckle.

"Mebbe," she relented, then went to the periscope to track the area. But sure enough, there they were, a half-dozen or so people wrapped in plastic like MRE meals, and standing on a sandy mound, the yellow runoff creeping steadily up the side of their dwindling island.

"What the hell is going on here?" Jessica growled, leaning into the windshield to try to get a look. "Some of his sec men left the wag?"

"Men or women?" Jake asked, flipping a switch to turn on the halogen headlights. The beams stabbed into the rain but were swallowed whole after only a few yards. "He's got all those damn wives, ya know. I heard it was a hundred."

"Only a few. But this looks like a mix," Kate said slowly. "Might be a kid and wrinklie, too. But I can't tell for sure."

Taking a rag from his pants, Blackjack wiped the inside of the blister to remove the thickening fog of condensation that the damn AC always caused. "Think it's a mutiny?" he asked, squinting outside.

"No," the Trader said, leaving the periscope. "No way that one APC could hold a dozen people even if they were stuffed in like cordwood."

"Might have been riding on top," Jessica suggested. "Then the rain came and they ran just before we used the missiles."

In spite of her gut feeling on the matter, Kate had to admit that did cover everything and made a damn lot of sense. The logical thing would be for them to start the engines and leave, letting the rain ace the strangers in its own way. Only that civie had spoken well of Ryan, and she had been hearing rumors of such a man who traveled the Deathlands chilling slavers, and such. That alone earned him a lot of ammo in her book. Mebbe even enough for a face-to-face.

"Hello?" the radio cracked once more. "You still there?"

"I hear ya," Kate asked bluntly into the comm, walking over to the front window. There wasn't much to be seen through the downpour. "So what do you want from me?"

"How about letting us in? We're getting chilled out here."

Jake and Blackjack both snorted rudely at that. At the door, the guard worked the bolt on his M-16 and tested the locks to make sure the hatch was firmly secured. Kate approved. Her people knew their jobs; hopefully so did she.

"You might get chilled in here," the woman replied, a touch of anger distorting her words. "It's just a question of my blasters, or the nuking rain. I got no reason to ace you, but then, I also got no reason to trust you. But tell you what. We'll shoot you if you like, and save getting melted from the chems."

There came a bitter laugh. "Okay, here's a new deal. We know where Gaza is. Fair trade. A ride for the info."

"Mutie crap. The baron is chilled," Jake said, but there was a trace of doubt in his face. "Gotta be. Look at that fucking wag!"

"If he was inside," Kate said, then raised the hand

comm to her mouth and pressed the transmit switch. "Deal sounds okay, but too many riding along. I only need one of you to talk."

"Nobody talks unless we all go," he stated firmly, the rain audible in the background. Somebody was coughing hard from the stink of the polluted water. "The deal is everybody rides, or nobody."

"You a family?"

"Close enough," Ryan stated.

Part of her ability to trade with barons and civies was the talent to tell a fucking lie from a masked truth. Kate could hear in his voice that he considered this the truth. That didn't mean it was—he could be insane—but she wasn't getting that read off the man, and made her decision.

"Okay, drop your blasters and come in, one at a time," Kate said. "Anybody gets fancy and my troops will cut you down."

"The dog has no teeth," he countered. "We keep the blasters and come in together."

"Then you don't come in!"

"Then you don't get Gaza!"

There was a long pause as the rain water slowly rose, the salty mix a murky white like pus flowing from an infected wound.

"Okay, final chance," Kate growled into the hand comm. "You come in with the iron, but take it off once inside. But keep your knives. That's as good as it gets. Take it or leave it."

"And how do I know we can trust you?"

About time he asked that. "Fair enough," she said, and released the transmit switch. "Jake, give them the lights."

The driver adjusted the controls and on the outside hull of the war wag brilliant electric lights came on illuminating the sides of the huge rig. Covered by several layers of clear acrylic paint salvaged from an auto body shop, was the carefully painted symbol of a lightning bolt slashing across a star.

"If you know anything, that says everything," she stated. "The word of the Trader is jack in every ville for a thousand miles along the New Mex and Panhandle."

"Yes, it is," Ryan said. "Deal. We're coming in."

"Use the back door," Kate added, and turned the radio off.

"Think we can trust them, Chief?" Blackjack asked, turning from the machine-gun blister.

"I don't trust anybody," she said, tucking the hand comm away and pulling out the Ingram to check the ammo clip. "Have armed guards meet them in the washroom, and if they cause us any trouble, blow them to hell."

Chapter Twenty

Sloshing through the foul water, the companions walked to the aft end of the imposing war wag. A door was already open there, bright lights showing from inside. The last to trundle into a small steel-lined room, Ryan closed the door and the companions drew in their first deep breath since the deluge had started.

"Now what?" Dean asked, the foggy plastic sheets dripping yellow water onto the stainless-steel floor.

"Use the hose," a voice said gruffly through a grille in the only other door. The stubby barrel of a rapid-fire showed through the opening, pointing their way. "Then hang the ponchos on the wall and dump your blasters in the iron box in the corner."

Dutifully, the companions rinsed themselves, the faint yellow water swirling into a drain in the middle of the floor. The original Trader had used something similar for folks set on fire from Molotov cocktails and the like.

When they were clean, the air smelled even better and it was much easier to breathe. Shaking out the plastic shower curtains, they hung them on the steel hooks welded to the wall and let them drip directly onto the floor.

"Now the iron," the voice behind the blaster insisted, and there came the telltale sound of a slide being racked to drive home the necessity of obedience.

Reluctantly, the companions shed their weapons, placing the arsenal of blasters into an old U.S. Army footlocker, the munitions bag barely fitting within the tight confines. The lack of weight around his waist disturbed Ryan, and he really hated to give up the weapons, but there was no other way. The companions had been caught without blasters many times before, and it always cost a world of pain to get them back. At least they still had some blades.

"Ammo, too," the guard ordered, and they complied. What good was one without the other?

Now the door swung open, and three men entered, short rapid-fires held in their hands, the blasters perfect for combat inside the cramped confines of a wag. One of the men held himself oddly stiff, his broad shoulders tense from some hidden ailment.

"That everything?" the guard demanded, looking them over carefully. "What's in the bag?"

Mildred opened the canvas satchel to display the collection of bottles and surgical instruments.

"You a healer?" he asked suspiciously.

She nodded, then added, "I bet that old busted leg hurts like a bitch in this kind of weather."

The stiff guard reacted in surprise to that, then let his face ease into a grim smile.

"Okay, you're a fucking healer." He chuckled, then motioned with the rapid-fire toward the open doorway. However, his index finger was no longer resting on the trigger. "This way. The chief wants to see you in the galley."

The sound of the rain grew less noticeable as they walked along a narrow corridor, a perfect killing zone for defenders in the vehicle to ace invaders trying to reach the rear quarters. Soon the rumble of powerful engines could be heard, as well as the high-pitched whine of an electric generator. But another set of doors closed off that section, and the engine room was left behind. Crew quarters came next, the bunks disheveled and personal items about, a lot of preDark girlie posters on the walls, some of them pure hard-core. Mildred tried not to blush, while Jak and Dean noticed the explicit pictures with frank approval.

A swinging set of louvered doors was chained open and the next room was warm, the air fragrant with the smell of a meat stew and black coffee. A long table was bolted to the floor, a bench on each side attached to the sturdy legs. Just like a submarine galley, Ryan noted privately, thinking of a stint with Admiral Poseidon. Everything firmly in place so that it wouldn't slide about in combat and get in the way of repairs, or an escape.

"Eat up," a slim woman announced, turning from

a small electric stove built into the dividing wall, the burners glowing red as molten lava. "I made plenty, so there's plenty for everybody."

Expertly, she placed scarred red plastic bowls and utensils on the tables and then thumped a heavy metal pot full of bubbling stew in the middle of the table. There were chunks of meat mixed with veggies, and the smell was a pain in the belly of the hungry companions. Their last meal had been breakfast in the museum about twelve hours earlier.

"Coffee next!" the cook announced, turning back to the stove. A parkerized revolver rode in a holster at the small of her back where it would be safe from bumping into a hot stove.

As the companions took seats at the table, the skinny guard with a mustache frowned in disapproval.

"Hey, Matilda, the chief didn't say they got a meal," he stated.

"No, she didn't," a new man said as he entered the galley, a large revolver riding snug in a shoulder holster under his left arm. "But I do. So shut up, Anders, and stay out of the way."

The gray-haired man was huge, not fat, just large, with a barrel chest and wide arms. The tendons on his hands were as pronounced as coiled cables under a tarpaulin, and his irregular nose had clearly been broken in countless fights.

Flashing in anger, Anders bridled at that, but then

backed down from the big man and left the galley in a huff muttering to himself.

"Damn fool." Matilda sighed, placing a huge speckled urn of coffee on the table along with a tray of tin cups and a handful of mixed packets of powdered cream and sugar from MRE meal packs.

"Hell of a tech on the engines, though," the giant stated, leaning against the wall and crossing his thick arms. "Okay, Ryan, you and your people grab some chow. The chief will be with ya in a tick."

Feeding us so the sec men have enough time to search through our possessions, he realized, pouring a cup full of the black brew. Seven holsters but only six blasters would give vital info to anybody with a brain. It was a bastard smart move, and he would have done the same thing himself in their position.

Pouring a cup of the fresh coffee, Mildred studied the fluid as it went into the cup, then sniffed carefully and took a small sip, holding the brew in her mouth for a moment before swallowing and nodding to the others. If there were any drugs in the potent java, they were beyond her ability to discern.

The companions divided the food into the bowls and dug in with gusto. While they ate, the big man accepted a steaming cup of java from the cook and took a gulp in spite of the boiling temperature.

"Blessed be, when you joined the convoy, Matilda," he said with a grin. "Our last cook could ruin food by opening the can, and his coffee was perfect for dipping pungi sticks into to poison muties.''

The woman merely smiled and returned to her work. With so many sec men in the convoy, her work was never really finished. Matilda was either starting a meal, serving it or washing dishes afterward. But this was still a hundred times better for her and Avarm than working in a ville. Almost a whole day had gone by so far and nobody had tried to rape her or steal Avarm to put him in slave chains. It was just incredible.

''Got a name?'' Ryan asked in a friendly manner, spooning more stew into his mouth.

''I'm Fat Pete,'' the man said, a hand resting on his thigh only inches away from the .357 Magnum S&W blaster riding at his side. ''I'm the top kick here. Now.'' The word was added to the sentence after a split second had passed, Ryan could make a guess what it meant. The XO for the convoy had been aced by Gaza, probably one of the bike riders dissolving outside in the mud.

''Nothing to do with us,'' Ryan said firmly. ''We're just trying to find the Trader, ace Gaza if we can.''

''I like that second part,'' Kate said, stepping into view from the corridor.

Laying aside his spoon, Ryan watched as the tall woman entered the galley. So this was the person using the name of Trader. The woman was clean and well muscled, with fancy boots and two wide gun belts

ing her ample hips; one sporting a big-bore revolver, the other carrying a hand comm. Her shirt swelled from a wealth of breast underneath, and her golden blond hair was tied off in a short ponytail with a strip of camou cloth. Her nose had been broken once and set poorly, and a band of scars circled each wrist. A former slave, eh?

Her skin was deeply bronzed from the Deathlands sun, and her eyes were hard, but not cold. There was still a trace of compassion in the expression.

"You the Trader?" Ryan asked, laying aside his spoon.

"Just Trader," Kate said, sliding back her Stetson hat until it hung down her back from the thong around her neck. "And inside these walls you can call me Kate."

"Ryan," he replied, indicating himself with a thumb, and then introducing the rest of the companions.

Leaning against the wall, Kate nodded at each in turn. They were lean and hard looking, but without that dead glint in their eyes of mercies or coldhearts. The redhead in the group was a real beauty, but she carried herself with a warrior's pride and nobody was telling her to get them things. All equal, eh? She liked that. Mebbe it had been a good idea to cut these folks a deal. Never enough friendlies out here in the Deathlands.

"Well, you're inside," she said as he finished. "So where the hell is Gaza?"

"Aced?" Fat Pete demanded, a note of urgency in his tone.

Pouring more coffee, Ryan shook his head. "The best way I read it, he's alive and down in the city. The APC was broken. Somebody ripped out some wires. He went down to find replacement parts."

Blowing air out his nose, Fat Pete glanced at the metal wall separating them from the city below. "Good," he said gruffly. "Then he's aced already and we can leave."

"Not yet," Kate stated. "Baron Gaza is tougher than he looks and luckier than any ten escaped slaves. Fighting Gaza is like blacksmithing iron—the harder you hit it, the stronger it gets. Harder to chill than the original Trader."

"Ain't that the bastard truth," Ryan growled in agreement.

"So how did you know him?" she asked. "The Trader, I mean."

"We rode with the Trader for years," Ryan said, indicating J.B. at the end of the table. "But we got caught in an ambush one day and the convoy was blown to hell. Sort of parted company after that." Which was all a hell of a big lie, but as close as the man would come to describing the chain of events that led to the discovery of the redoubts.

Just then, the rig shook slightly as the diesel engines kicked on for a moment to charge the batteries.

Kate could see nothing in the big man's scarred face, but she had a gut feeling he was holding some info back. She had encountered a lot of rumors in her search for the Trader, and the name of Ryan appeared often in the later years, but always as a staunch ally. Then she turned to study the wiry man with glasses and the hat. Yeah, so that had to be J.B. These were the men who stood by the Trader's side in that bad day in Mocsin and then into the Darks. Sounded like her search was over at last.

"And he's dead," Kate said as a question.

Pushing away his empty bowl, J.B. wiped his face on a cloth. "Don't know for sure," the Armorer replied honestly. "Last time we saw him, he and a friend were making a stand between a rock and a hard place. There was nothing we could do to help. They could have fought clear, but we just don't know."

"Did you know the first Trader?" Dean asked. "The real one?"

"We're all real traders," the woman said with a bitter laugh. "Just some more than others, is all.

"And, yes," she continued. "I met the man just once. When he came riding into my ville blowing lead in every direction. His sec men shouted his name as if it were a war chant. Aced every sec man there. Cleaned the place out."

Ryan scowled deeply at that. The Trader looting a ville? Bullshit.

"Then he set all of the slaves free," Kate went on, one hand stealing over to rub the scars on her wrist. "Left us all of the blasters, and even gave us some supplies and books, then went away. Took nothing but water, and we had plenty of that, so it was nothing to us."

"He did that a lot," Ryan said, leaning back in the bench. "The man had a bad itch about scratching slavers."

"Me, too," Kate said. After her release from the chains, the girl had fought hard to keep from going back into them as a gaudy slut in a brothel. But after a person had been to hell, no amount of whippings and beatings could make him or her go back. Soon she stole a blaster, then a horse and wagon and left on her own.

That was the beginning of her life as a trader. First acting as armed escort for pilgrims wanting to reach new lands, then exchanging goods for services, then goods for better goods. But always on the trail of the Trader to join with the man and work on freeing more slaves. A blaster and three live rounds bought her some info that proved to be all lies, but when she returned, a hot knife got her back the weapon and the truth.

Over the years, pieces of the puzzle fell into place and then she found it, one of the Trader's hidden depots where he cached supplies and fuel. There were a lot of blasters, grens, machine guns, all sorts of mil iron, and even a working wag that was now one of the small cargo vans of her armored convoy. But at the time it looked like a juggernaut from ancient legends. As unstoppable as a stampede and larger than the sky.

Now her wags sported a laser and dozens of missiles. Kate had a crew of fifty and three hidden caches of her own spread across the burning landscape. But still it wasn't enough to ever feel as safe as she had that day when the big man with an easy grin fired his blaster and blew open the locks on her chains, giving her the double-edged gift of freedom.

"So these are the outlanders," a newcomer said from the corridor. The scrawny man had wild hair, thinning at the top even though he seemed no more than thirty or so. His teeth were a disaster, badly crooked, and his left foot was obviously deformed, little more than a twisted lump at the end of his leg.

"Everything okay?" Kate demanded, all business once more.

"Sure, sure," Eric said, limping into the room. "I have the radar on full, and our belly armor is live with current. Nobody's getting in, or out, without our knowing. And we're not going anywhere until this storm subsides, so I decided to meet our guests."

"They ain't guests," Fat Pete stated firmly. "We cut a deal, and we're sticking to our side. That's all."

"Fair enough," Eric said. "Still never hurts to check and see if they got a tech in the group."

"You and those damn machines."

"Saved our ass at Hellsgate."

"This is Eric, our chief tech," Kate said, with a head bob. "He runs the comp that runs the show."

"Mutie shit," Jak said rudely, removing his sunglasses and folding them to tuck them away into a shirt pocket. "All comps aced." The teenager knew that was only true on the surface. In the underground redoubts, the bases were run by huge banks of comps that operated fusion generators and the mat-trans system.

"Comps are real as a kick in the belly, friend," Eric said amiably. "Quite a lot of comps still function okay. Oh, not if they were left running since skydark, then the last program is now burned into the system forever and is now the only thing they can do. But if not turned on, they're okay."

"If you need any help, just let me know," Mildred offered, passing her bowl to Matilda. "I know something about computers."

Eric arched an eyebrow at that word. The healer spoke old tech? "Convince me," he said.

Mildred thought about all the jargon she had learned in med school, but most of that was system specific. Something general would do. "Cold is better than hot," she said. "They go slower when they overheat. If you got comps here, then you also have some serious air conditioners to compensate for the heat of the desert.''

Erik stared at the woman in disbelief.

''Probably looted some software from an auto-body shop to monitor your engines,'' the physician went on, taking a logical guess. ''So what do you have on the start-up screen, clouds or an apple?''

''By God, you are a hacker,'' Erik said softly. ''Wanna see the nest?''

Nest. That was as good a term for every tangle of computer wires the woman had ever encountered.

''Sure,'' she said, standing. ''I can probably teach you how to defrag the hard drive. You would have to shut down for a while, but afterward it might double the processing speed.''

''Double?'' Kate said in sudden interest.

''And we'd be without the radar and such for how long?'' Fat Pete growled, uncrossing his arms. ''This could just be a trick to get us to weak our defenses for an attack.''

Thoughtfully, Kate rubbed her jaw. ''Or nuking save us in the next firefight.'' They could try that back at the depot, where they were safe from attack and far, far away from this battle zone.

''Hell, we could do it right now,'' she relented. ''There's nothing Gaza can do in this hellstorm. We're safe for a while from any more of his rockets. In fact—''

Whatever she was going to say was cut off by a

peal of thunder, the ground shaking under the war wag in a minor earthquake. Then it happened again, and again, steady and continuous as if a giant were striding across the world.

"It's me," Kate said into her hand comm. "What the hell is going on outside?"

"We don't know!" Jake replied over the crackling speaker. "There's a whole lot of explosions on the cliff, and the ground is starting to break about…there it goes!"

As he spoke, the war wag lurched into motion, wheeling backward with the diesels roaring with restrained power.

"Okay, we're clear," Jake said, panting. "Christ, that was close. A whole section of the cliff just broke loose and dropped into the city, but we're clear now."

Ryan scowled darkly at that and exchanged looks with the other companions. He didn't know how or why, but he knew it was Gaza.

"All stations report!" Kate snapped, and listened to the familiar voices announcing the status of the department of the war wag, and then the other wags. Only the second cargo van didn't respond.

"Duncan, have you got a visual on Little Sue?" the Trader demanded into the hand comm. "Duncan, can you read me?"

"It's gone," the man said, his voice sounding like something from the grave. "It's just vanished in a fireball. She's gone, blown to bits."

"Missile hit?" Kate demanded.

"Impossible. Radar showed clear."

"Must have been a lightning strike," Eric said hopefully.

"Six more chilled," Fat Pete said woodenly, his face a waxy pallor. "Sue, Jimmy, that new guy, Bones…"

Just then the pounding started once more, moving along the cliff, passing them by in powerful waves that rattled everything in the galley.

"Lightning strike, my ass. That's cannon fire," Ryan said, standing. "Better sound the alert, I think we're under attack!"

"We?" Kate shot back, a hand resting on her boxy rapid-fire.

Ryan looked the blonde hard in the face. "If that's Gaza, then we're with you all the way."

A long moment passed while the savage explosions continued, the rig shaking with increasing force.

"Deal," the Trader said at last. "This way to the control room."

Chapter Twenty-One

"Got 'em!" Baron Gaza cried as the small vehicle on the monitor violently detonated.

"Confirmed," the tank replied. "That was a kill."

"There are more, a larger one. Find it!" Gaza demanded, leaning into the vid screen. On the control board was a vid screen with a view of the cliff. The angle was bad, and he couldn't see much past the edge, but just that glimpse of the wag was enough. The robotic tank responded instantly to his command and blew it apart with the main cannon.

"Second target has been acquired," it stated in the flat voice, bringing another van into sight, this one only visible halfway up from the desert ground. It seemed to be moving fast from the rain sheeting off its chassis, but the wag stayed in the exact center of the monitor as if nailed there.

"Ready on your command, sir."

Gaza bared his teeth in a feral grin. "Kill them," he whispered.

The turret traversed a small arc, and then the main gun fired, the barrel pulsating with a high-pitched hum. A split second later the black hole appeared in its side and the wag flipped over sideways as if exploding from within. Bodies and wreckage flew into the storm, a tire going over the edge of the cliff and falling from sight.

"Target has been eliminated," the machine said, patiently waiting for the next command.

The metal voice was getting clearer constantly, as if knocking off the dust of a hundred years of sleep. That made sense to Gaza. If you built a machine this complex, what the hell difference was there between it and a living thing? None that he could see.

"Anything else? Is there a large wag, covered with guns and missiles?"

"Wag?"

"Vehicle, truck—is there any other enemy transports? Any further movement on the cliff?"

There was a brief pause, as vid screen flicked along the visible length of the cliff, large sections hidden behind the preDark buildings. Only a few of them still had fires burning in their guts. The rest were cold and dark, many beginning to crumble from the combination of fresh air, fire damage and the acid rain. The preDark city was dying before his eyes. In a few days this would be only a hole in the ground filled with rubbish and bones.

"Negative. The perimeter is clear. Mil-sat relays inoperative for unknown reason."

Try the end of the world, tin brain. "Well done," the baron complimented. "Stay razor."

There was a long pause. "Razor, sir?"

Fuck! "Stay…sharp and on alert," Gaza said carefully, feeling a trickle of sweat flow down his face. Damn, he had to be more careful than that.

"Roger, order confirmed, sir. Alert status will be maintained at razor level."

Unnerved, the baron arched an eyebrow at that but forced himself to say nothing. So it learned, eh? That was both good and bad. He was riding a wild mutie here, but there was no other way out of this hellhole but this behemoth.

Hunched in the gunner's chair, Kathleen held her eyes closed tight, hands over both ears. She was clearly terrified by the sentient machine. Gaza sneered—well, too fucking bad. There were lots of sluts in the world to replace her, but only one behemoth. Yeah, good name.

"Alert, change of plans," he decided. "We shall leave the area and begin digging efforts. But shoot anything you see. The…enemy has a lot of missiles and they must be stopped."

"Confirmed."

Setting the tank in motion, Gaza was first startled, then delighted at the smoothness of its ride. Somehow the machine adjusted itself to always stay level, even as it rolled over the preDark cars. On the side monitors, the machine was passing dozens of stores ripe for the looting. But that wasn't pressing at the moment. There was a stash of MRE packs in the tank, enough for him and Kathleen for a few days. After that, he could get all he needed from the Trader. He knew that she had hidden depots across the Deathlands filled with fuel, food, rockets, everything. The tank was powered by some tech thing called a fusion reactor, so didn't need any fuel, but the rest would come in handy as rewards for his new army of sec men.

As it cleared a squat monolithic structure, the western face of the cliff came into direct view and now the turret swung around and hummed again, a fireball instantly exploding on the rocks.

"Is this what we're firing?" the baron asked, lifting a plastic cube in his hand.

"Confirmed," the machine responded as the cannon hummed again, and then again.

The baron turned the object about so that it reflected the rainbow lights from the complex control boards. At first he had thought it was sort of paperweight or target marker. The thing was only a greenish cube about the size of his fist. There was no brass, no C-4, not anything that he recognized as dangerous.

"Explain how this works to my civilian wife," the baron said, pronouncing the old words carefully and glancing at the woman cowering in the chair.

The machine started into a tech talk involving kinetic energy and caloric conversion that was far beyond his understanding of such things. But he slowly got the idea. Yeah, a strong man could hold a bullet in his hand and throw it at you with all of his strength and it wasn't going to do anything. The bullet wasn't dangerous; it was the speed of the lead. This thing took those cubes and fired them so nuking fast they hit like bombs.

"How many more in storage?" he demanded, placing the cube aside with some reverence.

"Four hundred nine." The cannon hummed. "Four hundred eight."

And the truck in the park was filled with thousands of them. Once he got out of this fucking city, there was nothing and nobody in the world that could stand before this monster war wag.

"Hit the new cliff lower so the rocks pull themselves down," he directed. "Then hit the fresh fall high to widen the destruction. Gotta have a wide path for a wag...for a tank of this size."

"Confirmed, sir," the machine replied, and the cannon shifted its angle, humming and humming as fresh sections of the rocky cliff exploded into pieces, the rubble tumbling into the sinkhole and slowly building a wide sloping ramp that was reaching for the surface and freedom.

The cannon hummed, and whole new sections of the cliff came tumbling down, the pile gradually growing in width as the rainy desert sands began to flow down into the city.

Gaza was pleased it responded so well. Mebbe he was getting good at this tech talk. But he had to stay double razor, keep everything simple and try to talk as if he was preDark. Treat this as his new wife and the world would be his command!

Once he got out of this fucking pit.

IN THE CONTROL ROOM of War Wag One, the group of people listened to the thick silence coming from the ceiling speaker. Only a second earlier it had been the driver of Cargo Van Three, then there was an explosion and nothing.

"War Wag Two has confirmed," Jessica said, a radio receiver held to her ear. "Three is gone, blown to pieces."

"Aced, a dozen of us like muties in a pit," Blackjack said, frowning at the concept.

Standing in the doorway, Anders said nothing, but his face was a mask of controlled terror. Twice, he started to speak, but decided to remain quiet.

"Yeah, but aced us with what?" Kate demanded angrily, slumping into her chair. "What the nuking hell hit us?"

"It came from the city," Jake said hesitantly. "Or at least, I think it did. Damn thing moved so fast I couldn't really track it in flight. Only the afterghost on the screen showed where it had come from."

"Impossible! Nothing moves that fast," the Trader snapped. "Check the screen."

"I did," he stated firmly. "It's working fine."

"Laser?" Dean asked.

"Nothing on the thermal scanners," Jessica stated. "Cold and clear."

"Rain hide heat sig," Jak suggested.

The woman shook her head. "The downpour only makes the air colder and increases a heat sig. This was no rocket."

"Armbrust rocket fires silent and cold," J.B. said hesitantly.

"The ear didn't hear any cannons firing or rockets flying either," Eric's voice said from the speakers. The comp tech was back in his air-conditioned blister of tinted plastic, with Mildred standing nearby, the two of them surrounded by a maze of wires and cables.

"Armbrust makes noise flying. No way around that."

"It's a coil gun," Ryan said, rubbing a fist into a palm. "Gotta be. That's the bastard thing that makes sense. Trader found one a long time ago."

"Somewhere down there, Gaza found a fucking coil gun, a portable one like a bazooka, or an APC," Krysty said, then scowled. "Mother Gaia, he was going for spare parts for his busted APC and found an armed one!"

"Hopefully, one that cannot drive," Doc added in a bass rumble. "If he achieved mobility with such a weapon, the baron would become a most formidable opponent."

"A coil gun," Kate said slowly. "Those are just legends, mag guns firing plastic balls so fast they hit like skybombs. That's just a fairy tale to scare the littles.''

''Plastic cubes, actually,'' Mildred said over the PA system. ''That form gives a better caloric yield on impact.''

Kate gave Ryan a hard disbelieving stare.

''If Mildred says that's what it is, then you can load that into your blaster and start shooting.''

''Eric?'' Kate asked meaningfully.

''I agree, Chief,'' the man said. ''But it's only a guess on my part. She knows things. I'd say listen to the healer.''

''Accepted, then.'' The Trader nodded. ''Okay, Mildred got any clever suggestions?''

''Coil guns are purely line of sight,'' Mildred said. ''Have to be because their prime function is pure velocity. The cubes can't track like a missile or arch over a hill like a rocket. Think of them as fast bullets and you understand.''

Listening from her chair, Kate almost smiled at that news. Good, so there was the flaw. Excellent. ''Jess, tell the others to stay way from the cliff, the more distance the better. Down in that hole he can't see up here. We stay clear, he can shoot all day and wouldn't hit a nuking thing.''

''And neither can we,'' Jake replied from the control board. ''We just going to leave him down there?''

Kate snorted. ''Not a chance in hell. Can we get a reading with the radar?''

"Not into the city. It's designed for the sky, not to scan down into holes."

"How about change the angle?" J.B. asked.

"Not in this," the man said, gesturing at the ceiling the sound of rain on every side. "No way."

"Can we hit him with the L-gun?" Blackjack asked, swiveling about at the machine-gun blister. With the enemy down in the sinkhole, he had nothing to guard for a moment.

"Angle is wrong. Never planned on shooting down a goddamn well," Kate replied with a frown. "We could do it, but we'd have to be right at the very edge of the cliff. A sitting target for his coil gun."

"You have a working laser?" Ryan asked.

"Bet your ass we do. We made it ourselves," she admitted with pride. "Or rather Eric did. Took us a year. Uses diamond dust as a light source. He is an ace tech, and can make anything."

"Shit lousy blaster shot, though." Blackjack smirked at the blister.

Behind the tinted plastic, Eric made a rude gesture in response.

J.B. mused on that. Burning diamonds was clever. Jewelry was without value these days, and so a lot of it could still be found in the ruins. Diamonds were merely coal, after all. Probably used thermite to ignite the diamond dust and then watch out, the stronger the source, the hotter the laser.

"Heads up," Eric announced suddenly, his voice

distorted with static as lightning flashed nearby. All conversation stopped for a moment as the thunder rolled over them shaking the wags.

"The ear has a series of explosions to the north," Eric continued reporting. "A lot of them, very fast, very strong."

"Is he fighting somebody else?" Dean asked hopefully.

Jak replied, "Mebbe it only thinks it's us."

"Bah, the feeb has gone blaster-happy," Blackjack muttered. "Just shooting for the sound of it."

"Or he's clearing the line of sight," Ryan corrected. "Once those few standing buildings are gone, he'll be able to track the entire rim of the cliff from one central location."

"Fuck it," the door guard said with conviction. "Let him keep the city. He'll be ass deep in muties for the rest of his life."

Then Eric spoke, "No, he *is* shooting at the cliff. I hear rocks falling, but no glass shattering, or anything else breakable. This makes no sense."

Frowning in thought, Ryan turned. "J.B., you took a recce of the rim while we were on top of the building."

"Yeah. So?"

"Is the north face of the cliff the lowest point?"

"Sure," the Armorer said, then realized what that meant.

"He's digging a path out," Kate growled, slamming

a fist onto the arm of her chair. "Using the coil gun to blow down the cliff and make a ramp of solid rock to reach the surface!"

"If he achieves open ground with that APC," Mildred started.

"Tank," Jessica interrupted. "During the lightning I got a brief vid of the city and saw it. Big monster, five, six times the size of any APC. It's a goddamn tank."

"Nuking hell!" Anders whispered, slumping his shoulders. "Gaza with a working preDark tank."

"If the baron escapes from the pit in that behemoth, he'll take over the Deathlands in a year. He was a major danger with just an APC, but with a full operational preDark tank—" Kate paused "—he'll be unstoppable. We got nothing that can even dent that big bastard until it's close enough to blow us to bits."

"The bastard has all of the advantages," Fat Pete said, speaking at last.

"Except one," Ryan stated, going to the windshield and looking at the pouring rain. "Think any of those motorcycles might still work?"

"Sure," Blackjack said, leaning on the .50-cal, making the belt of ammo jingle. "They've survived acid rain storms before. Why?"

"We'll need a lot more plastic sheeting," J.B. said, tilting back his fedora. "And a hell of a diversion. But if these folks have enough cable and a good winch, we can use the ravine and ledge we climbed before to get back down into the city.''

''A ground attack?''

''Yeah. Gaza may be blasting the cliff to make a path out,'' Ryan said with a grim smile, ''but we already know the way down, and the very last bastard thing he would ever expect at this point is a strike from behind.''

''And above,'' Kate said, tossing the man her personal hand comm. He made the catch. ''Only use the even channels. Jump each time you make a call. We'll hit him together.''

''Allies?'' Ryan asked.

''Partners,'' she agreed. ''Deal?''

The one-eyed man nodded at that and started along the corridor, pushing Anders out of the way as he and the rest of the companions started toward the washroom and their battered ponchos.

In the tumultuous sky, the chem storm raged away, completely unconcerned with the very human battle about to begin on the muddy ground below.

Chapter Twenty-Two

Rumbling, tumbling and rolling madly, the pieces of the shattered cliff cascaded into the city, crushing cars and smashing into the sides of small buildings.

Gaza watched impatiently as the loose material shifted and slid about in the pale yellow rain, the salt and sand mixing into a vicious mud that flowed as thick as snot from the desert above. Damn. There was no way he could roll the behemoth through that mess without becoming completely quagmired, a sitting target for the Trader to shoot apart at her leisure. Fuck that nonsense.

Again and again, the cannon hummed, discharging new projectiles at beyond the speed of sound. Each time, the power gauges on the control board swung high toward the redline, but never reached the danger zone. After his initial zeal of discovery, it was soon apparent to the baron that the mil wag wasn't in as good a shape as he had originally believed, but it was still better than that patchwork wag the Trader drove. Clearly, some minor adjustments would have to be made to his master plan, but nothing serious. And the beginning was exactly the same—get out of the hole, then kill the Trader.

Steadily, the ammo count dropped, as more and more of the cliff was blown loose and the sharply sloped mound of rubble expanded into the ruins, becoming less angled, easier to climb, wider, flatter, stronger.

Soon freedom would be his, very soon now.

AT THE BOTTOM of the cliff, the rain was splattering juicy and hard on the plastic ponchos of the men, their three bikes equally draped with as much plastic sheeting as they could carry as some extra protection against the deadly rain. Only three motorcycles had been recovered, the rest damaged from shrapnel. Three bikes meant just three riders. Only Ryan and J.B. were going, along with Fat Pete, the goliath insisting a member of the convoy ride with the outlanders for obvious security reasons. The rest of the companions were in War Wag One, helping with what they could.

Despite his blunt demeanor, Ryan didn't think the big man liked the companions, and especially the way the Trader looked at Ryan when she thought nobody else would notice. The one-eyed man had wanted a ride from the Trader, but not that kind, and was no threat to the love-stricken man. But the big hardcase didn't see the matter that way, finding it difficult to believe that everybody didn't want to be with the Trader.

Well equipped, Ryan and J.B. had their personal blasters back, plus a lot of secondary stuff from the Trader's considerable supplies, along with the only two functional LAW rockets. And that was it. They had to do the job with two, or else the mission was a bust and Gaza would bring a new meaning of hurt to the helpless world above.

"Let's go," Fat Pete said, checking the sawed-off double-barrel at his side. The scattergun had been Roberto's, rescued from the acid puddles soon enough that the firing mechanism hadn't been damaged. The shells were doubtful and he had tossed those, but now the loops of the gun belt were full of slick cartridges sprayed with the silicon lube they used to protect the hoses of the bikes.

Twisting the hand grips and kicking the starters, the men got the Harleys sputtering into life, and worked the fuel and clutch awhile until the engines grew warm and finally smoothed out. Slipping into gear, the three drove carefully through the rocks and rubble until reaching the flat city streets. Now they fed the hungry machines juice and leaned into the acceleration, dodging potholes, skeletons and wags, often going onto the sidewalks to avoid the motionless traffic jam of the dead.

Staying in a triangle formation to keep from splashing one another with their wakes, the three men urged the motorcycles on ever faster, staying low behind the cracked windshields.

In their wake, stickies rushed to the empty windows attracted by the noise, then hooted loudly as the acid rain washed over their naked forms. The flesh bubbled, falling away in gooey strings, with their thin blood pouring out until the beating internal organs simply fell onto the dirty floors.

High above the sagging metropolis, lightning flashed and the thunder rumbled but the rain was coming with less force, the brunt of the terrible storm already over. Soon, the peace of the desert would return and what scant cover the hellish tempest offered the desperate people would be gone completely.

"MOVE OUT!" Kate ordered, and War Wag One lurched into motion.

Driving at top speed, the massive rig churned through the stormy desert, staying a good distance from the edge of the cliff, navigating purely by the fire-lit skyscrapers within the sunken city.

"Where the hell is Anders?" Blackjack asked, returning from the main corridor. "The bastard said he would watch my blaster while I took a whiz."

"But he left right after you," Jessica started, then her face sagged as she realized the truth. "Oh, no."

"So the coward finally ran," Kate said, uncaring of any hurt feelings the truth might incur. "Good riddance, waste of fuel hauling his useless ass along."

"Damn right," Jake said, reaching out to pat the

other tech on the shoulder. "Stay razor, pretty lady, we got a job to do."

Jessica slumped at the pronouncement and returned to her work in sad silence.

However, nobody else was really surprised, and had been expecting it for a long time. If Kate could, she would find the bastard and hang him from a tree, but they had a fight to finish first. Hopefully, the rain would chill the dirty bastard and save her the trouble of tracking him down.

"Missiles are primed and ready, Chief," Jake reported briskly, his hands moving across the controls. "Four in the pod and that's everything. The rest were with Susie in the cargo van."

Kate merely grunted at that.

"The L-gun is fully charged," Eric announced over the speakers, "but we only have one full shot, mebbe two short ones, so make it count, Chief."

"That was the plan," the Trader muttered, listening to the gentle rhythm of the softening rain. The woman had gone into battle with less and emerged alive. Hopefully, she could manage to pull that off one more time.

GNAWING ON A RATION BAR from an MRE pack, Kathleen jerked up her head to listen as a strident crashing shook the behemoth and banks of lights flickered in rippling rainbows.

"Son of a bitch," Gaza said, leaning into the monitor. That last shot had really done the trick. A good hundred yards of cliff had broken free to fall into the city, crushing several one-story buildings. Loose rubble spread across the widening gap of destruction, forming a gentle ramp to the rougher sections of the ragged cliff. By the nuke, this was going to work!

Just then, a whole section of the board lit up and a soft beeping sounded a warning as the turret traversed a sharp arc, the cannon stopped humming as the side-mounted rapid-fires cut loose. A split second later, the tank rocked as something slammed on the roof with triphammer force, silencing the twin .50-cal machine guns.

"Report!" Gaza barked, starting to rise from his chair, then stopping, unable to decide what to do or where to go.

"Source unknown, possible rock splinter recent collapse," the tank reported with machine calm. "Zero penetration to primary hull, but both antipersonnel machine guns have been disabled. The service droids have not responded and may also be damaged. Should I call for assistance?"

Snapping fingers for his attention, Kathleen touched her throat and shook her head hard. Gaza nodded in understanding.

"There is to be no communication to anybody except me," the baron commanded, feeling a touch of fear in his belly. "Total silence. Got that?"

The damn thing was old, but smarter than most humans. He didn't want it trying to talk to anybody else, mebbe learn the truth that the war was over for a hundred fragging years and this was a private fight.

There was a pause that grew to uncomfortable length.

"Acknowledged," it said. "Communications blackout is now in progress. Active relay via geosync satellite has not been achieved. Only passive monitoring will continue."

"Good. Now keep digging," the man directed. He added, "But if anything appears on the cliff, even a lone person, use the main gun to kill on sight."

Unfortunately, without the .50-cal, the tank had only the main cannon and that was needed for the cliff. Suddenly, the baron wasn't so sure that it was a chunk of rock that had hit the tank. Might have been a gren. Could they be under attack? It seemed unlikely. Only a feeb would attack a preDark tank with anything short of an implo gren. No, it was a rock splinter, nothing more.

"Confirmed," the tank said, and the main cannon hummed once more, another acre of rock blasting loose to tumble onto the growing mound.

THE BIG HARLEY purring between his spread legs, Ryan braked to a halt behind a thick brick wall and thumbed the transmit on the hand comm.

"Okay, I got the machine guns with the pipe bombs," Ryan said quickly. "Now light 'er up!"

"Bet your ass we will," Pete growled in response. "Roger that," J.B. added.

Tucking the comm into a pocket, Ryan fed the Twin-V 88 some fuel and rode down the block, arching around the tank to a new position. A few seconds later, the exact spot he had just transmitted from loudly detonated. Yeah, he had expected that would be the reaction to a radio broadcast this close. Once Gaza figured it wasn't muties running about, he would be forced to use the big gun, which slowed his departure and bought the Trader more time.

But the bastard cannon was fast! Wouldn't have thought something that large could move so bastard quick! And he had faced such a titan before. The damn mil wag was a GE Ranger, a comp-operated tank very similar to one they had fought back in Ohio. It had taken a suicide run to stop that war machine, and he sure as nuking hell hoped it wouldn't require such a sacrifice again here in Texas.

Suddenly, a flame flickered from a second story and a burning object arced through the drizzling sky to hit behind the tank, forming a pool of fire. As the main gun swung that way, Pete drove the Harley down a flight of stairs and deeper into the ruins. The tank hummed and that area exploded. J.B. then popped up on the other side and threw another Molotov that landed on top of the Ranger, and Ryan added a third in front of the machine. As they raced away, Pete tossed in a fourth, sealing the war wag in a ring of flame.

Steering with one hand through the scattered rain, Ryan pulled out the hand comm and hit the switch. "Okay, she's hot as an oven! Do it now!" he cried out. But there was no response, only the crackle of static.

"I was afraid of this. We're too bastard far!" J.B. cursed. "The Trader can't hear us!"

Ryan glanced at the buildings rising in the center of the city. "And they sure as hell can't see us—that's for damn sure. Got no choice. One of us goes back!"

"On it!" Fat Pete cried and roared off, shouting into the hand comm.

The tank fired at the departing man as he took a corner and an entire side of a bank blew out, masonry tumbling into the puddle-filled street, crushing cars and trucks.

"We have to keep it busy," Ryan said, driving and talking at the same time. He paused to take a pothole, the impact jarring his spine and kidneys hard. "Keep talking and moving! It'll track on us and ignore Pete!"

"You hope!" J.B. replied over the crackling comm. "Sure as hell wish we could use the LAW rockets, but they wouldn't dent this monster!"

Rolling out of the pool of flames, the tank hummed again, the radios crackled from the electromagnetic impulse of the coil gun cannon. Another section of the ruins detonated, a roiling fireball throwing rubble skyward.

"Fireblast, it moved!" Ryan raged. "Any more Molotovs?"

"No!"

"Then we use the satchel charge!"

"Too late!"

Glancing upward, Ryan cursed as he saw the fiery outline of the heatseekers from War Wag One arc over the city and plummet straight down toward the empty pool of fire. Then a pair peeled off to separate and strike different buildings still blazing, a furniture warehouse and a chemical factory. But the rest dived toward their target and impacted on the vacant street, throwing chunks of pavement in every direction, the staggering blast toppling dozens of additional ruins.

"We were too slow!" Ryan snarled. "Okay, we use the backup plan!"

Killing their radios, Ryan and J.B. rode to new locations and parked in the penumbra of jagged structures that hopefully would hide them from the sensors of the Ranger. Stepping off the bikes, the men unlimbered their LAW rockets, pulled the pins and extended the tubes to swing the launchers toward the tallest remaining skyscraper.

In a whooshing roar, the rockets launched and climbed on hot contrails to slam deep into the structure, the double explosions blowing out the Plexiglas windows on the middle floors.

Even as the shiny plastic fell, there was a brilliant strobe of light from the cliff as the L-gun of War Wag One stabbed out a short shimmering beam of destruction that hit the building and cut it in two, finishing the job the rockets merely started. As the slab of floors fell away, the war wag now had a direct line-of-sight view of the Ranger.

Even as the tank swung its main gun toward the enemy on the high ground, the homemade laser stabbed out with a sustained beam of shimmering energy that lanced straight through the machine like a burning sword. As the chassis glowed red-hot, the coil gun hummed one last time as the Ranger flashed rads from the violated DU armor, flooding the vicinity to lethal levels. Everything flammable in the tank vaporized into superheated steam, and there was a brief human scream as the reserve ammo for the machine guns ignited, heaving the ruptured vehicle into the air, a halo of shrapnel brutally peppering everything in sight. Tumbling in the air, the tank crashed back down as a flaming meteor, secondary explosions cooking nuke batteries and adding to the general annihilation.

Then impossibly, incredibly, the electric motors roared with life and the Ranger tried to rally once more until lightning crackled from the engine compartment and the fusion reactor scrammed, shutting off all power. Crackling in flames, the demolished war wag sat there for a few calculated seconds, just long enough to draw an enemy closer, and then the self-

destruct charges welded inside its sturdy frame detonated. The four hundred pounds of thermite flaring
incandescent, creating a nimbus of searing blinding
light.

As the hellish inferno slowly dimmed and vision
returned, there was nothing remaining of the preDark
tank but a steaming crater in the ground and a very
great deal of molten steel scattered about sizzling on
the damp ground.

"Hello?" the hand comm crackled. "Anybody
there?"

Ryan pressed the switch. "I'm okay, Pete. How
about you, J.B.?"

"Alive and kicking," the Armorer replied.

Looking to the cliff, Ryan frowned when he
couldn't find the war wag. "How is Trader?" he asked
urgently. "Did they take a hit?"

"She...she's aced," Fat Pete said woodenly. "Everybody else got out in time, in case the attack failed,
but she stayed to aim the laser."

"The Trader is chilled," Ryan said softly, raising a
gloved hand to shield his face from the raging inferno
of the dying tank. PreDark lampposts on the distant
corners were starting to soften and bend over from the
heat like melting icicles, the sidewalks shattering into
rubble, bricks crumbling into the ash they were forged
from again.

"No way she could have escaped?" J.B. prompted
hopefully.

"None," Fat Pete said in a tight voice. "Duncan saw it happen from War Wag Two, which I guess is now One, and I'm the new Trader." There was a pause filled with only the sound of his controlled breathing.

"Which means you fucking outlanders aren't welcome here anymore," Trader snarled in barely controlled rage.

Epilogue

As morning came, words were few and the mood was solemn as the people picked through the steaming wreckage of the destroyed war wag to find anything they could salvage. It would be a very long drive to the closest depot and their next cache of supplies. The decision had already been made in the morning light to accept a deal from an Ohio trader who needed help reclaiming a huge war wag from the side of a mountain. How it got there, nobody could say, but it was packed with weapons and in prime condition. With their share, they could be back in business again, and there would be some trading along the way. Some chilling, too, most likely, but then that was life.

"That everything?" Jak asked, strapping the water can to the side of the motorcycle. The air was clean this morning, the stink of the acid long gone with the sun, leaving the desert feeling clean and renewed.

"Everything I can think of taking," Ryan answered, checking the hoses on the big Harley. The hog needed a good cleaning, but aside from that it was fit for travel. Whoever the recent owners were, they had taken excellent care of the bikes.

"Nice of the Trader to let us have these," Dean said, wiping off the seat with a damp rag. The saddlebags were full of food and water, and even a few of the pipe bombs. They would be able to reach the redoubt on the Grandee without any real problems.

"Nothing courteous about it—the bikes let us leave faster," J.B. explained, checking his Uzi machine pistol. "I guess he loved her a lot. Mebbe too much. Damn fool should have said something while she was still around."

"'Love oft ties the tongue as steel can bind a hand,'" Doc rumbled.

Spread before the companions, the Texas desert was flattened into a mosaic pattern of raindrops hits, the landscape even more barren and desolate than before.

"Looks like the surface of the moon," Mildred muttered, hefting her med kit. She had shared what she could of the recent acquisitions from the city with Matilda, who was now the healer for the convoy. It left them both short on supplies, but each came away with a few items they didn't have before. A fair exchange.

"How know moon?" Jak asked, topping off the oil in his machine.

"Saw it on TV."

"Vid?"

"Live broadcast."

"Doesn't matter. We're all here and still breathing,'' J.B. said with a warm smile. ''I guess that doomie was wrong, eh?''

Krysty gave him a grin, but didn't comment in return. The message in blood had only said what would happen, not when. She still felt the hand of death among them and knew it would strike soon. Maybe not today or tomorrow, but soon.

Several techs and sec men for the convoy were inspecting a tire on the small cargo van, Fat Pete among them, so Ryan took the chance to walk over to the giant who now called himself Trader. The name was being passed around a lot these days, but the two so far had been worthy of the title.

''We'll be leaving now,'' Ryan said. ''Heading south to the Grandee.'' The one-eyed wanted to say more, but knew it wouldn't be accepted well.

''Good,'' the giant replied gruffly.

With a shrug, Ryan turned, but the man stopped him.

''Hellfire, look, there's no blood lost between us, outlander, so if we cross paths again some day, there won't be a bounty on your head. Might even be welcome, if enough time has passed.''

Ryan said nothing, merely nodding, knowing this speech wasn't for him, but for the man giving it, a way to say things he couldn't say in private. Nothing special about it: wounds needed to bleed before they could heal was all.

Exhaling deeply, the Trader went on, ''But right

now I can't stand the fragging sight of you. Go while you can, and I do mean now.''

"Guess I'd feel about the same if you got aced," Ryan said as Krysty climbed onto the rear of the bike.

Holding open the door to the war wag, Jake offered a hand to Jessica, and the woman smiled as he climbed inside. The hatch closed with a bang, followed by metallic thuds as the bolts were thrown, sealing it tight.

"At least some folks learn from the mistakes of others," Mildred said. "I wish them good luck."

"Amen," Doc rumbled. "Farewell and adieu."

Black smoke streamed up from the big diesels, then turned gray and the armored transport started moving away. Watching the two battered wags roll for the horizon, Ryan wished Pete luck.

"Pity you can't ace folks twice," J.B. muttered, revving the engine slightly to clear the carburetor. "If anybody deserved a hard death, it was Gaza. He went far too quickly for my taste."

"But you can do as many times as you wish, my friend," Doc Tanner said, tucking his ebony stick into a saddlebag where he could easily reach it in case of trouble. "I remember in detail the deaths of Cort Strasser and Silas every night before I sleep. Very soothing, indeed."

"Not healthy to always dwell in the past," Krysty said softly.

"Ah, but dear lady, it is always the past," Doc answered, climbing onto the bike. "There is no other time than the eternal memory of now."

Starting his battered motorcycle, Ryan led the others southward toward the closest known redoubt.

STUMBLING ALONG through the desert, Anders tripped on something and went flying, face to the ground. Slowly standing, he saw that it was a leather bag of some kind. Checking the contents, the sec man was delighted to find it full of water, clear, clean water. A godsend!

Drinking deeply from the tip of the bag, he felt giddy with excitement with the find. Then he became drunkenly silly, and he clumsily missed his own mouth, the tainted water stinging as it washed into his eyes.

Cursing in pain, Anders dropped the bag and slumped to the ground, moaning in pain, then soon wailing in madness as the *jinkaja* poison flooded his body.

Lost in his world of madness, the man never saw the Core members rise up from the damp sands to reclaim the bag and leave again, abandoning the invader to the brutal mercies of the desert.

CLIMBING DOWN the hill, Larry found the two-leg making bubbling sounds as it feebly waved its arms and legs. Coming closer, the little mutie took a rock conveniently nearby and bashed the big thing in the side of the head. The two-leg dropped still, only its lips and fingertips moving to show it was still alive.

Now with gleeful intent, Larry took the precious glass dagger from his bag and began cutting away the clothing of the norm until the flesh was laid bare to the sun. Then he quickly sliced the tendons in the legs and arms so the food couldn't escape and settled in for a good meal, all the while singing the praise of his departed mate and child as he filled his belly with the hot, red flesh.

The screaming lasted for a very long time, and when he was done, Larry slipped away into the growing night, at last satisfied that the anguished spirits of his mate and child had finally been set to rest. But then, the desert always found a way to balance the scales of revenge, and death.

James Axler
Outlanders®

MAD GOD'S WRATH

The survivors of the oldest moon colony have been revived from cryostasis and brought to Cerberus Redoubt, leaving behind an enemy in deep, frozen sleep. But betrayal and treachery bring the rebel stronghold under seige by the resurrected demon king of a lost world. With a prize hostage in tow to lure Kane and his fellow warriors, he retreats to the uncharted planet of mystery and impossibility for a final act of madness.

Available February 2004 at your favorite retail outlet.